GOTU

Mike McNeff

Booktrope Editions
Seattle WA
2011

Copyright 2011 Mike McNeff

Cover Design by

Edited by Rachel Leach

ISBN 978-1-935961-38-3

Library of Congress Control Number: 2011960956

DEDICATION

This book is dedicated to Pilot/Officer Thomas McNeff and Paramedic/Officer Richard Stratman of the Arizona Department of Public Safety who were killed in the line duty on October 2, 1983 after rescuing over thirty people from raging flood waters, and to all law enforcement officers who have given their last full measure protecting and serving their communities all over this world.

ACKNOWLEDGEMENTS

Writing a novel is a journey with many stops at way stations to rest and calibrate your compass. At each way station there are people who offer help and encouragement. My writers group, Just Write on the Coupeville Wharf, was and is a major way station. Bob Mayer got me focused on my writing, as he has done for hundreds of writers. My critique group, Rowena Williamson, Mare Chapman, Hanna Rhys Barnes, and Audrey Mackaman are a source of unrelenting honesty about my writing. Rowena and my sister, Cathy Shaw, each helped shape the original manuscript into something with promise. Ken Shear and my Booktrope team made the book the best it can be. Most importantly, my wife Linda has loved me for over thirty-four years no matter what new direction my restless mind decides to wander.

ONE

S CRAMBLE! SCRAMBLE! We have a target!" The intercom blared through the U.S. Customs Air Support offices.

Sergeant Robin Marlette, supervisor of the Arizona Department of Public Safety Narcotics Special Enforcement Unit, jumped up from his desk and ran to the steel door leading to the flight line. He could hear the rush of footsteps behind him as his squad and the U.S. Customs crew poured out of other offices and the ready room. He hit the metal bar on the door and burst into the warm Phoenix summer night, then ran down the dimly lit tarmac to the sinister-looking UH-60 Blackhawk helicopter. He fervently hoped for a jump on a drug smuggler, his favorite thing to do as a cop.

When he reached the chopper, the mechanic had the doors open wide. Robin could just make out the name "Jumpin' Jack Flash" on the nose of the Blackhawk. He climbed in and moved to the middle OD green canvas seat of the first row facing the rear of the aircraft. Robin picked up his Galil ARM 7.62 mm rifle from the seat and sat down.

The smell of JP4 jet fuel added to the aroma of a military aircraft permeating his senses—a comfortable smell to him. He put on his intercom headset and hit the toggle switch, slipped on his tactical vest, and locked in the buckles. A quick check confirmed all of the gear on his vest was secure. Robin snapped himself into his seat harness.

The other six men of the squad and two U.S. Customs agents were doing the same thing. The two Customs pilots already pushed the throttles to full power as they quickly completed the scramble checklist. Two Customs Air Interdiction Officers manned a 7.62 mm Mini-gun in each gunner's window.

Robin listened as the pilot, Jack Moore, better known as "Jumpin' Jack Flash," talked to the control tower at Sky Harbor Airport. The heat inside of the Blackhawk drew sweat from Robin's pores.

"Sky Harbor, Lima Two-One advising law enforcement scramble for one-eight-zero."

"Roger, Lima Two-One. Cleared for immediate departure, one-eight-zero. Winds calm, barometer two-zero-zero-niner...and good hunting."

"Lima Two-One, roger."

Robin gave his team thumbs up and got thumbs up from all members.

"Robin, we ready?" Jack asked.

"Ready, Jack. Blast off."

The big bird, now screaming with the combination of its twin jet engines and rotors, bounded off the ramp into the night sky.

"Lima Two-One, Quarterback." Jack called the U.S. Air Force Airborne Warning and Control System (AWACS) aircraft tracking the target on radar.

"Go ahead, Lima Two-One. This is Quarterback."

"Lima Two-One, Quarterback, requesting target info."

"Lima Two-One, your target is an aircraft that crossed the border at Lochiel, Arizona at two hundred and fifty feet doing one hundred and fifty knots. Target is currently eight nautical miles northwest of Patagonia. Poppa One-Nine is locking on to him now. Your current intercept is one-five-zero for sixty-one miles."

"Roger, Quarterback. Copy intercept one-five-zero for sixty-one miles."

Robin knew Poppa One-Nine was a U.S. Customs Lear Jet equipped with the same look-down, shoot-down radar used in the F-16 fighter jet. He felt the Blackhawk bank as Jack turned to intercept the target aircraft.

"Poppa One-Nine, Quarterback. We have target locked now twenty-eight nautical miles south of Tucson at five hundred feet doing one hundred and fifty knots. Heading is three-three-five."

"Roger, Poppa One-Nine. Your target is confirmed."

"Roger, Quarterback. We also have the target on FLIR. Target is a Cessna 210 running dark."

"Roger, Poppa One-Nine. Lima Two-One, you copy Poppa One-Nine?"

"Lima Two-One, Quarterback, we copy Poppa One-Nine and will start com with him."

"Roger, Lima Two-One. Quarterback out."

Robin breathed in cooler air as the Blackhawk gained altitude. The radio traffic told him the Customs Lear Jet chase plane locked the same target on their radar as the AWACS had on theirs and watched it through a Forward Looking Infra Red sensor. The AWACS made the transfer of the target because it flew a "training" mission. The Air Force couldn't officially do interdiction missions in the Continental United States due to the latest court interpretations of the Posse Comitatus law. Robin briefly contemplated the obvious absurdity. The target, flying at a low altitude and running dark without its navigation lights on, was likely a drug smuggler.

"Lima Two-One, Poppa One-Nine. Do you have us on radar yet?" Jack asked.

"Lima Two-One, give me a squawk for positive ident."

"Roger, Poppa One-Nine. Lima Two-One squawking one-two-one-zero now."

"Okay, Lima Two-One, I've got you standby."

Jack didn't reply to the chase plane. He sounded almost bored on the radio, but Robin knew from past experience Jack had a short fuse for chase planes not giving frequent updates on intercept headings. On two occasions, a suspect aircraft got away because the Blackhawk jumped the strip too late. More than a few seconds of "standby" pegged Jack's patience.

"Poppa One-Nine, would you mind giving us intercept distance?" Jack's irritation crept in to his previously calm voice.

"Poppa One-Nine, Lima Two-One. Intercept heading is still good distance is fifty-six miles."

"We're going dark," Jack told his co-pilot Oscar Leighton over the intercom. The Blackhawk now flew without navigation lights.

"Poppa One-Nine, Lima Two-One. Target just went into a steep climb. Standby, standby Lima Two-One, the target is now at four thousand feet. Lghts on!" Excitement raised the pitch in Poppa One-Nine's voice.

"What do you think, Robin?" Jack asked.

"Sounds like the ol' pop-up trick to me. This guy's a definite target."

"Looks good to me," Jack agreed.

"Roger, Poppa One-Nine. Advise us at five miles," Jack told the chase plane.

"Roger, Lima Two-One."

Robin quickly went over his equipment again. He hit the bottom of the magazine in his rifle to make sure it was seated correctly. His heart beat against his ballistic vest. At a closure rate of over three hundred knots, things would begin to happen fast. Eight minutes later, Poppa One-Nine's voice crackled over the radio.

"Poppa One-Nine, Lima Two-One. Target is now five miles from you, at four thousand feet, lights still on. He should be coming down your left side."

"Lima Two-One, Roger," Jack replied.

Everyone on the helicopter began searching the night sky for the suspect aircraft. Robin watched as the men nearest the windows strained in their harnesses to get a better view. Suddenly, Oscar's voice came excitedly over the intercom.

"I got 'em at eleven o'clock low."

"I see him," Jack said.

A few seconds later, Robin felt the Blackhawk go into a diving left turn. The helicopter began pulling "G's," pushing Robin into the seat. Jack maneuvered the Blackhawk behind and slightly below the aircraft, putting the chopper in the target aircraft's blind spot.

"Robin, we are passing Casa Grande on the left," Jack advised. "If we keep on this course, my bet is he's headed for Rainbow Valley."

"That would be nice," Robin replied. "Like doing a jump in our own back yard."

Robin's squad and the Customs agents made many arrests and follow-up investigations and spent hundreds of hours conducting surveillance in Rainbow Valley. They knew every inch of the desolate desert area in between the Sierra Estrella and the Maricopa Mountains, southwest of Phoenix. Hundreds of places to land an airplane made it a favorite destination for air smugglers.

"Target is losing altitude and turning west," Oscar said.

"It looks like he is going to land," Jack observed.

"Are his lights still on?" Robin asked.

"That's affirm," Jack replied.

"He may be doing a decoy landing at Casa Grande airport," cautioned Robin.

"Roger," Jack answered.

"Either of you guys have the night vision on?" Robin asked.

"Yes, Mother Marlette," Oscar replied in a sarcastic voice.

Robin saw Burke Jameson flipping the bird towards Oscar's position up front. Robin turned in his seat only to see Oscar giving *him* the finger. Robin blew a kiss to Oscar, who chuckled and shook his head as he turned back forward. The helicopter's roar buried the team's laughter, but it eased the growing tension.

"The target is on final for Casa Grande," Jack said.

"Poppa One-Nine, Lima Two-One. It looks like the target is landing," the chase plane said.

"Standby, Poppa One-Nine," Jack replied. "He may be faking.."

"Roger, Two-One."

"He's gone dark! He's gone dark!" Oscar said with elation.

"There's no doubt about it now," Robin drawled. "Some time tonight that boy is going to get a gun screwed in his ear."

"Amen, brother," Jack replied.

Oscar watched the suspect aircraft through the night vision goggles and said, "The target is now headed west-northwest from Casa Grande."

"Poppa One-Nine, Lima Two-One. What's your read on the target?" Jack asked the chase plane.

"Lima Two-One, Poppa One-Nine, the target is heading two-niner-niner at five hundred feet, doing one hundred and ten knots and accelerating."

"Roger, One-Nine."

Robin breathed more quickly now, his heart still beating against his vest. His eyes moved over his team. Even in the dimmed cabin lights, he could the see the anticipation in his men. Each man fidgeted with equipment, making sure to be ready for the jump out of the helicopter. They only knew Jack would position the load of drugs at twelve o'clock off the nose of the helicopter—nothing else was certain. The team called it "jumping into the Twilight Zone."

"Lima Two-One, Poppa One-Nine. The target is slowing down."

"Roger, One-Nine. I'm going into a hover. Let me know when the target appears to be final." Jack dropped the Blackhawk down to one hundred feet and hovered. This standard tactic prevented alerting any ground crew waiting for the air smuggler to the presence of the Blackhawk.

"Lima Two-One, the target is circling about four miles north of you," the chase plane advised.

"Roger, One-Nine."

"Robin, it looks like he's trying to land at Alvey's," Jack said.

"I'll take your word for it, Jack, because I can't see where we are."

"Sorry, pal. I keep forgetting you can't see what I see."

"It's okay, Jack. If you're wrong, I get your wife and first born."

"No, no," Jack laughed, "not my first born!"

"Lima Two-One, Poppa One-Nine. Target appears to be on final and there are two pairs of headlights on the strip."

"Roger, One-Nine. Here we go, gang," Jack added on the intercom.

G-forces pressed Robin into his seat as the powerful Blackhawk surged upward. He reached to his forehead and pulled his goggles down over his eyes. He then pulled the straps of his seat harness tight.

"I got com," Robin said as calmly as he could.

"Roger," Jack responded.

"Assault team," Robin began, "this will be a full team deployment. We have one aircraft and at least two vehicles. The strip is Alvey's. Anybody not understand?" Nobody spoke up. "Go to portables," Robin ordered. All team members removed their headsets and hung them from the hooks on the helicopter ceiling. They kept their portable radios off until they left the aircraft. Robin communicated by hand signal now because he stayed plugged into the intercom so he could talk to Jack.

"Target is down," growled Oscar as he watched through the night vision.

The Blackhawk raced towards Alvey's strip at maximum speed, skimming the desert floor with a payload of armed and determined men. Robin looked at his squad. Their faces locked on him, waiting for his signals. No one laughed now. This was a dangerous time.

TWO

The Blackhawk hit the ground in what Jack liked to call a controlled crash, jarring the men in the troop compartment. "Searchlight on!" Oscar advised.

Robin was reaching for his harness release when the chopper shot back into the air and went almost into a ninety-degree bank. He looked out the left window and saw the big rotor blades just barely clearing the sagebrush and mesquite dancing in the rotor wash. If Robin didn't have the utmost confidence in Jack's and Oscar's flying abilities, he would' probably be more than just a little concerned for his life. Still, an awe-filled "Jesus Christ!" fell from his lips, only to disintegrate in the roar of the Blackhawk's engines and rotors.

"Hang on," Oscar yelled. "We're having to herd these fuckers!"

Jack flung the Blackhawk all over the sky. The men in the troop compartment were slammed against seat and harness. From past experience, Robin knew the vehicles on the ground were attempting to run, but Jack maneuvered the Blackhawk in front them, trying to force the suspects to abandon their vehicles. After sixty seconds of being herded by the madman in the giant, angry Blackhawk, the suspects bailed from the trucks.

The Blackhawk's landing gear slammed into the ground again. "Go! Go! Go!" Jack yelled into the intercom.

"Roger!" Robin yelled back. Robin moved his arms out to his sides and pointed to the doors on both sides of the chopper. Immediately both doors slid open and men jumped out in prearranged sequence. Robin, the last man out, tossed his headset, popped his harness, and turned on his portable radio. As he came to the door he charged his rifle, engaged the safety, and jumped out the left side of the helicopter into a thick, stinging swirl of dust kicked up by the chopper's rotors. The Blackhawk's three million candlepower searchlight illuminated the dust. It all merged with the screaming jet engines, making Robin feel like he had jumped into hell.

The whole assault team knelt down on one knee in front of the Blackhawk. Each man covered his face and the action of his weapon to protect him from the whirlwind of dust. This gave Jack and Oscar a chance to do a head count and verify all men on the assault team did get out and were in front of the chopper. Jack pulled on the collective lever and the Blackhawk jumped back into the sky.

"Wedge formation! Emmett, you're point!" Robin ordered. The team quickly formed a wedge with Robin in the middle and started moving forward.

"Shots fired! Shots fired!" Someone screamed into the radio.

Robin started to press his mic button to talk, but several men transmitted at the same time, causing a garbled mess of static and half-words to come over the headset. He did make out somebody saying "two o'clock," so he looked over to his right. He then heard gunfire and saw flashes about forty yards away. The sickening snap of a bullet went by his ear.

The right flank of the wedge returned fire. Robin dropped to one knee, thumbing the safety as he raised his rifle to his cheek. He lined up the three glowing dots on the tritium night sights and put them where he saw the last flash. The rifle punched his shoulder as he fired two rounds. He dropped into the prone position and popped out the bipod on his rifle. Pointing his weapon at the last place he saw the suspect, he looked over the sights.

Robin pushed his mic button and started to talk, but he had to clear his dry throat before he could speak.

"Two Nora Six, all units! Hold your traffic! Hold your traffic! Lima Two-One, we are taking fire from a suspect about fifty yards from drop-off, at two o'clock. Get the light on him!"

"Roger, Nora Six."

The Blackhawk's searchlight illuminated the aircraft and a pickup truck near it because the load of drugs would most likely be there. Jack moved the Blackhawk so the searchlight illuminated a Chevrolet Blazer and the right gunner could cover the vehicle with his Minigun. Robin waited for more fire from the suspect, but none came. From his prone position, he could see under the Blazer and could just make out the feet of a person. They were pointed up.

"I think we have one suspect down," Robin said into his mic. "I want the right flank of the wedge to cover the Blazer. Emmett, take the left flank forward and secure that pickup."

"Ten-Four, Sarge."

Robin watched as Emmett Franks rose off his knee and waved the left side of the wedge forward. Emmett raised his MP5 to his shoulder and moved in a crouching walk towards the pickup. Doug Ariel followed at Emmett's left, but slightly behind him. Mike Collins and John Lucheck, a customs agent, made up the rest of the left side. Mike nudged John forward. They stopped the front of the pickup, while Emmett and Doug went to the rear.

The Blackhawk moved so most of the light shone on the Blazer, although the pickup remained partially illuminated. Jack positioned the jump so the left side of the pickup faced perpendicular to the team. The truck appeared to be a Ford with a camper shell on the back. As Emmett and the others moved toward the truck, they appeared to be strange shadow creatures gliding across an eerie, hostile landscape of glowing, swirling dust with the screaming jet engines and rotors of the Blackhawk giving the effect of howling alien monsters.

When the men reached the truck, both pairs crouched down by their respective wheel wells. "We'll go first, Mike, to avoid cross fire," Emmett said over the radio.

"Ten-Four."

Emmett crouched at the middle of the tailgate while Doug positioned himself under the window of the camper, to form an "L"-shaped kill zone. Doug switched to his Colt .45 with his flashlight in his left hand while Emmett used the light attached to his MP5. Suddenly, both men jumped up, shining their lights into the camper. Then they instantly dropped down, their lights going out. Robin saw the two men confer briefly at the left rear corner of the truck and then take a cautious, but longer look.

"Camper's clear. Your turn, Mike."

"Ten-Four."

Mike slung his Galil on his back and drew his Smith & Wesson .357 revolver and his flashlight. John kept his Steyr-Aug ready. Mike crouched at the rear of the driver's window, while John stood at the front door post. They both made their move, Mike shining his light into the cab.

"Front is clear," Mike said over the radio.

"Ten-Four," Emmett replied. "Let's secure a perimeter."

Both pairs disappeared to the other side of the truck. Thirty seconds later Emmett told Robin the truck was secure and loaded with dope.

"Right flank, follow me to secure the Blazer," Robin ordered. "Rick, I'm going to cover the suspect. You and Matt take the front. Burke, you and Mark take the rear." Robin looked at the men as he said this. They gave him a thumbs up to show they understood. Robin turned and started for the Blazer. He put his Galil to his shoulder and moved forward in a crouching walk, also known as the "Groucho Walk." When he got to the front of the Blazer, he knelt down next to the wheel well and waited for Rick Santos and Matt Howe, the other customs agent, who got there a second later. He noticed bullet holes in the Blazer and a flat left front tire. Robin moved around the front of the Blazer and positioned himself by the right front headlight, with the right front wheel between himself and the suspect. He aimed his rifle at the suspect's chest. In the glow of the searchlight, he saw no movement.

A half minute later, Rick came around and told Robin they had cleared the Blazer. Robin told Burke and Mark Warren, the other member of Robin's team, to scan the area on the other side of the Blazer. He and Rick did the same. It looked clear.

"Okay, guys," Robin said, "It seems one of us got lucky and hit the suspect, because he looks deader than a door nail. But we'll go through the drill. I'll do it. Cover me."

"Roger-dodger, Sarge," Burke responded.

Robin moved out parallel to the suspect, until he passed the man's head. He dropped to one knee and scanned the area for any movement around him. Clear of threats, Robin moved to ten feet from the suspect's head. He put his rifle on safe and slung it over his shoulder. Drawing his Colt .45, Robin started for the suspect. When he reached three feet from the suspect's head, he saw the man's eyes were open and he had been hit in the neck and upper chest. In the glow of the Blackhawk's searchlight, Robin looked over a Hispanic man, about twenty years old, with a round, chubby face. He wore a loose-fitting silk shirt and what appeared to be tailored pants. Rattlesnake-hide boots were on his feet.

The suspect's empty hands lay at his side. Holding his .45 six inches from the suspect's head, Robin reached and felt for the carotid artery. Finding no pulse, Robin holstered his pistol and rolled the suspect over to handcuff him. When he saw pieces of lung hanging out of the back, he decided handcuffing was unnecessary. He searched for weapons on the body and found a Czech 9mm pistol. He cleared the pistol and put it and the magazine in the leg pocket of his flight suit.

Robin used his flashlight to look for the suspect's primary weapon. Just underneath the Blazer, he saw an AK-47. He reached under the truck and drew an outline in the sand around the gun with his finger. Robin picked up the rifle, removed the magazine, and cleared the action. He retrieved the live round he ejected, placed it back into the magazine, and put the magazine into his other leg pocket. Robin laid the weapon back into the outline.

"Two Nora Six, Lima Two-One."

"Go ahead, Nora Six."

"Lima Two-One, we've secured the two vehicles here. I need you to go on state frequency and notify DPS that Two Nora Six squad has been involved in a shooting with one suspect down and no officers injured. We need Two Nora and a shooting team at this location."

"Roger, Two Nora Six."

Suddenly Robin remembered the target aircraft. He turned to look at it and saw the pickup now parked next to the plane.

"Emmett, is the plane secure?"

"Ten-Four, Sarge."

"Thanks for taking care of that."

"Well, Mike took charge. We knew you were busy."

"How much dope we get?"

"I figure about two hundred or so kilos in the truck and about fifty more still in the plane."

"Coke?"

"Looks like it."

The Blackhawk now flew higher and in ever increasing circles around Robin's team, searching the area with its light. Rick Santos and Burke Jameson covered Robin and Mark Warren as they began to search the body for identification and documentary evidence.

"Lima Two-One, Two Nora Six."

"Go ahead, Two-One."

"Be advised your immediate perimeter appears clear. DPS has been notified and is responding per your request."

"Roger."

"Also, Nora Six, be advised the FBI is responding for our side of the shooting."

"Roger, Two-One."

Robin turned to Burke and his team. "You three guys start cutting for sign."

"You got it, Boss," Burke said.

Robin then called Emmett on the radio. "Nora Six, Nora Six-Two."

"Six-Two."

"Emmett, you and Doug start cutting for sign from there. Mark and I will stay with the body and the load."

"Ten-Four."

The eight men assigned to cut sign searched for the tracks of the suspects who ran from the scene. Robin looked at his watch. The team had been on the ground for approximately twelve minutes. It felt like an eternity.

"Rob, you better look at this," said Mark Warren in an ominous tone. He handed Robin a Mexican driver's license. It bore a picture of the dead man. When Robin read the name, he whispered an involuntary, "Son of a bitch!"

"Nora Six, Nora Six-Two," Emmett's voice crackled over Robin's headset.

"Nora Six."

"We've got one in custody."

As Robin made his way to Emmett Franks and John Lucheck, the name Ramon Jesus Rodriquez-Lara caused his brain to run in high gear. His team had killed the brother of the number one drug lord in Mexico! Robin knew some people were going be happy and some would be pissed off. But the question: *Why did Ramon Rodriquez show up on the ground crew of a smuggling deal?* seared into his mind.

Robin walked up to Emmett and John, eyeing the slender, blond, white male between them.

"Who do we have here?" Robin asked.

"Well," Emmett began, "we have one Eric Newman, who just walked up to us and announced he flew the target airplane. He wants to talk to the man in charge. I've placed him under arrest and advised him of his rights."

Robin looked at Newman, who appeared tired but not visibly upset about being arrested. He stood tall, about six feet, with a mustache and a two-day growth of beard. He wore expensive Western clothes.

"Why'd you give yourself up?"

"Running around in the middle of the desert at night ain't my thing."

"Fair enough. I'm Sergeant Robin Marlette, Arizona Department of Public Safety. What can I do for you?"

Newman laughed. "Sergeant! I want to talk to someone higher than you!"

"Boy," Emmett drawled, "you don't want to piss this man off, because there ain't nobody higher or lower who can help you more than the Sarge here"

"It's okay, Emmett," Robin interrupted. He moved closer to Newman. "Look, I don't have time to screw around. I run this show. *I* decide who gets breaks and who doesn't. In this particular deal, since we just waxed Ramon Rodriquez-Lara, I decide who lives and who dies. Now, either you start talking to me or you can wait for a higher ranking officer."

As soon as Newman heard Robin say they killed Ramon Rodriquez, his eyes grew very large. In the glow of the flashlights, Robin thought Newman became deathly pale. Emmett and John looked surprised by the news, but were much happier about it. John slapped Emmett's upheld hand.

"You've got to protect me," Newman blurted out. "Miguel will kill everybody here tonight!"

"You mean Miguel Rodriquez-Lara?" Robin asked.

"Hell yes, that's who I mean! It's bad enough you got the money, but killing his brother. Oh, God!"

"Slow down, slow down," Robin said. "What money?"

"What money?!" Newman almost screamed. "You idiots think there's dope on that plane?!"

Robin grabbed Newman by the arm and walked him to the Cessna. When they got to the plane, Robin reached in and picked up one of the packages. Using his Swiss Army knife, he cut the package open, revealing a stack of U.S. currency. Robin pulled Newman over to the pickup and sat him down on the front bumper.

"Okay, Newman, all you've told me is that Rodriquez is going to be pissed—which I already figured out for myself—and we have load of money and not dope, which I would have found out soon enough. Tell me something I *need* to know."

Newman, who had been looking at the ground, slowly raised his head and stared at Robin.

"Why should I trust you? For all I know you're just another dirty cop."

"You don't know jack shit about me or my men and we don't know jack shit about you. So on that account we start out even, but right now I hold the rest of the cards. It's up to you to tell me why I should give you a break and frankly, since I've got one dead drug big shot and a whole lot of seized cash, I really don't give a damn what you do."

Robin leaned toward Newman and began speaking in a measured tone. "I'll tell you this. You better make up your mind about what you're going to do before the cavalry gets here, because once the word's out we nailed you, you're not worth a tinker's damn to us."

Newman stared at Robin as he turned and started walking to the airplane. "All right, All right, I'll talk," Newman muttered.

"What?" Emmett asked.

"I'll talk, I'll talk," Newman said raising his voice.

Robin turned and faced Newman. "Give me the name of the first person on this side of the border you can make a case on."

Newman looked at Robin for a moment more and said, "Carl Walton." Robin and Emmett looked at each other, their eyes meeting in gleeful shock. Robin was about to speak when Burke Jameson called him on the radio.

"Two Nora Six-One, Two Nora Six."

"Go ahead, Six-One."

"It looks like there were two suspects around the Blazer. Someone came to the Blazer from the area of the pickup and then headed out in the desert. We are going to start tracking."

"Ten-Four."

Robin turned toward Emmett. "Emmett, you and John take Newman and the money to DPS. Process and impound the money. I want the wrappers processed for prints. When you're done with the money, take Newman to the Casablanca and start debriefing him until he can't stay awake. I'll get you security relief as soon as possible."

"Here goes another marathon run," Emmett sighed. He waved John over.

Robin turned to Newman. "Are the wrappers on the money special or marked or a signal in any way?"

"Nah, they're just butcher paper."

Robin's mind worked on a plan. "The money is supposed to go to Walton, right?"

"Yeah," Newman answered.

"For payoffs?"

"Five million dollars' worth."

"Who is supposed to deliver it to Walton?"

"Me and Ramon."

"How many people were here tonight?"

"I don't really know. I came alone in the plane."

Robin knew his plan would be tough to get by the brass, but that never stopped him before. He put his hand on Emmett's shoulder. "Get going, Emmett. Don't talk to anyone. Refer them to me."

"You got it."

Emmett and John got into the pickup, putting Newman between them. Doug and Mike had already loaded the rest of the money from the plane. Emmett started the engine and looked at Robin, his large, round, ebony face showing a broad grin.

"You love this shit, don't you?"

"Working for you is never dull, Sarge."

"Get outta here before I think of something else for you to do." With Emmett's thumb sticking up out of the window, the pickup went bumping into the dark desert morning.

"Two Nora Six, Lima Two-One."

"Lima Two-One," came back Jack's happy voice.

"Go to TAC 4." Robin was telling the pilots to switch to one of the ten tactical frequencies the team used.

"Roger."

"Lima Two-One on TAC 4."

"Jack, the pickup is leaving the scene. Just ignore it."

"Pickup?" I haven't seen a pickup all night. How 'bout you, Oscar?"

"Me? I've been asleep all night."

Robin laughed as he looked up at the Blackhawk. "You guys are a real comedy team, you know that?"

"That's what they say about our flying, too," Oscar said cheerfully.

"Roger," replied Robin as he shook his head.

When he switched back to the ops frequency, Burke advised him they had found a definite suspect trail.

"Two Nora Six, Two Nora Six-One," Robin called Burke.

"Go ahead, Sarge."

"Talk the chopper over to you so they can light up the area ahead of you."

"Ten-Four. We can use it."

"Two Nora Six, Lima Two-One."

"We copy, Nora Six."

As Burke started talking to Jack, Robin walked over to the airplane and climbed in the passenger seat. He looked at his watch. They had been on the ground for almost forty-five minutes. Robin shook his head. It turned out to be one hell of a deal so far. His thoughts turned to Carl Walton.

Walton, a prominent Phoenix attorney and senior partner in a large law firm, held high office in the state Republican Party. He actively lobbied in the state legislature and in Congress. Carl Walton was also a crook.

Robin ran into Walton several times during his career. Each time the meeting resulted in verbal confrontation. When Robin became a detective, he started picking up information about Walton. Sources revealed Walton's illegal activities included money laundering, bribery, and even extortion. Unfortunately, Robin couldn't find anyone to testify about Walton's illegal activities. People were definitely afraid of the man. Having already pulled out his notebook and pen, Robin began writing a prioritized list of things needed to be done to make the plan to nail Carl Walton work.

"Nora Six-One, watch it! There's a suspect at one o'clock laying in a wash sixty yards out!" Oscar warned Burke.

Robin jumped out of the plane and looked anxiously into the distant night. The Blackhawk's searchlight glowed brightly about a mile and a half away.

"Roger, Two-One," Burke answered. He ordered Rick Santos and Matt Howe, who were the security flankers for the tracking team, to move forward and flank the suspect.

"Nora Six-One, Lima Two-One. The suspect is standing up. He is armed with a rifle."

"Nora Six-Five is in the wash," Rick advised.

"Twenty-Two Ten also," said Matt.

"Suspect is now running west," Oscar said tersely.

"Six-Five has him in sight. He's coming towards me."

"I'm headed your direction, Rick," said Matt.

"Hurry up, Matt," Rick almost whispered. "I'm going to jump this guy."

"I'm coming, I'm coming," Matt breathed heavily.

Rick Santos crouched behind sage brush as he watched the suspect rush toward him in a desperate attempt to get away from the searchlight. The suspect held his weapon at port arms, exposing his lower abdomen as a target for Rick's shoulder. Rick laid his rifle down, his heart pounding and his senses exquisitely alert. When he saw the man four strides away in the searchlight, Rick lunged like a ground-hugging missile and buried his right shoulder into the suspect's gut.

"Six-Five has the suspect down and Twenty-Two Ten is with him," Jack said.

"Suspect in custody," Matt breathed into his radio.

Robin felt the tension leave his body. It was harder for him to listen to his men in action than to be in the middle of it with them. He leaned against the plane and took a deep breath. Looking up, he saw the desert sky shimmering with millions of stars. The night cooled so much, it was almost cold. Robin tasted dust in this mouth. He pulled one of his canteens and took a long drink, soothing his dry throat.

Robin looked over at Mark, who was maintaining security over the body and the Blazer.

"That guy giving you any trouble, Mark?"

"Naw, Rob, but it's for damn sure he ain't a conversationalist."

"It looks like we missed the excitement."

"That's okay with me. I've been shot at enough for one night."

"Can't argue with that," Robin laughed. He looked at his watch—they had been on the ground for a little over an hour and thirty minutes. Robin figured it would take the brass and the shooting teams another forty-five minutes to get to his location.

The Blackhawk picked up the tracking team and the captured suspect and landed at the original drop-off point. It kicked up the usual dust storm. Robin cursed as stinging sand engulfed him. He turned his back to the helicopter and hunched his five-foot-ten inch frame down behind the airplane. Robin expected the Blackhawk to shut down; instead, it lifted off again. He watched the chopper's navigation lights head out to the northeast, over the Estrellas.

The team headed over to him. When they were close, he noticed the suspect bent slightly and limping.

"What's with the 'Hawk?" he asked Burke.

"They gotta go pick up the Feds' shooting team."

"How many trails did you see out there?"

"Just dipshit's here," Burke replied, nodding to the suspect.

Robin worried about other suspects in the area. The Blackhawk provided their top cover and light, as well as their communications link. The team's portable radios could not hit any repeater towers from Rainbow Valley and therefore couldn't talk to the DPS communications center.

In his younger years, Burke tracked animals as a hunter and later he tracked men as a Green Beret in Vietnam, so Robin knew if Burke said there were no trails, there were none.

The suspect Rick caught appeared to be a Hispanic man, about five-foot-eight with a stocky muscular build. He was covered in desert sand and dust. The spine clusters sticking out of his legs were evidence he had tangled with some cholla cactus, a definite hazard when you try to escape in the desert at night. He wore a neatly trimmed full beard surrounding a handsome face. Robin noticed the man watching everything closely, not frightened or nervous. Instead, Robin could sense the suspect making mental notes.

"Do we know who this guy is?" Robin asked Rick.

"He has Mexican ID on him that says his name is Manuel Garcia-Galbodon."

"You don't sound convinced that's who he is, Rick."

"I'm not, Rob. This guy's accent is strange. He hasn't said much except that he doesn't speak English, and he shut right up when he found out I speak Spanish. He said enough, though, to make me think this guy ain't Mexican. I think this asshole is Cuban."

"Did you check his hands for Marielito tatts?"

"Yeah, I did. Negative."

"Check his upper arms."

Rick rolled up the suspect's right sleeve and looked at his upper arm with his flashlight, revealing a four-point star with lines running out from it.

"Well, well, well," said Robin. "It looks like we got ourselves a terrorist."

"Jesus! This is getting to be one helluva night!" Burke said, shaking his head.

The symbol for the terrorist organization known as the "Path of the Shining Star" was familiar to Robin and his men from their training in the Special Operations Unit of DPS, the department's SWAT team. Robin's squad comprised Team Six of SOU. In addition, Robin and his men had previous information about a connection between narcotics traffickers and terrorist groups from two informants they worked with south of the border. The team had never caught dope smugglers and terrorists together before. Robin's mind churned questions and theories.

"What kind of rifle did Manny baby have?" Robin asked.

"A full blown AK-47," said Burke. "And Sarge, he had the selector on semi-auto."

Certainty formed in Robin's mind. The suspect used tactics of a well-trained and disciplined operator. He also had experience with combat action because he didn't panic and start shooting aimlessly. The suspect kept his weapon on semi-auto for aimed fire and to conserve ammunition. The guy probably knew how to defeat standard U.S. police procedures.

"Rick, double cuff this asshole and loop a plastic cuff around the handcuffs and his belt and link some a plastic cuffs around his ankles and watch him. He is probably pretty good at hand-to-hand combat."

"I'll stay with him, too," said Burke, "just in case he gets frisky." Robin smiled at Burke's suggestion—he'd trained primarily in hand-to-hand combat in the Green Berets.

As Rick and Burke started to lead the prisoner to a clear spot, Robin stopped Burke.

"Burke, try to get the guy to talk. I'm willing to bet he's the guard for the money, but there is more to this boy than that. I'd like to know just how close he is to ol' Miguel."

"I'll try, Sarge, but he looks like a tough nut."

Robin looked at the six-two, solidly built officer. "So are you. So get with it."

"Okay, okay," Burke said, grinning as he walked over to Rick and the suspect.

Robin turned to Mike Collins and Doug Ariel. "One of you guys go relieve Mark. He's been babysittin' that stiff long enough."

"Okee dokee, Sarge." Collins headed off towards the Blazer.

A few seconds later the Cuban started talking in a raised voice. Burke called Robin over to where he and Rick guarded the prisoner.

"The boy wants to talk to you, Rob," Burke told him.

"What's your problem?" Robin asked the suspect.

Rick was starting to translate into Spanish when the Cuban spat at Rick's feet and said, "I speak English, Puto!"

Robin grabbed the Cuban by the shirt and pulled him up so they were face to face. "Don't you insult my men, you dirt bag!"

"I demand to be treated as a prisoner of war! I am a Colonel in the Army of the Path of the Shining Star!"

"You may think you're some goddamn shining soldier, but you're just another asshole doper to us so sit down in the dirt where you belong!"

With that comment, Robin threw the Cuban down on the ground, half kneeling, half sitting on the desert floor. Robin could feel his face flush with anger. Visions of the many lives he witnessed shattered by cocaine and heroin over the last six years flooded his brain. The fact that this man considered himself above a scum drug smuggler enraged Robin. He wanted to kick the prisoner in the teeth, but Burke's strong, gentle hand on his shoulder held him in check.

"Rob, let it be. He's just another asshole."

"I'm not a criminal!" yelled the Cuban.

"The fuck you're not!" Robin yelled back. "You're worse than the rest of them because you hide behind a cause. You still take most of the money for yourself and your little asshole buddies so you can keep your coke whores happy and play the big shot! But you forgot one thing"

At this, Rick held up his hand to Robin and unbuckled his tactical vest. Slipping it off, he unzipped his flight suit and turned his back to the Cuban. Then, peeling off the top part of the suit, he revealed the back of a dark blue tee shirt. Burke shined his light on Rick's back. The top of the shirt displayed the word POLICE. Underneath, a scene of outer space, complete with planets and a shooting star, sat above the prominently printed words *Guardians of the Universe*. The words "Special Enforcement Unit" were at the bottom of the scene.

Rick turned around and spoke to the prisoner in Spanish. "You see this?" He pointed to the left side of his breast. "Don't you ever forget this," he said with a big grin.

Rick pointed to the star of the Arizona Department of Public Safety. Above the star was the word "Police." Under the star large letters spelled "GOTU." To the uninitiated, it meant "Guardians of the Universe." To the Guardians, Robin's squad, it meant just what it said GOTU. Rick wanted the Cuban to remember.

The Cuban stared at Rick for a moment and then turned to Robin. His eyes flashed a look of realization and recognition in them. "The Guardians," the prisoner spat. "You and your men are already marked for death."

"Well, you are not in such good shape yourself," Robin shot back. "You were supposed to guard the money, and we got that. *And* I imagine Miguel wanted you to take care of his dear little brother, Ramon."

"You have captured Ramon?"

"Oh, don't you wish," Robin taunted. "No, we didn't capture Ramon. We blew his ass away."

The Cuban's back straightened as if someone stuck a knife in it. Robin looked down at him.

"Yes, sports fan, you heard right. Ramon is dead."

The Cuban stared at Robin, his eyes filled with hatred and a hint of fear. Robin seized upon the fear. "Oh, I know. You're hoping Miguel will understand, but I'm telling you he won't. You and I both know Miguel Rodriguez-Lara is nothing but a vicious, low-life doper, and he is going to kill you for this little fuck-up and every relative of yours he can get his hands on."

The Cuban said nothing, but Robin could tell he hit a nerve. He also could tell the Cuban wasn't going to talk. "Watch this asshole, guys. He has a lot more to lose than he first thought he did."

Robin turned and started walking back to the airplane with Matt Howe leaving Burke and Rick with the suspect. The distant sound of a helicopter filtered across the desert. "Shooting team," he said to himself. Matt, who joined Customs a little over two years ago, shook his head. "What in the hell have you gotten me into, Marlette?"

"Welcome to the wonderful world of dope, Matt."

THREE

Captain Tom Pearle, commander of the DPS Narcotics Enforcement Division, stared out the window of the helicopter at the pale desert glowing in the light of the half moon. He saw his ghostly reflection in the plexiglass. Pearle's blond hair, unusually tousled this early morning, topped tired blue eyes. He felt the stubble on his square jaw. His thoughts rested on Robin Marlette and his men. Some of the brass thought Marlette was uncontrollable, but the man had turned a bunch of burnt out cops into the best narcotics squad in the state.

As one supervising agent of the FBI put it, "Marlette's squad is the cutting edge of narcotics enforcement in the state of Arizona."

A great asset for Arizona, but a headache for Tom Pearle.

When Pearle created the Narcotics Special Enforcement Unit, he did it with Robin in mind. Robin reported to Pearle a few weeks later, and Pearle's orders to Robin were simple: Go after the most dangerous narcotics violators in the state. He didn't care what Robin did to nail them, just as long as he kept it legal. Robin was a lawyer, which made Pearle confident there would be no problem in that regard. He smiled as he remembered the grin on Robin's face and the gleam in his eyes.

Despite the fact that the men assigned to Robin's squad had either been in trouble or were close to it, they kicked ass ever since the SEU started to work. In the first year of operation, they arrested fifty-three suspects, all of whom had been involved in violent acts of some kind. Men who hated their jobs now couldn't stay away from work. Each year their numbers of arrests and seizures grew larger.

Pearle looked to his right at Lieutenant Les Hammel as his head nodded in sleep. When Pearle formed SEU, he put it in Hammel's district. Pearle also told the lieutenant it would take both of them to keep up with Robin. Hammel emphatically told Pearle he could handle any sergeant, including Marlette. He asked Pearle to let him do his job and not interfere. The captain agreed, but told Hammel he would be back in a while to ask for the "secret" in dealing with Marlette.

Hammel went for nine months before he walked into Pearle's office one Tuesday afternoon. Hammel told Pearle he thought Robin and his men were out of control. "Why do you think that, Les?" asked Pearle with an almost whimsical smile.

"I don't know, sir, it's just"

"Have they screwed up any cases?"

"No sir. The prosecutors like their cases."

"Are they violating any policy?"

"Not really. Sometimes Marlette stretches policy, but I think a good sergeant has to, occasionally."

"So do I, Les. Look, Robin is a unique leader. He took six men who were not producing and turned them into the best narcotics unit in the state. He's doing it his way, that's for sure. As long as he's doing it legally, why should we get in his way? And *that,* by the way, is the secret to handling Marlette. Don't get in his way."

"Well, maybe I'm wrong, but even though Robin and his men are doing a good job, I think they may be hurting themselves. They work ten to sixteen hours a day, six or seven days a week. Two of them are separated from their wives. It seems to me they are living for the job. That's not good."

Pearle stared past Hammel at a picture on the wall of himself and Robin when they were partners working narcotics back in the early seventies. Pearle and Robin had done two or three buys or arrests a night and at least two search warrants a week. They worked twelve to sixteen hours a day. As Tom Pearle looked at the picture, he envied Robin. Robin knew after the rank of sergeant, work meant riding a desk. So, he never tested for lieutenant. Tom Pearle did. Now Pearle worked as a deskbound manager while Robin did police work.

"Let it be, Les," Pearle told the lieutenant. "They may be a streaking comet, but let them burn bright while they can. They must figure the ride is worth the price."

"Yes sir," sighed the lieutenant.

As the helicopter began to land, Pearle looked at Les Hammel. "A good man trying to do a good job," he thought. "I'm glad he's on my team."

Robin watched the DPS Bell Jet Long Ranger settle onto the desert in a cloud of dust. The whine of the jet eased as the pilot shut the engine down. The paramedic jumped out and assisted the passengers, who Robin recognized as his captain and lieutenant. Although he didn't ask for Pearle in his shooting notification, he had a feeling the captain would show up. He smiled to himself at the incongruity of Tom Pearle's muscular six-foot frame next to Les Hammel, who stood five foot seven and was more round than muscular. Hammel also wore a mustache that never seemed appropriate for his appearance or demeanor.

"If you two are the shooting team, they're scraping the bottom of the barrel," Robin greeted the two men.

"Rob, your respect for command authority never ceases to amaze me," Pearle replied. "The shooting team will be coming in on the Blackhawk."

"Robin, are you and your men okay?"" asked Hammel.

"Yes,sir. Rick may have a sore shoulder from playing high school football star, but other than that we're all fine."

"I assume it is a good shooting?" Pearle asked.

"The shooting is the easy part of the deal. From then on everything gets very serious and very complicated." Robin went on to relate the details of the jump to the two commanders. The two men grew more serious with every event. It didn't take a mental giant to see the Guardians made a spectacular jump with very dangerous implications.

"Well, it looks like your squad did it again," said Hammel." You guys will be famous once more."

"Slow down, Les," cautioned Pearle. "I've seen that look in Marlette's eyes before." Pearle gave Robin a hard look. "Okay, hotshot, let's hear what you're thinking."

Robin took a deep breath. "I want to deliver the money to Walton."

"Goddamn it, Rob! Now you've really gone nuts!" blurted Pearle. "How in the hell do you expect me to convince the chief and the director to let you give away five million *forfeitable* dollars?!"

"I don't fucking care how you do it! That's your job"

"Hold it! Hold it!" yelled Hammel. "Damn! Working in between you two guys is a gigantic pain in the ass!"

Suddenly Robin began to laugh, a deep, spontaneous belly laugh. Pearle started to laugh the same way. Both men laughed so hard they held each other up. Hammel joined in the laughter. Robin reached over and put his hand on the lieutenant's shoulder.

"Lieutenant, Tom and I worked for a sergeant back in the seventies who used to tell us the same thing. I guess some things never change." The three men started to settle down.

"Look, the captain has a point. It's going to be a real tough idea to sell. On the other hand, Captain, you're the one who told me Marlette does it right and we should let him run with the ball."

Pearle looked at Hammel, then at Robin. "Tell me why I should put my neck on the chopping block again."

"Walton is getting five million dollars to make payoffs to some very important assholes. If everything goes right, we have an inside man. Once the delivery of the money is made, we can monitor Walton by surveillance, wiretap, and grand jury subpoena. In the end, we may be able to nail some of those important assholes along with Walton."

Pearle rubbed his forehead as if he was trying to ward off pain he knew loomed ahead.

"I think it's worth it, Captain," volunteered Hammel.

"Since when have you gotten so wild-assed?"

"Well, sir, if Robin and his men are going to keep on working like they have, it might as well be for cases that mean something."

Pearle looked off into the stars blanketing the desert sky, as if looking for a sign to tell him what to do. Then he faced Robin. "I guess I brought you into the division to go after the most dangerous assholes in the business and that's just what you are doing. I don't know whatever possessed me to think it would be easy for me."

"Bullshit. You knew you would have to cover me. You're the politician, not me."

"You don't have to remind me. That's why a lot of commanders don't want you around."

"They just can't handle the pressure," said Robin, grinning. "You know the ol' saying, 'Little deals, little headaches...big deals, big headaches no deals, no headaches,'" Pearle chimed in.

"Okay, okay, Rob. Go get 'em. Just make it right."

"Always."

"Come on, Les," Pearle said to Hammel. "Let's go get one last good breakfast before we get our new ulcers."

Hammel looked at Robin. "Keep me posted on your progress."

"Yes, sir, Lieutenant."

Pearle and Hammel walked back to the Jet Ranger and after a brief conversation with the crew, they all got into the helicopter. Just before the pilot started the engine, Robin heard the Blackhawk coming back. He keyed his radio.

"Two Nora Six, Lima Two-One."

"Lima Two-One."

"Lima Two-One, you might hover out south for a minute. We have a Jet Ranger about to lift off."

"Roger, Nora Six."

Robin figured if the Blackhawk got close enough to the Ranger when it started to lift off, the power of the Blackhawk's rotor wash could be disastrous for the light Jet Ranger. No use in taking any chances.

The Ranger now powered up and was starting to lift off. The pilot banked the agile chopper to the east and headed back to Phoenix.

"Lima Two-One, Two Nora Six, we're coming in."

"Roger, Two-One."

Robin hustled back to the Cessna and got inside to protect himself from the inevitable dust storm. Matt Howe already hunkered down there. They watched the flashing navigation lights of the big helicopter coming towards them. It flared out and touched down. The dust storm created by the rotors rocked the Cessna. Robin heard the engines start to wind down.

"Come on, Matt. Let's go see who we've got to deal with." Robin and Matt climbed out of the airplane and started walking to the Blackhawk. Chris Fleming of the FBI stepped out of the chopper first. A new FBI agent, whose name Robin couldn't remember, followed Chris.

After the FBI agents, came Sergeant Mike Hayes and Officer Tim Becker of the DPS shooting team. Jack opened the pilot's door and gave Robin a casual salute with a big grin. Robin returned the greeting.

"The brass is in here cussin' your ass, Rob," Jack called.

"My brass has already been here, so all they get is leftovers."

"I heard that, Rob." Robin recognized the voice of Bill Grassley, the U.S. Customs Resident Agent in Charge of the Phoenix Office of Investigation. He jumped out of the Blackhawk with Russ Martin, the supervisor of the U.S. Customs Phoenix Air Support Office, behind him. Robin took a deep breath. *More brass to convince.*

Bill Grassley usually agreed with Robin's plans. In fact, the more innovative Robin got, the more Grassley liked it. Robin didn't know what Bill would think about letting five million dollars walk, and he tried to gauge Bill's mood this early morning.

Grassley's green eyes seemed to scan the environment inquisitively. Keenly intelligent, he was much like Robin—get to the point and leave out the bullshit.

The group of men gathered around Robin and Mark. Robin went through the events of the night for a second time, knowing he would have to do it a hundred times more. He did not go into the future plan. Operational security mandated the DPS officers, and the young FBI agent didn't need to know. Robin needed Chris Fleming's help, but first he wanted to privately brief Grassley and Martin about the plan.

"Are all the shooters here so we can interview them?" asked Fleming.

"Yes they are, Chris. Feel free to talk to any of them." Robin reached into his left leg pocket and retrieved the Czech pistol and magazine. He handed them to Chris. "These were on the stiff's body." He then reached into his right leg pocket and retrieved the AK magazine.

"This is his AK magazine. The top rounds in both mags were in the breech of the respective guns."

"Good. Okay, folks, whaddya say we get started. We'll talk to you last, Rob." The four men in the shooting team walked over to the Blazer, where Mike Collins kept the body company.

Robin looked at Bill Grassley. "Bill, we have a chance to turn this jump into one hell of a conspiracy investigation."

"Lay it on me, Rob."

Robin told the details about Newman, Walton, and the money and his own plan to nail the intended payees. Bill Grassley listened intently. When Robin finished, Russ Martin let out a low whistle. Jack and Oscar, who were standing behind the two supervisors, grinned and gave Robin thumbs up, but Bill Grassley had to make the decision and he stood with his arms folded, looking at the ground for a full minute. Finally, he looked up at Robin.

"You know it will take at least three weeks just to get a wiretap authorization, even on an emergency application."

"I know, but I can get state authorization in six days and be up in ten and since the state statute is the same as the federal one, it will fly in federal court. So, we apply to both at the same time, start with the state wire, and convert to the federal when it's authorized."

"I can buy that." Grassley looked over at the Cuban. "How are you going to keep him quiet?"

"I'll need a minute with Chris Fleming to see if I can handle that."

"Whatever backing you need from me with the Bureau, you got it," Grassley replied.

"You think you'll have any trouble getting approval to walk the money?"

"Hell yes, I'm going to have trouble, Rob; at least as much trouble as your brass. But, I have some stock built up. I think I can swing it. Your probable targets will be worth it in my mind."

Robin smiled and put his arm around Grassley's shoulders. "Someday, Bill, you'll be running U.S. Customs."

"Only if you don't screw this case up," Bill replied with a chuckle.

"I'll go talk to Chris and get the Cuban taken care of."

As Robin started walking towards the shooting team, Jack Moore called out to him. "You better make sure Air Support is involved in this shindig."

"I'm going to fly your ass off, Moore," Robin called back. Jack and Oscar high-handed each other and grinned into the night.

As Robin walked over to where the shooting team worked, his mind mulled over troubling thoughts. Walking five million dollars would not be popular with the brass in his department or the Feds in Treasury and the Department of Justice. All law enforcement agencies worked to get large seizures to supplement their beleaguered budgets. Eighty percent of the money seized by the DPS Narcotics Division went to the Highway Patrol Bureau under one pretext or another. The law directed the seized money must go back to the department for narcotics enforcement. The brass decided the Highway Patrol made narcotics arrests, so they got the money. In reality, the patrol got the money because they ran short due to overtime, vehicle maintenance, and the price of gasoline. As the high profile guys, the department had to keep them running up and down the highway.

Robin felt partial to the Highway Patrol himself. He started his career there and he planned to finish it there. In Robin's mind, however, the battle against the drug smugglers and dealers was critical now. Third world countries were behind a large part of the narcotics distribution in the United States, for the express purpose of destroying America and financing terrorist activities. The apparent lack of interest in this knowledge by higher authorities greatly disturbed Robin.

Robin and his men were in the front lines of this war, and they needed money to carry it on. Right now they needed the five million dollars to take down some very powerful men in the act of betraying their country in the war against drugs just to make a buck.

"Yo, Rob."

Robin's thoughts were interrupted by Matt Howe's voice. "Hey man, you're going to have to slow down so I can keep up with you. I know I'm new at this game, but if I just stand around with my thumb up my ass while you do all the work, Grassley is going to ship me to the Ajo Inspection Station to work the graveyard shift." Even in the light of the half moon, Matt looked young to Robin. His closely cropped blond hair and blue eyes were a perfect match for his freckled face. Matt looked like the picture of youthful freshness. Robin thought of how this work would erode that freshness in a few years.

Robin didn't slow his stride. "Matt, I don't mean to leave you out, but I don't have the time to baby you. I'm not slowing down. You have to keep up. Be assertive and jump in anytime. You won't hurt my feelings."

"Look, Rob, I don't know one tenth what you do about this business. I watch you work and I'm dazzled. Hell, I've talked to your guys. You dazzle them! I want to be productive and I want to learn. I can't do it when you leave me out."

Robin smiled and put his arm around Matt's shoulders. "Now that's a load of bullshit, Matt, but flattery will get you everywhere. Come on. Let's go see if we can get something for nothing from the FBI without destroying them as an institution."

"Think we can pull that off?"

"Hell, no," laughed Robin.

The men were laughing when they walked up to the shooting investigators. "Chris, we need to talk to you," Robin said.

Chris Fleming looked at the two men and shook his head with a knowing look. "I detect a conspiracy here."

Robin and Matt pulled Chris aside. "The suspect we have in custody over there is Cuban. He is also a member of the Path of the Shining Light terrorist group."

"Well I'll be damned. You guys really did do a good jump, didn't you? What do you need from me?"

We need you to take the Cuban into custody under the National Security Act, so we can keep him quiet."

"Whoa, brother! You're asking for the whole world. I can't just do that without some damn serious justification."

"Well, then pipe down and listen, Chris." Robin described the details of the night. Chris listened, obviously getting more interested by the minute. Robin knew Chris figured this to be one hell of a public corruption case. In the federal system, the FBI had primary responsibility for investigating those kinds of cases. Chris would want in as the FBI case agent.

Chris Fleming was a twenty-six-year veteran of the FBI and an excellent investigator. Five years experience on the FBI Hostage Rescue Team also made him a good man to have around when the shit hit the fan. Not arrogant or condescending as some FBI agents could be, Chris understood how valuable local cops were in providing information and help on investigations. Local cops were also a good source of federal cases to the savvy FBI agent.

Robin liked Chris because like Robin, Chris had little ambition in terms of promotion. Both men just wanted to put criminals in prison. They loved working in the field. A desk would be a prison to them.

Robin finished giving Chris the details of the night. He knew he sold the case enough to Chris to start the ball rolling on taking the Cuban into custody under the National Security Act. Of course, Chris had a mountain of administrative bullshit to plow through to make the custody status stick, but he maintained a lot of contacts. If anybody could do it, he could.

"Okay," Chris said, "When we get the Cuban to Sky Harbor, I'll get on the phone and get things started. Just remember, I'm in."

"I know, I know. Any other agent but you and I wouldn't have said anything. I'm glad you're in."

"Hell, I wouldn't want to miss one of your shit storms."

As the two men laughed, the fire of another Arizona-scorched desert day began to glow on the horizon.

The shooting team worked on their investigation while Robin's team finished processing the aircraft and vehicles for evidence. In addition to photographs, Rick Santos worked on a diagram of the scene. The team videotaped most of the evidence processing. Mike and Mark changed the tire on the Blazer and found no leaks coming out of the engine from the bullet hits on the vehicle. When the teams were finished, they gathered around the Blackhawk.

Robin scanned his team assembled before him. They were all coated with a mixture of dust and droplets of mud formed by the sweat on their uniforms. "Okay, folks," Rob began. "Nobody talks about what happened out here to anyone. I'm sure there will be lots of people asking questions. Refer them to me. A loose tongue could jeopardize any follow-up investigation. All reports will be disseminated on a need to know basis only." Robin turned to Mike Hayes. "That goes for the shooting team also, Mike."

"You got it, Rob."

"Good. Jack, Burke and I will take the Cessna in. Follow us if you would." Jack nodded in agreement. Both Robin and Burke Jameson were private pilots.

"Rick, you and Mike take the Blazer to the Sky Harbor office."

"Ten-Four, Sarge."

"Chris, are you assuming responsibility for the body?"

"Yeah, and I'm formally taking custody of the Cuban now at least until I'm told otherwise."

Robin smiled at Chris. Chris wouldn't do that unless he had the whole thing figured out.

"Okay, let's do it, troops," said Robin. "We'll work out the rest when we get to the office. Now mount up! We're burning daylight!"

FOUR

R obin's squad worked another ten hours before all the loose ends were tied up. The mounds of paperwork he needed to do, when he could hardly keep his eyes open, was the hardest part of deals like this. He fought sleep with gallons of coffee. The coffee itself did not necessarily guarantee he would stay awake, but the fact that he had to urinate every thirty minutes did.

Robin's immediate priority focused on the security of the operation. Within four hours of landing at Sky Harbor, the heads of all the agencies involved ordered the strictest secrecy be maintained on the case. The chain of command became simplified, with Robin in tactical command subject only to the orders of Assistant United States Attorney Jim Adams, who spoke for the joint agency chiefs. For a cop, it doesn't get any better.

The jurisdictional issues worked out well for Robin. DPS assumed lead agency for the investigation. It would be a joint state and federal Organized Crime Drug Enforcement Task Force (OCDETF) prosecution. Because the case involved public corruption, the FBI had primary authority over that aspect federally. U.S. Customs had primary authority over the money smuggling. Although the FBI and Customs could both do the money laundering investigation, Robin all but insisted the IRS do that part of the investigation. They were by far and away the best at it.

At this early stage, Robin thought he had a chance to keep DEA out of the investigation. Robin did not like DEA and DEA did not like Robin because he had kicked them off two prior OCDETF cases for not being willing to do the grunt work. He knew DEA would be snooping around to find out what happened and try to get into the case because it involved Rodriquez-Lara's cartel.

Robin's thoughts were interrupted by the ringing of the phone. When he answered it, Emmett's happy deep voice greeted him.

"Hey, Boss, you still awake?"

"Yeah, how 'bout you, cowboy?"

"Shit, Rob, what this guy has told us will keep us all awake for a long time."

"Good stuff, huh?"

"Sarge, this is going to be the biggest case we ever dreamed of doing. This guy is going to do some very big assholes."

"Okay, Emmett. I should be there in about an hour."

"No hurry, Sarge. We're comfortable."

"See ya."

"Bye."

Emmett's phone call reminded Robin he needed to get some relief troops to watch Newman. *Time to call the crazies of Victor Thirty-Two squad.* Robin picked up the phone and punched squad Sergeant Ernie Jackson's home number. The phone rang.

"Jackson residence, Judy speaking."

"Hi, Judy. This is Uncle Rob. Is your Dad home?"

"Hi, Uncle Rob. Dad's home. I'll get him."

"Thanks, Judy."

A few seconds later, Ernie came on the phone. "Yo, Rob! What's up?"

"I need help, Ernie."

"Will it be worth my while?"

"Well, asshole, since Sunday is your day off, you'll at least get overtime."

"Good point! When and where?"

"I need you and two of your guys at our hideout as soon as you can."

"Okay, but just tell me this. Is this another one of your wild-assed marathon shit storms?"

"It looks like it."

Robin could hear Ernie take a deep breath. "Goddamn, Marlette. I don't know why I let you get me into these things."

"You do it because you're a hard chargin,' raggedy ass street cop like me, Ernie. So quit fuckin' around and get moving."

"Okay, dickhead. We'll see you in about an hour or so."

"Good. Adios."

"Bye."

Robin finished his paperwork and walked out to the undercover van the department issued him, a new 1988 tan one-ton Chevrolet complete with built-in surveillance equipment and gear lockers built to Robin's specifications. Ten minutes later, he pulled into the parking lot of the Casablanca Motel. The owner of the Casablanca let the Guardians have two adjoining rooms for free. At one time, the owner's daughter became hooked on cocaine. The Guardians put her dealer in prison for fifteen years.

Robin went to room 268 and knocked twice, paused, and knocked once. Emmett answered the door, his muscular six-four frame filling the opening.

"Where is Newman?" Robin asked.

"He's asleep."

"Jackson and two of his guys are on the way to relieve you."

"Sounds good."

Robin looked over at John Lucheck, sound asleep in a chair.

"He tried to stay awake," shrugged Emmett, "but he just couldn't overcome his federal training."

"He'll be all right," chuckled Robin.

Emmett walked over to the small refrigerator in the room and took out two beers. He tossed one over to Robin. Emmett lifted his can as a toast and said, "To celebrate the start of a great case." Robin lifted his can and took a swallow of the cold beer. He pulled out his .45 and laid it on the table. When he wore street clothes, as he did now, he carried his gun in a Bruce Nelson Summer Special holster worn inside his pants. Taking the gun out eased the pressure around his waist. Robin sat down in one chair and propped his feet up on another. He could feel the tension leaving his body.

The two men sat at the table and discussed the general strategy of the new case. Emmett's report of Newman's debriefing impressed Robin. The several people he named were very powerful in politics and business. Newman acted as the bagman for the payoffs to these people. If they could get the additional evidence they needed to make this case airtight, it would be the best case yet.

Although both men were relaxing, they were alert to sounds outside the room, listening for anything out of place. Once, somebody walked by the room and both men silently and swiftly moved into defensive positions. The footsteps stopped momentarily and then moved on. Robin and Emmett sat down again after visually clearing the outside through the windows and the peep hole in the door.

About a half an hour later, they heard more footsteps. Emmett moved behind the wall that separated the bathroom from the main room. Robin stood against the door jam. Both officers had their weapons ready. The confidential knock sounded through the door.

"Yo!" said Robin.

"Yo ho, mate!" Robin looked through the peephole to see Ernie making ridiculous faces on the other side. Robin opened the door to let Ernie in, along with Rocky Barnett and Marv Allen of Ernie's squad. As they walked in, all three men's eyes were sizing up the environment of the motel room. Emmett came from behind the wall, to Rocky's and Marv's nods of approval. Rocky looked at John Lucheck, still fast asleep, and said, "fucking Feds." He went over and kicked Lucheck on the bottom of his foot.

"Wake up, Special Agent Lucheck, time to go home." Rocky did not say "Special Agent" with the reverence which some federal officers are fond.

Robin began to brief Ernie Jackson and his two men on the case to date. The men's flashing eyes and broad grins showed their obvious excitement. Good cops always want to get the big fish. Robin's faith in these men as good cops had paid off before. He could see it paying off again.

Necessarily, Ernie Jackson's enthusiasm for the Guardians' new case came from a different perspective than the men of his squad. While assisting the Guardians on a short-term basis did not pose a problem, committing his squad to a long-term investigation did. It took the brass to approve a long-term commitment. Ernie wanted to be on this case, so he had to sell it to his brass. Even though he could see the Guardians latched on to one hell of a case, selling his brass on working with the Guardians would not be easy.

In the past cases when Victor Thirty-Two squad worked with the Guardians, the results were always great. The cases were also laced with controversy, however, and very few high-ranking officers want controversy—especially when the case is initiated by another department. Everybody knew taking down the big fish meant inquiries from political figures. These suspects used the high-powered lawyers and the political connections to cause interference. Since some high-ranking police officers harbored the fragile dream of successfully running for political office after retirement, to them controversy floated like a fart in the car on the first date. So, Ernie had his work cut out for him. As he listened to Robin, he planned his approach to the Phoenix Police brass.

Ernie's and Robin's squads began training together on a regular basis when the Phoenix PD gave Ernie's squad functions similar to Robin's. The men soon became a tight-knit group. Robin and Ernie became close personal friends and did family outings together. Soon the two squads were doing joint investigations with the FBI and U.S. Customs, with the Guardians and Victor Thirty-Two squad forming the core of the investigative team. By the intensity of the fire burning in Robin's eyes this day, Ernie knew the new case looked to be the largest joint investigation yet. When Robin and Emmett finished bringing the Phoenix officers up to date on the case, Rocky let out a low whistle.

"Ol' Miguel is going to be one pissed off son of a bitch."

"You're right, Rock," said Robin. "There is no doubt he'll be throwing shit into the game."

"Fuck Rodriguez," growled Ernie. "We're all trained on how to handle assholes like him. It's the other targets that are going to make my brass real nervous about letting us get involved in this shindig."

"Aw, come on, Sarge," said Marv angrily. "There's no way you can let those bastards keep us out of this case."

"Whose side are you on?" Ernie asked Marv with a pained voice.

"Marv's right, ya ol' fart," chided Robin. "You know you can pull it off. You always have before."

"Yeah, and that's why I've got gray hair and ulcers and you're no help either, asshole," said Ernie, pointing an accusing finger at Robin.

By now everybody in the room laughed at Ernie's perceived predicament. Ernie looked around and then hung his shaking head in frustrated resignation. This made everyone laugh louder. Robin laughed so hard tears were welling in his eyes. A forceful knock at the door connecting the adjoining room interrupted the laughter. Emmett jumped up and opened the door, revealing a haggard and bleary-eyed Newman standing in his underwear.

"Am I going to get some sleep or are you guys just going to fuck with me?"

"It's okay, buddy," said Emmett, "You needed to be up to meet these guys anyway."

Emmett introduced Ernie, Rocky, and Marv to Newman, who acknowledged the introduction with a wave and a grunt.

"Can you guys keep it down so I can get some sleep now?" Newman asked in a surly tone.

"Yeah buddy, hit the rack," replied Emmett.

Newman turned and shuffled off toward his bed as Emmett closed the door gently behind him.

"Hey, that's some asshole you're givin' us to babysit," said Rocky.

"Just remember he's on our side for now, Rock," said Robin.

"I know, I know," Rocky replied, smiling at Robin as he stood up. He told Ernie he would be right back and walked out the door. Ernie then launched a soliloquy about how Robin and the Phoenix Police brass were giving him ulcers because he was always in the middle of their disputes. Robin just smiled as he stood up and got ready to leave with Emmett and John. Emmett opened the door just as Rocky returned with an innocuous Cordura case everyone knew contained a Heckler & Koch MP5 submachine gun.

"Rocky, I thought you and your Sig .45 could handle anything," kidded Emmett.

"We can handle any amount of assholes up to ten. After that we require only minimal assistance."

"Heeeey," said Marv in a hurt voice.

"Excuse me, Marv. I'm, of course, speaking for my associate also."

"So you and Marv can only handle ten assholes at once?" Robin asked innocently.

"We are simply trying to be modest," said Rocky with a sweeping bow.

"Gentlemen, your modesty is overwhelming," said Robin with a return bow.

Everybody broke out in laughter again. Robin gave an informal salute and closed the door behind the leaving officers.

"Do you think that's really necessary, Rocky?" asked Ernie, pointing to the MP5.

Rocky looked at his sergeant with a serious look. "Maybe not today, Sarge, but as pissed off as Rodriguez is gonna be, it won't be long."

Ernie took a long, deep breath and nodded.

FIVE

Robin fought to stay awake. The engine and the air conditioner droned hypnotically as he drove through sparse traffic on the freeway. He turned up the police radio so the incessant chatter would annoy him. It didn't work very well. Normally, Robin maintained awareness of his surroundings, but not at this moment.

A constant replay of the recent events streamed through his mind, evoking a rainbow of emotion: the excitement and satisfaction of a good bust, the anticipation of the upcoming investigation, the disquiet of Rodriguez's possible revenge. The stream stopped and Robin's mind focused on Rodriguez. He wondered if Rodriguez knew about his brother yet. Robin mulled over his possible reactions and wondered how he would find out. Who would be the unlucky messenger? Robin didn't doubt Rodriguez could throw some serious shit into the game. "Well, Miguel," Robin said aloud, "you better make it good, because we're going to take your ass down and take it down hard." A grim smile formed on Robin's lips.

Robin turned the corner onto his street. It worried him slightly that he did not really remember driving the last couple of miles. He parked his van, turned off the engine, and just sat there for a minute. Exhausted, he opened the door and slowly climbed out. As he started for his front door, a loud, young voice yelled "Dad!" from behind him. Robin turned around and saw his ten-year-old son Eddie rocketing towards him on a bike. When Eddie got close to his father, he slammed on his brakes and skidded to a halt with a giant grin. One look at Eddie positively proved his lineage. It made Robin intensely proud.

"Hey Dad, remember you said we were going to play some baseball today?"

"Yes, I remember, Eddie."

"Well, can Aaron and Bobby play too?"

Robin felt pangs of guilt he'd felt far too many times before. "I can't play right now, son. I've been up all night and I need some sleep."

"Ahwww, Dad!"

Robin could see tears building in his son's eyes. He put his arms around Eddie, who buried his face into his father's chest. "We were very busy last night. Let me get some sleep and if it's still light out when I wake up, we'll play some ball. It will be cooler then anyway."

Eddie looked up into Robin's eyes. "Okay, Dad." He got back on his bike. "Did you catch any bad guys last night?"

"We caught some big time bad guys last night."

"Radical, dude! Well I gotta go, Dad. Love you."

"Love you too, son," said Robin as he watched his son rocket back up the street.

Robin walked up his driveway to the door of his house, a modest single story home in the Ahwatukee neighborhood of South Phoenix. The home had a white stucco exterior and a double car garage with desert landscaping in the front yard. Robin hated desert landscaping, but it made the yard easy to maintain. At least a large palo verde tree provided shade. When he reached the door his wife, Karen, opened it from the inside.

Robin's wife stood two inches shorter than him, with medium length auburn hair surrounding a creamy smooth face. Her deep green eyes projected an intensity accentuated by an expressive mouth with inviting lips. Robin perpetually believed those lips begged to be kissed, which he did. *How I love this woman!*

"Hi, babe," he said. She hugged him tight. "What's the matter, honey?" Robin asked.

"What's the matter? You don't come home last night. I stay awake all night long worrying about you. Then you call me at seven in the morning and tell me you've been in another shootout and you ask me what the problem is."

"I'm sorry, honey. I didn't mean to scare you."

"Robin, this makes three shootings for your squad in five years. It makes five shootings for you since you've been a cop. How long do think you can keep this up before you get shot?"

"I can keep it up as long as we do as well as we did last night. Everybody did what they were supposed to do and none of us got hurt."

"Damn it, Robin. I know your squad is good. The whole damn world knows it. But you have told me yourself that a lot of it is luck—and luck can run out."

"So what do you want? Should we quit and just let the assholes have a free run?"

"Who is 'we'? I'm talking about you. I'm not married to anybody else. You're a lawyer, for God's sake. You can be a prosecutor and fight the criminals that way. At least you won't have to get shot at."

"I've told you before. The cases are made in the street. If the cops do it right, the case is good. If the cops fuck it up, then the case is fucked up and there's nothing a prosecutor can do about it. That's why I'm a cop."

"You're a cop because you need the identity the badge gives you. There is something inside of you that needs the stupid, macho bullshit of being a cop."

Robin fought to control his temper. He and Karen had been over this ground many times before. He knew she spoke partly out of fear. He also knew she meant what she said. Whenever they got into these arguments, nobody won.

"Karen, I don't want to argue with you. For now, being a cop is my job. I'm dead tired right now and need sleep. I'll end this conversation by just saying I love you."

Robin kissed Karen on the cheek, feeling the stiffness in her body. He squeezed her hand and headed for the bedroom. Karen had already closed the blinds, turned on the ceiling fan, and turned Robin's side of the bed down. He took off his gun, handcuffs, and extra magazines and put them up on his closet shelf. He took off his clothes and let them drop in a pile at his feet. It felt so good to get them off.

As he climbed into bed, he heard Karen crying in the kitchen. He started to get up to go to her, but then thought better of it. He didn't want the fight to start again. Robin lay back in the bed. Wearily, his mind started to float

"Rob, honey, it's all right. You're having a nightmare." Robin's mind struggled for consciousness as Karen's voice filtered through the terror gripping him. He breathed fast, his right hand closed tightly.

"Robin, wake up. You're having a nightmare." Robin looked around him and realized he was in his bed, Karen shaking him. He put his hand on her arm to stop her. His body relaxed and he lay back down.

"What were you dreaming about?"

"These guys were coming at me, shooting. I tried to shoot back, but my gun jammed"

Karen put her arms around his neck and kissed him. "Robin, I love you. I'm sorry about the fight."

Robin pulled her to him. "It's all right, honey. I know it isn't easy for you."

"I'm proud of what you do, Rob. It just scares me. I don't want to lose you. I need you."

"I love you more than anything, Karen and I need you a helluva lot more than you need me."

Karen raised her head and smiled at Robin. "Are you hungry?"

"What time is it?"

"Six o'clock. You've been asleep a little over four hours."

"I'd better get up or I'll never get to sleep tonight."

"Oh, by the way, there's three little baseball players waiting for you out front."

"The kid never gives up, does he?"

"Of course not. He takes after his father."

"Well, I promised him, so I better get with it." Robin gave Karen long, deep kiss. "I love you, Karen."

"I love you to, Robin."

Robin got up and put on a pair of shorts and his "Staff" tee shirt from the DEA Command School. Despite the battles Robin fought with DEA, they still asked him to do a presentation on how to supervise narcotics officers. Robin felt a sort of satisfaction from the fact that DEA still thought enough of his abilities to ask him to teach other agencies about narcotics enforcement.

Robin went into the bathroom and splashed water on his face. As he dried off, he looked at this face in the mirror. His forty-two years were beginning to show in the form of gray flecks in his black hair and crow's feet at the corners of eyes. Speckles of white colored the dark stubble around his strong jaw. He gave his hair a quick once-over with a brush. Karen often said she wished he had more vanity. He wanted to believe she was kidding.

He walked into the kitchen where Karen had set out rice, baked chicken, and a beer for him. Robin quickly ate the meal. Afterward, he leaned back in his chair, holding his satisfied stomach. "That was good."

"How many times have I told you that you eat too fast?" chided Karen.

"You'd get this way too if you had only a thirty-minute meal period."

"Robin, you only had thirty-minute meal periods when you were on patrol, and you haven't been on patrol for five years."

"Old habits are hard to break."

"I know. I've been trying to break one for twenty-two years."

"That wouldn't be the one that's twenty-two years and four kids old, would it?"

"What if it is?"

Robin took Karen into his arms. "I hear it's an impossible habit to break."

"Right now I think that depends on how happy you make a certain ten-year-old."

"Right! Well, I guess I'll be off on that mission then."

Robin kissed Karen and went back to the bedroom and got his baseball glove. He walked to the front door and opened it to see a very serious marble game in progress. Eddie looked up and saw his Dad.

"Anybody here interested in a little baseball?" asked Robin.

Three little boys immediately scrambled to pick up marbles and gather up baseball gear. Robin chuckled to himself as Eddie grinned so widely his face threatened to break. The group started to leave when Robin's seventeen-year-old son, Casey, drove up.

"Hey," Robin yelled to Casey. "You want to help me give these heathens some baseball practice?" Casey gave the typical teenage dubious look back to Robin.

"Look, I promise to make it a state secret if you do or I'll get it certified 'cool' by the current favorite rock group of the day."

"Dad, you're such a dork," Casey laughed, and shook his head. He reached back into his '73 Volkswagen Bug and retrieved his baseball glove. Upon realizing both his father and his big brother were going to play baseball, Eddie's grin grew even more. The group gathered up and headed for the elementary school baseball field. Somehow, Robin and Casey ended up carrying all the gear.

"Where's Laurie?" Robin asked about his sixteen-year-old daughter.

"She went to band practice today," replied Casey.

"Why on Sunday?"

"Because they really screwed up at last night's game."

"How's she getting home?"

"Chad Wilson will bring her home."

"Oh, great! You just stand by and let a boy bring your sister home?"

"Get real, Dad," Casey said, rolling his eyes.

Robin laughed. "It's okay, son. I'm just kidding, I think."

Robin watched with amused wonder as the three little guys wandered all over the street on the way to the ball field. They inspected almost every rock, stick, and bug with great curiosity and conversation. Robin considered the fact that the boys probably inspected each one of these items a thousand times before.

When the group arrived at the school ball field, Robin took up pitching duties and Casey did the catching. The three boys took turns batting and playing the field. After an hour, the boys said they were tired and went off to play on the monkey bars. Robin and Casey sat down at one of the several lunch tables.

"Well, son, you'll be graduating in one week. Feel any different?"

Casey's steady blue eyes met his father's. "No. Should I?"

"It's not mandatory, but a whole lot of new things are going to be happening to you. You need to be thinking about them."

Casey adjusted the ball cap that seemed to be an integral part of his nature. "Dad, I'm ready for college. Besides, it's not like when Cathy went to the U of A. I'm only going to be a couple of miles away."

Casey won a baseball scholarship to Arizona State University. Casey's ready smile immediately engaged most people he met. It belied his exceptional physical strength and agility. He was an outstanding player for his high school team, and an honor student to boot. Robin knew his son to be an intelligent, capable young man. He also knew Casey was starting to feel his oats, and Robin felt some words of caution were in order.

"It may not be as easy you think, son. You'll be making your own decisions, and what's more important, you'll be responsible for them. You've done a good job in high school and got yourself into the college you wanted. Now you have to pay attention to college because it means the rest of your life."

Casey looked at his hands folded on the table. Robin could see the muscles in his son's jaw working.

"I'm not trying to piss you off, Casey. I've been in the world a little longer than you, and I've made many mistakes. I don't want you to make the same ones. I'm trying to let you benefit from my experience."

"You couldn't have that many mistakes. You and Mom have us in a nice house and have raised a pretty damn nice bunch of kids. You're an outstanding cop and a pretty famous one too; at least your name's in the paper a lot."

"Believe me, son, I've made plenty of mistakes and I'll guarantee you that having your name in the newspaper isn't a good measure of success. I guess what I'm trying to say is that whenever you can, think about what you're doing before you do it."

"You mean like always check your back trail?"

Robin looked at his son, puzzled for a minute, and then laughed.

"You see, Dad, in your own way you've already taught me the things you're talking about. All the camping and hiking trips, the shooting lessons, all the lessons on hand-to-hand combat. These gave me the two things you've always harped on - confidence and discipline. I believe in those principles, Dad. You did a good job."

Robin looked at his son and realized Casey had indeed been giving the future some thought. Maybe Casey should be a little cocky right now. It might help him get through some of the hard lessons all young adults have to go through.

. "Okay, Casey. It looks like you've got some of this figured out. Just remember your Mom and I will always be here if you need us."

"I know, Dad."

"Well, let's round up the heathens and head home."

The night crept in as Robin called to the younger boys. The heat of the day still lingered, but the relief of not having the sun beating down always felt good. The boys did not want to stop playing, but Robin gently gave them no choice.

During the walk back home, the boys got themselves goosey by making up ghost stories. Casey really got them going. Robin looked up at the sky. The Phoenix city lights dimmed the blanket of stars he marveled at last night. He wondered if Miguel Rodriquez knew about his brother's untimely demise yet. He also wondered if the Guardians could really pull this deal off. It promised to be the most ambitious operation they have ever attempted, and a million different things could make it explode in their faces. Robin mentally shrugged. *That's life in the fast lane.*

A Phoenix police car pulled alongside the group driven by Sergeant Gabe Martinez. Robin and Gabe had become friends when Robin worked patrol on the Phoenix freeway system. He and Gabe worked the same area and had backed each other up numerous times. When Gabe promoted to sergeant, he became the supervisor for the area where Rob lived. He often stopped by for a cup of coffee.

A giant of a man, Gabe stood six-two and lifted weights every day. Robin noticed the boys gawking at Gabe's biceps.

"Hey, Rob! What's up?"

"Gabriel! Good to see you. Need a cup?"

"Naw, we're short-handed tonight, so I gotta keep movin'. I saw you and just wanted to say hi."

"Well, I'm glad you did." Robin walked over closer to Gabe and leaned closer to the window.

"Gabe, we are in an investigation involving some pretty bad dudes. We killed one last night. I would appreciate it if you could keep an eye out around here."

"Not a problem, my friend. You know we do anyway, just for drill. But I will heighten the awareness factor. Anybody in particular we should be looking for?"

"Mexican nationals in the area would be a tipoff."

Gabe looked at his friend. "Rob, you really look worried."

"I am, Gabe. I am."

"Hang tough, amigo. We'll do anything we can."

"I know, buddy. Thanks."

With a wave to the boys, Gabe drove off.

When Robin and his sons walked into the house, Karen was watching the news. She turned to Robin. "They talked about your shooting on the news."

"Did they make us sound good or bad?"

"It sounded as good as killing somebody can sound, but they also said at least one person escaped. You didn't tell me that."

Robin just answered with a grunt. He opened the refrigerator and got a beer, opened it, and sat down next to Karen. He put his arm around her and looked into her eyes. She knew he didn't tell her everything.

"I wonder what it would be like to be married to a more passive woman."

"That's something you will never find out, my dear."

"Oh well," Robin sighed, smiling and calm on the outside. Inside, the disquieting thought of Rodriquez's revenge chilled him. If the news covered the shooting, then Rodriquez knew about his brother. The party was about to begin.

SIX

Juan Trinadad-Nunez stared straight ahead at the fire in the large stone fireplace. Although anger rose inside of him, he did an admirable job of controlling it. It had been a very long time since a man talked to him like this and lived. Since Miguel Rodriguez had made Juan a very wealthy man, however, Miguel would not die for his harsh words. Juan knew Miguel's tirade flowed from his brother's death at the hands of the troublesome "Guardians." Juan couldn't be sure grief fueled Miguel's anger. More likely, Miguel's belief that his power over the world had been severely breached contributed to his state of mind. Of course, the missing money did not help.

Miguel told Juan the lawyer Walton, who had called only a short time ago, informed Miguel about his brother's death. Walton learned of it on a television newscast. A case of unfortunate timing caused Juan to be visiting Miguel when the call came. Miguel threw an Inca sculpture, smashing it to pieces against the wall, as his first reaction to the news. He began screaming at Juan. The screaming continued.

"I trust *you* to make sure these deliveries get done right! I *trusted* you to take care of my brother! All I see is a fucking failure!"

"This kind of delivery has been made many times before, Miguel, without problems. I will find out what went wrong and fix it."

"Fix it! *Fix it!* How are you going to bring my brother back?!"

"Miguel, I pleaded with you not to let your brother go. He was not ready."

Rodriguez slammed his fist down on the desk next to Juan. Juan did not flinch. Miguel's long thin face loomed a foot away from Juan's; both men were looking into each other's eyes. Miguel's eyes burned with an angry madness. Juan held his steady, without fear. After several seconds of silence, with only the crackle of the fire and the cool hiss of the refrigeration coming through the vents, Miguel's shoulders slumped and his head hung over his chest. He slowly straightened up, turned to the chair across from Juan, and fell into it, staring at Juan with vacant eyes.

Juan looked at his employer. Very few people in Mexico could compete with Miguel's power, but Juan knew a good deal of that influence came from Juan's own ruthlessness. In fact, Juan believed he held the power. He only let Miguel head the organization because Juan did not want the headache. He already had more money than he could ever spend in his lifetime. Why bother?

Miguel looked pathetic. The "most powerful man in the world" doesn't slump in a chair with a blank stare. For a second Juan thought he might kill Miguel and take over the organization. No, it would be too much trouble, he thought. Instead he would appease the man and prove again *he* held the power.

"Miguel, I bear the death of Ramonito heavy in my heart. Although not my brother in blood, I loved him like a brother as I love you. Let me exact revenge upon these common policemen."

Miguel's upraised hand interrupted Juan. Miguel leaned forward in his chair, his hands folded on his knees. He spoke in a hoarse and conspiratorial voice.

"I want you to learn everything you can about these men. Find out which one them killed my brother. I want them dead, but first I want them to be in anguish. I want them to feel a thousand times more pain than I feel. Find out how to do that, my friend, and we shall have our revenge. That is your mission."

Juan's eyebrows rose at the word "mission." It meant Miguel was playing freedom fighter again. Juan got up from his chair and stood somewhat at attention.

"I will take care of it, mi Jefe."

Miguel stood up and put his hand on Juan's shoulder. "I know you will, my faithful friend," he said solemnly.

Juan turned and walked out of the room, feeling awkward. Once outside, though, he relaxed and thought of the irony of his "mission." Juan had always thought Ramon was an idiot; he cared nothing about his death. Getting rid of him equaled getting rid of a painful pimple on his ass.

Juan walked down the large, red tiled hallway, his footsteps echoing off the walls. He approached a guard, who stood out of respect. Juan nodded in acknowledgement. He turned Walton's words over in his mind. The news media had reported Ramon's death, but said nothing about Newman or Carlos or the money. *This is very interesting. If the police captured them, they would have announced this as well. So perhaps they escaped. They did say that at least one person escaped. They must have also escaped with the money, or the American police would have definitely bragged about such a seizure. Maybe things aren't so bad after all.* Juan felt better already.

Juan walked out on to the veranda. He could see the entire south side of the "ranch." Actually, its thick walls and fortified buildings made it a formidable fortress. From his second-story view he could see no less than twelve heavily armed guards he and Carlos personally chose and trained. In all, over forty men guarded the complex twenty-four hours a day. Currently, twenty-five tons of marijuana, eight thousand kilos of cocaine, and three thousand kilos of heroin sat in two large barn-like buildings on the premises. The guards were necessary.

The sound of an aircraft engine starting up prompted Juan to walk to the corner of the veranda. He gazed at the airstrip just south of the compound wall. In the fading light of dusk, he saw a twin engine Beechcraft taxiing. The aircraft bore a Canadian registration number. Juan leaned forward and rested his forearms on the veranda railing. The Canadians developed almost as great an appetite for cocaine as the Americans, he thought. Juan smiled. They were also willing to pay more.

The Beechcraft reached the end of the runway and turned around. The pilot revved one engine, then the other. Then both engines gathered power in unison as the plane strained against its brakes. The aircraft started to roll forward and quickly built speed. Juan lost sight of it as it went behind the buildings on the east side of the compound. He walked back around the corner in time to see the Beechcraft in a steep left bank. It rolled out to a northerly heading at about two hundred feet off the ground. *Crazy pilot,* he thought, shaking his head.

Juan watched the plane disappear into the twilight. He kept his eyes to the north, even when he could no longer see the aircraft. He stared into America. *The absurd Americans believe their country is the most powerful in the world. Yet they are powerless against this ranch, only fifteen miles south of the border. Every day the organization sent more and more of the most destructive force in the world into the United States, and every day the very fiber of that country grew weaker.* A proud smile formed on Juan's lips. He felt great pride in his contribution to the destruction of arrogant America.

Juan deeply breathed in the warm, Sonoran desert night air. He must tell Maria that Carlos would be delayed in returning from Arizona—not an unpleasant task for Juan. Maria's beauty took him the minute he saw her. Her mere presence in the same room excited him. Maria, being the wife of Carlos, complicated his feelings. He respected and truly liked Carlos—he was one of the few men Juan did respect. This, however, did not deter him from trying to impress Maria. In fact, Juan wanted to win Maria for himself, friendship notwithstanding.

Juan walked downstairs from the veranda and out to the east side of the main ranch house to the house where Carlos and Maria lived. Juan felt his quickened heartbeat fueled by anticipation as he approached Maria's door. He quickly straightened himself out and ran his hands over his hair. Juan gave three sharp knocks on the door.

When the door opened and Juan saw Maria, he became nervous and unsettled. She did not glow or smile as usual. Maria's face looked drawn; her eyes empty and exhausted. She did not say anything to Juan, but simply stared at him.

"Maria, I…I just wanted to tell you Carlos will be late in getting back from across the border." Juan cursed himself for stammering.

Maria's eyes brightened. "Carlos is safe?"

"Of course, my dear," said Juan, making his voice mask his uncertainty.

Maria seemed to almost collapse at this news. Juan reached out and took hold of her arm as support. She in turn held on to his arm.

Looking up, she smiled weakly at him, her dark brown eyes meeting his with gratitude. Juan's heart pounded and his mouth became dry. He had never been this close to Maria before.

"I am sorry for my weakness, Juan. I fear I have spent too many nights waiting for my husband to come back from somewhere."

"Maria, you talk nonsense. Carlos is clever and strong. Nothing could ever happen to him." Juan realized an opportunity and added an afterthought. "*I* would not let anything happen to him."

Maria lowered her head as if in supplicant thanks. At least Juan viewed it that way. She smiled again, and, stepping back, quietly closed the door. Juan continued to stand in front of the door for a frustrated minute. He sighed deeply, turned, and walked away, angry with himself for not being more assertive about getting inside the house. He trudged off to the guards' quarters. He needed a strong drink and the company of strong men.

Maria moved through the house, turning off the lights. When she reached the bedroom, she fell on to the bed, sobbing and exhausted. Maria both worried about her husband and cursed him for leaving her in the company of such scum as Juan Trinidad and Miguel Rodriguez. Living her life for the "good of Cuba" no longer mattered. She wanted only a quiet life with her husband and to be a mother. She realized neither of these wishes.

Maria rose and sat on the edge of the bed, holding her head in her hands. The curls at the end of her flowing black hair tumbled into her lap. The excitement of marrying an intelligence agent deceived her. She had thought it would be glamorous diplomatic gatherings laced with intrigue. There were glamorous positions in Cuba's intelligence community, but not for Carlos. A dedicated agent, he wanted only those assignments that directly contributed to the goals of his country. The main goal was to destroy the United States of America. Encouraging and feeding America's narcotics habit contributed to that goal. Carlos facilitated the flow of narcotics into the United States. He used the narcotics smuggling apparatus to get Cuban and other third world agents across the border. All of this disturbed Maria for reasons she did not fully comprehend.

Maria stood up and removed her robe, placing it on the foot of the bed. The glow from the perimeter security lights filtered through the window, allowing Maria to see herself in the mirror across from her. She worked hard at keeping her youthful beauty intact for her husband. She very much wanted him with her so he could enjoy her charms. This thought caused the tears to flow again. Maria fell into the large bed, so lonely without Carlos. She eventually cried herself to sleep.

Robin looked at Karen lying naked before him. The shimmering moonlight came through their bedroom window and warmly illuminated her body. Strands of her auburn hair lay across her dark, smoldering green eyes. Karen's pink lips parted slightly as her breath began to quicken. *God, I love this woman!*

Robin lay down next to her and pulled her close to him. His hand moved slowly, caressing her hip as he kissed her gently on the lips. He lightly ran his fingers over her forehead, first across and then in gentle circles. He kissed her upper lip and then her lower lip and the corners of her mouth. Then he kissed her on her mouth and their lips parted to accept each other's tongue. There they lovingly played.

Robin's hand wandered over Karen's breasts and stomach and between her legs. He lightly tickled her inner thighs, gradually working up to where they met. Ever so lightly, he played there until Karen's passion began to rise. His fingers began to gently massage and separate, moving to where he knew her sensitivity felt most exquisite. Karen strained against his hand, her tongue eagerly searching for his. He played there until she could no longer stand it.

Robin kissed his way down Karen's body. He kissed her breasts and nipples. He loved her breasts. They were not large and not small, but perfect. *I love this woman so much.* He kissed down to between her legs and nibbled at her thighs, alternately working his way up them to where all of her curves met. He worked his tongue there and brought her to repeated heights of pleasure until she told him she could do no more.

Robin lay down next to her. Karen rose half up and pushed him down and straddled him. She kissed him with intense passion and then began to kiss his neck and down his body. She lingered at his nipples, causing him to rumble with approval. Karen moved down his body, loving him with every kiss. She took him, pulsating, into her mouth, working her tongue and lips around him. His body arched. He urgently needed to be in her. He pulled her up on top of him. She kissed him and rocked back, using her hand to guide him into her. He gasped as he went deeper and deeper. Karen moved her hips in a way that nearly drove Robin wild. His eyes beheld the most beautiful woman he had ever seen, the woman who owned his heart and soul. He rolled them over and knelt over her, his thrusts moving to satisfy his desire and to please her. Karen wrapped her legs around him and he went deeper. Robin, lost in his wife's love could hold it no longer and came in spasmodic thrusts accompanied with a kiss long and deep and loving.

Karen drifted closer to sleep. She felt so safe when Robin was home, especially when he snuggled against her back, his genitals nestled in the crevice of her buttocks. She enjoyed the afterglow of their love. Although Karen knew Robin was exhausted, she felt a little annoyed he fell asleep so quickly. They hadn't talked enough; she wanted to talk to her husband about a hundred different things. She knew this would be her last chance for days, maybe weeks, with this new case starting.

Karen wondered why she loved this man so much. He focused on saving the world and didn't spend enough time with her or the kids. She knew he loved them all dearly, but she didn't understand why the dopers received more of his attention than his family. Karen felt herself slipping into sleep and decided to let herself go. She never slept well when Robin's work took him away. She might as well get a good night's sleep while she could.

Miguel sat dark and still in the large leather chair in front of the fireplace. He sipped his fifth glass of whiskey as he watched the fire consume the mesquite with its hypnotic dance. The large mirror in on top of the fireplace revealed the flames lighting his eyes with a crimson flicker and surrounding them with undulating shadows, giving his face a demonic cast. Miguel's breath came slow and deep.

His chest felt like it would split open. Ramon was the only person Miguel loved in his life. Their parents were killed when Miguel was ten and Ramon six. Since that time, Miguel had clawed, fought, bribed, extorted, and murdered to gain control of the world around him and keep the brothers together and away from the authorities. Miguel had even sold himself to older men for sex, because they paid good money—especially when he turned around and blackmailed them for more. It got the brothers out of cardboard shacks on the street and into decent apartments. Miguel cried no tears for Ramon. Whatever tears Miguel possessed dried up by the time he turned fifteen.

His mind fixed on the name Robin Marlette—the man responsible for the loss of millions of dollars and several good men of Miguel's organization. Miguel had previously considered having Marlette killed, but had been dissuaded by Juan and Walton. They insisted such an act would cause a massive crackdown on the organization, including a shutdown of the border. Many people who relied on the open border protected and helped the organization because of Miguel's generosity. If the border shut down, they would turn against him.

Miguel would be dissuaded no longer. He held Robin Marlette responsible for the death of his brother no matter who actually shot Ramon. Of course, they all must die, including Newman and Carlos, but Marlette must be made the example to all the American pigs. They all would learn Miguel Rodriguez-Lara was the most powerful man in the world. He would see this lesson would not be forgotten.

SEVEN

Burke Jameson's feet hit the pavement in a rhythmic beat at four-thirty in the morning—"oh-dark-thirty," as the saying went. Burke pushed himself through his workout an hour earlier than usual. He knew the minute he walked in the office Robin would ask if the pen registers were up. The machines record the numbers dialed by Walton and the numbers of his received calls. Burke wanted to be able to reply in the affirmative. Robin could get cranky when things didn't move fast enough.

Burke smiled to himself as he thought of his sergeant. In all his time in the Army and DPS, he never knew any leader who could motivate men better than Robin. He remembered when Robin took over the squad. The rumor proved true that a new squad would be formed out of the existing squads in the division. The other sergeants didn't want to give up officers who were producing, so they gave the lowest producers to the new squad. Robin got the burnouts and the misfits, Burke one of them.

His life in shambles and divorced for the second time, Burke had hit a low point in his life. Work simply angered and frustrated him. He thought the department and everybody else fought the war on drugs in a stupid way. All the low-level street dealers were busted while the big guys went untouched. Burke also drank too much. He came to work hung over more often than not, and didn't produce much in terms of cases. The rest of the new squad felt about the same as Burke.

Everyone expected the typical hardass bullshit a lot of new sergeants feel is necessary to show authority. Instead, Robin walked in and calmly introduced himself. He spoke directly without being overbearing. Robin told the men he knew why they had been selected for his new squad. He also told them he didn't give a damn what they did in the past. He only cared about what they did while they worked for him.

Next, Robin told them the squad's targets were the most dangerous narcotics violators in the state. At this news, Emmett Franks and Doug Auriel stood up and started to walk out. Burke also stood up.

"The job bother you guys?" Robin asked.

"It sure as hell does!" Burke shot back. "This department is too fucked up to tell a squad to do something like that. There isn't anybody in the narcotics division who knows how to do that job, let alone some over-educated desk jockey like you." Franks and Auriel stopped dead in their tracks. They decided to stay for the show they knew Burke would give.

"You're right about the department not doing it right in past, Burke, but this squad is proof they want to do it right, and I know how to get the job done," Robin said calmly. "What I need are a few guys who are willing, with the energy to get trained and the guts to do the job and stay sober enough to do it."

Robin stared directly at Burke, who glared back at him. Burke walked slowly from his chair, his face flushed with anger and his fists clenched.

"While you sat on your fucking ass in law school, I killed Viet Cong in a stinking fucking jungle. I did three goddamned tours for God and fucking country. So don't be telling me about fucking guts!"

"I have a great deal of respect for your service in Vietnam, Burke, but Vietnam is history. What counts is now."

Robin looked around at the men in the squad room. "This is a volunteer squad. The captain realizes it is a dangerous assignment. I'm not one to fuck around or dish out bullshit. You guys are on the shit list. It's either this squad or back to the Highway Patrol writing tickets. If you'll give me a chance, I'll show you it can work, but it's your choice."

"What happens if you don't make it work?" asked Emmett.

"Well in that case, I buy all of you a steak dinner with all the whiskey you can drink the night before I go back to the patrol."

Robin never had to buy that steak dinner.

Two hours later, Burke sat in front of the typewriter at his desk, pounding out an affidavit for pen registers on Carl Walton's home and business phones. At eight o'clock sharp he sat in the waiting room of Judge Cecil Roman, the presiding judge of the Superior Court. Judge Roman stepped off the elevator and noticed Burke waiting for him.

The judge walked up to and shook Burke's hand with a firm grip. Standing about three inches shorter than Burke, Judge Roman wore a neatly tailored navy blue suit, his closely cut hair dusted with gray. He constantly smiled with his eyes and projected a thoroughly professional demeanor.

"Morning, Burke. Robin must be cracking the whip again," the judge said.

"He never stops, Judge. He just treats us like slaves." Burke swallowed the last word and looked helplessly at the black judge.

Judge Roman shook his head and laughed. "Well, your squad is the happiest bunch of slaves I ever saw."

Burke relaxed. He thought about how, before he met Robin, he hated all lawyers; before he met Judge Roman, he hated all judges. He loved Robin like the brother he never had, and thought Judge Roman should be the President of the United States.

Burke handed the judge the affidavit. As Judge Roman read through the pages of the affidavit, his face became a grim visage. When he finished, he laid the affidavit down and looked out his office window.

"Burke, do you know how hard it is for a poor black boy from South Phoenix to get to be presiding judge of the Superior Court?"

"Is it anything like being a poor Indian boy from Neah Bay in Washington State, sir?"

The judge smiled at Burke. "It's probably the same for any poor boy. You know, I wouldn't sign this order unless I had complete trust and faith in the officer presenting it. You're going after one of the most prominent attorneys in the state, if not the nation. I know you guys are the best cops around, so I'm going to sign it. If you're wrong, we'll all be looking for work." With that, the judge signed the order for the pen registers.

Burke took the order from the judge. "Judge, you know Robin. We'll get these guys. All you'll have to worry about is being Chief Justice of the U.S. Supreme Court!"

Judge Roman laughed. "Get out of here before I change my mind."

Burke drove to the U.S. West security office and dropped the order off with Norm Walls, the Chief of Security. Walls gave Burke the location of the switch boxes where Burke had to do the tie-ins to the DPS pen register lines and the line codes for Walton's lines. Burke told Walls he would be out doing the field work that day, so Walls could cover any inquiries.

Burke went back to DPS headquarters and got the "telephone man" van, painted exactly like a U.S. West telephone repair van, only it bore the company logo of Central Communications Services, one of several undercover companies operated by DPS. Burke put on a hard hat similar to ones worn by U.S. West repair men and clipped on an I.D. card identifying him as an employee of Central Communications Services.

He began with the junction box servicing Walton's home. He picked this one first because he knew Walton was probably already at his office. Burke made sure by doing a drive-by first. Previous surveillance of Walton showed he always parked his car by his front door on the circular driveway. As Burke went by, he confirmed the absence of Walton's Mercedes.

He located the switch box a block away at an intersection not too busy with vehicle or foot traffic. Burke parked the van, set out some orange cones, and got to work. It took about twenty minutes for him to complete the hook-up, leaving a red law enforcement tag on the new switch. The tag told regular repairmen not to touch the line without first checking with Norm Walls.

After completing the house, Burke drove to Walton's office building in downtown Phoenix. He parked in front of the building, set out his cones, and strode through the front door with an air of confidence. He went to the building superintendent's office and told him he came to install a service. The superintendent asked him who purchased the service, but Burke just gave him a line number. When

asked what kind of service, he replied that he couldn't release
confidential information to protect the privacy of the customer. The
superintendent bought the explanation and told Burke where to find
the box.

This complicated box took Burke a good hour to hook up. He
had to sort out all the lines in the high-rise to find Walton's private
office line. A dedicated fax line also complicated the installation.
When Burke finished, he checked out with the superintendent and
headed back to the office.

Robin sat in his office when Burke walked into the DPS North
Central Narcotics District Headquarters.

"Hi, Rob," Burke greeted his sergeant.

"Pens up?" Robin's replied.

"Am I not your faithful Indian companion?"

This made Robin laugh. "Yeah, you are, Burke. I will allow you
one cup, make that two cups of coffee, before I give you a bunch of
more shit to do."

"That's okay, I drink real slow."

Robin watched as Burke got a cup of coffee and then sat down at
his desk to write a tech report on the installation of the pen registers.
He remembered how other narcotics sergeants told him he would
fail because all of his men were lazy assholes. They didn't say that
anymore, because his men weren't lazy and wanted to do a good
job—they just needed leadership.

Mark and Doug were writing the rough draft for the affidavit for
the wiretap. Rick and Emmett relieved Rocky and Marv at the
Casablanca. Robin worked out wire room and surveillance schedules
with the other supervisors of the different agencies. The squad
hummed and Robin felt content.

EIGHT

Juan Trinidad waited impatiently on the phone. Finally, on the other end the female voice said, "Department of Public Safety, Narcotics Division."

"Agent Molina, please."

"Just a moment." A few seconds later, another voice came on the phone.

"Agent Molina."

"It is Juan."

The voice on the other end turned into a hoarse whisper. "Are you crazy! I told you never to call me here! Jesus"

"Shut up, you idiot!" Trinidad shot back. "You belong to me and you will talk to me whenever and wherever I tell you."

Molina remained silent.

"Now, you find out who killed Ramon. Find out what happened to the money and to Newman and Carlos."

"Marlette is no idiot, Juan. Nobody is talking here. He has a lid on everything."

"You find out!" Trinidad barked. "And you will find out everything you can about Marlette's family."

"What the fuck do you mean, 'Marlette's family?'"

"Listen to me, Jose." Juan made his voice cold and threatening. "Do not be stupid. Miguel is very, very angry. Either Marlette will pay the consequences or you will."

"Okay, okay." Molina's voice trembled.

"I will call tomorrow."

"All right." Molina choked out the word.

Juan felt contempt for Molina. He thought he was weak. Molina loved to take the money for information, but he was afraid to take the risks to get information from the Guardians. Before Marlette came, the organization could maneuver around the police and get their product in without much interference. Molina's information ensured that success. When Marlette started the new squad, things changed. Molina worked on the street narcotics squad and was not cleared for the information worked by the Guardians. This forced Molina to snoop around and ask questions, which he didn't like to do. Sometimes Juan thought Molina feared Marlette as much as he feared Miguel and himself.

He told Molina to get on Marlette's squad. Since nobody left the squad to make an opening, no transfer appeared possible. Plus, Marlette controlled who came into his squad more than most other sergeants, according to Jose. Of course, the main problem, to Juan at least, centered on Marlette not liking Jose. He'd probably never let him in his squad. Juan understood, because he did not like Jose either. Juan decided he must supplement Jose's activities.

Molina sat at his desk with his head in his hands. He felt lucky he came in early to finish some reports. Alone in the street squad office, nobody could see him trembling. He desperately wanted to vomit, but choked it down. His eyeballs felt like they were going to explode as he held back the flood of tears.

Molina jumped out of his chair in a suppressed rage, a stream of obscenities gushing from his mouth in a hoarse whisper as he stomped around the office. *I hate Trinidad and his fucking big shot attitude. I hate that lunatic Rodriquez. I really hate that goddamn motherfucking Marlette for completely fucking up the sweet deal I have going.*

Molina sat back down. He took a deep breath. He really hated himself for falling into this trap. He knew now they were going after Marlette and his family. Despite all the warnings, anti-corruption training, and seeing what happened to bad cops who got caught, he never believed it would go this far for him. Trinidad made it sound like Jose's information just helped the poor people of Mexico, like his parents' families. Of course, the extra five thousand dollars a month didn't hurt.

Molina knew he had to do what Juan wanted or he and his own family would be hurt instead of Marlette and his family. *Marlette doesn't like me anyway, why should I care what happens to that stupid, gung ho asshole?*

Molina leaned back in his chair and rubbed his eyes as he thought. He knew Marlette had a wife and four kids from the pictures in his office. He needed to get his address. The division call out list only showed telephone numbers. Molina leaned forward as he remembered the Guardians giving Marlette a ration of shit about his daughter and Ernie Jackson's kid going together at the U of A. Maybe that kind of info would keep that asshole Trinidad off his back. He needed to learn more about that little deal.

Molina got up and walked down the hall to the restroom. He did not see anyone else there as he looked into the mirror. The image looking back at him had a pale face with puffy, red eyes. Molina could see a glint of fear in those eyes. A cold shiver shook his body. He turned the water on and splashed his face over and over, as if he were hoping to wash the fear away.

"You going swimmin', Jose?"

Molina jerked up at sound of the voice. He saw Rick Santos coming out of a stall. Molina turned off the water.

"Uh, well, I had a long night and short morning."

"I hear that, amigo," chuckled Rick.

"From what I hear, you guys are doing the same."

"It's SOP when you work for Marlette."

"You guys going to get medals for blowing that creep away?"

Rick zipped up and walked to the sinks. He turned on the water, soaped his hands, and then looked at Molina.

"You've never been in a gun fight, have you, Jose?"

"You know I haven't, Ricardo," answered Molina, looking down.

"It is not necessarily something you want a medal for, especially when someone dies."

"It wouldn't bother me."

Rick looked at the younger man for a moment and then said, "Maybe it wouldn't, Jose. Maybe it wouldn't." Rick then turned and walked out the door.

Molina went out after Rick and walked back to his office. He tensed with anger. He took a couple of deep breaths and decided to pay Marlette a visit and get some information.

Robin was listening to Chris Fleming talk on the phone about the status of the Cuban when he noticed Molina walk into the Guardians' squad room. Every time he saw the young officer, he got an uneasy feeling in his gut. He couldn't pin down why, but he just didn't trust the kid.

Chris had just finished up telling Robin he had Garcia held under the National Security Act and that the FBI had transported the prisoner to Quantico Marine Base in Virginia. Chris gave his assurance he was the FBI case agent for Garcia and nothing would be done without Robin being consulted. Robin hung up as Molina made his way to Robin's office.

"Hi Sarge," Molina greeted Robin.

"Hi Jose, what brings you to our humble digs?"

"Oh, just my regular begging session to get into your squad."

Robin forced a smile. "The first thing you have to do is get one of these old farts to transfer or retire."

"Sheeeit, these guys know a gravy job when they see one."

"Well, in my opinion, they are either crazy or too stupid to figure out what I really got them into."

"Seriously, Sarge, I really want to work for you. You guys are where the action is. That's where I gotta be."

Robin noticed Molina did not look well and acted nervous as hell. Robin did not consider himself to be an intimidating person. He wondered what the hell made this guy so weird, other than being a total dumbass. He decided to let the kid down easy.

"Look, Jose, I'm just a sergeant in this vast organization. If I could have enough slots in my squad, I'd love to have a hard workin' cop like you. But the brass, as usual, has different plans. I'm not getting any more positions, just more work, but I'll keep you in mind."

"Thanks, I appreciate it. By the way, I got a brother who is interested in going to the U of A. He is trying to figure out if he should live on campus or rent an apartment. I know your daughter goes there and I wondered if you had any suggestions."

"I don't know what I can tell you. My daughter lives on campus right now, but she wants to move off campus. I'm not for the move and since I pay part of her rent, she is kind of stuck. It really depends on your brother's preferences and budget."

"Yeah, I can see that. Well, does she live in a co-ed dorm or the good old-fashioned kind?"

"She lives in a women's dorm, which is precisely why she wants to move."

"Uh, oh, I see a jealous dad."

"You're goddamned right. Wait 'til your daughters grow up."

"I can wait on that score. Speaking of scores, you scored big last night."

"We did, all right. Look, Jose, I've these damn evaluations to get done."

"Okay, Sarge. We'll see you later."

Molina left and Rick appeared at Robin's door. "What did that dickhead want?"

"Your job."

"Fuck him! What a little weasel. You know, every chance he gets he tries to pump me for information about our cases. Just a little while ago he told me it wouldn't bother him to kill somebody. He bugs the shit out of me."

"Maybe he looks up to you."

"Why, because we're both Mexican?"

"It's just a thought, Rick. You are older and more experienced. He may be trying to impress you."

"Rob, you're talking like a lawyer again."

"What do you mean?"

"You're full of shit."

Burke walked in and told Robin the squad was ready to meet for a status check on assignments. Rob and Rick joined the rest of the men in the squad room. This meeting required each man to report his progress in the last twenty-four hours.

Emmett Franks started the briefing. "I got Newman pretty much all set. Security is being handled by Lucheck, Victor Thirty-Two squad, and myself. Newman has been advised of the rules for informants and shown how to properly wear and operate a body wire. I've completed the report on Newman's debriefing."

"Great work, Emmett. What about you, Burke?"

"The pens are all working fine. Walton is calling up a storm, but no calls to Mexico yet. Norm Walls promised to get subscriber information on the numbers Walton dialed as fast as he could. I talked with Jim Adams at the U.S. Attorney's Office and got two fifteen-minute shots at the grand jury every day for the next two weeks. We will have subpoenas for other phone companies, banks, credit companies, and other places flying outta there." The squad laughed.

"Just don't drive Jim crazy."

"Hell, he's a lawyer—he's already crazy!"

Robin shook his head. "Doug, how are you and Mark doing?"

"Mark and I have the surveillance schedules set up. Those of us not on "Newman duty," the FBI, IRS, and U.S. Customs will be doing surveillance on Walton and others as the cast of characters grows. Oscar and Jack are itching to fly."

"Thanks, Doug. Mike, how's the wire room coming?"

"I am lining up the off-site wiretap room location and getting the wiretap equipment together and making sure it is in good working order. I got a location picked out; I'm just doing a little negotiation with the owner over the rent."

Robin laughed. "Don't get hung up on the rent. It's not your money."

"I know, but this guy thinks he's got a big fish and I just have to cut down his expectations."

"Just remember, time is the most important thing right now."

"Don't worry, I'll have a deal by tomorrow."

"Good enough. Rick, I take it you have the rest covered?"

"I'm available to respond to and coordinate any SOU calls or marijuana garden reports. I'll also remain contact man for our two informants in Mexico, since those guys can only make contact when they are clear of bandits."

"That's good. Those two informants' butts are hanging way out. I don't want to let them down in any way."

"I've got 'em covered."

"You are a good man, Rick."

"Okay, guys, as usual this case is going to crunch us for time. Still, we have to take care of our smaller cases and keep all our informants happy. That means we will have to cover for each other at times. Be flexible and don't be afraid to speak up if you are getting spread too thin."

Robin coordinated all aspects of the case and reviewed applications for the wiretap and the overall case report. Of course, since the Guardians were responsible for narcotics intelligence, Robin maintained those reports also.

Burke raised his hand. "That goes for you too, Sarge, right?"

"If I need help, you'll be the first to know."

Robin smiled broadly and was starting back to his office when Lieutenant Hammel came into the squad room.

"Rob, the lab just confirmed the ballistics on the bullets that killed Ramon Rodriquez came from your gun. Nice shooting." The men murmured their approval.

"We also just got an anonymous call on a possible marijuana garden." Robin's good feelings turned to all too familiar frustration.

"Goddamn it," he muttered. "Oh well, Rick, check it out. If you need a recon, Mike will be your second man. Doug, I'll cover for Mike on surveillance."

"I can handle a recon by myself," Rick responded.

"Don't fuck with me, Rick. No solo recons. That's the rule."

"I'm just trying to help, Rob."

"You being hurt or dead is no help to me."

"Game time, boys," Burke interceded. "Let's do what the Sarge says."

Hammel handed Santos a piece of paper with the information on it. The lieutenant looked over the squad. "I don't know what to do about you guys. I think you're all crazy. You do the work of three squads; leave your families for weeks at a time; half of you are on the verge of getting divorced; you all look like shit; and the thing is, you don't have to be doing this. It's just a job."

Robin stared at the floor, resisting the urge to strangle his lieutenant, when Burke spoke up.

"That's the fucking problem, Lieutenant. You think it's just a job. *We know it's a war.* And because of your kind of attitude, we're losing this war. I'm sick and fucking tired of losing wars. If I have to follow Sergeant Marlette to fucking hell to win this one, then I will, by God. I'll work a hundred hours a week if he tells me to. So will every man here."

Robin looked at his squad. They were all looking at Lieutenant Hammel defiantly. Hammel quietly turned and walked out of the squad room. The men all turned and looked at Robin.

He fought back his emotion. He could not find the words to describe the love he had for these men. They faced death simply because he said so. They put their family lives at stake because they came to believe in his war. And now they said they would follow him into hell, if that's what it took. He would give his life before allowing one of his men to be hurt or killed.

"Thanks guys," Robin said. He took a deep breath and looked at his men. "We're kind of in this alone. Everybody thinks we're crazy for working like we do, but they all want part of our action, because we are doing it right and kicking ass. As this new case progresses, it's going to get even more lonely. The closer we get to politicians, the more nervous the brass is going to get. Even if we're successful, we won't be on their dinner list. I hope nobody here planned on being director."

"Fuck it, Sarge," Emmett said in a low voice. "We're in this for us. We were all burned out before you came. We had no leadership. None of us were doing much of anything. Now we're being cops, damn good cops. I'm proud as hell to be a member of this squad. I don't really give a fuck what anybody else thinks."

"That goes for all of us, Rob," said Mike.

"Well then," Robin said as he stood up. "Let's quit fucking off and get to work!"

"Now there's a real sentimental son of a bitch for you," said Doug, laughing.

Robin looked at his men. "I guess since we are all such macho men, I shouldn't say this—but I love you guys like brothers."

Burke put his arms around Robin's shoulders. "We know Rob but you're still a son of a bitch."

The men broke up the meeting laughing and joking with each other. Robin went back to his office and began reviewing his plan for the case. The time came to have Newman call Walton and set up a meeting. This would give the Guardians some time for pen register info and surveillance when Walton would be making contact with people to tell them the money was safe. Hopefully, it would be enough info for a wiretap order.

Robin wondered how careful Walton would be with Newman. Newman told Emmett that Walton liked him—they did some hunting and fishing together. Newman thought Walton would do anything to make his wife happy, and since he married Newman's sister, everything would be okay. Robin still worried because Walton was no dummy.

For sure, Walton would be somewhat loose until he got control of the money. Criminals' greed is a police officer's friend. Robin believed Walton couldn't control his greed for five million dollars...especially, when the money would buy the other thing Walton wanted - power. The combination of these two things was the key to making Newman's contact successful.

NINE

Cathy Marlette raised her eyes from her psychology book and looked at her boyfriend, Andy Jackson. He focused on an engineering book, immersed in mathematical calculations on a complicated problem Cathy didn't even want to understand. They occupied a study room in the U of A library. Cathy reflected on how she enjoyed the quiet and the closeness she felt with Andy as they worked toward their common goal: graduation and marriage.

She returned her attention to her psychology text book, but couldn't maintain concentration. Her mind wandered back to when she and Andy first met. Cathy remembered her dad announced they were going on a picnic at Apache Lake with another family. Seventeen at the time, a family picnic did not rank as one of her top ideas of a great time. Her dad mentioned the other family included an eighteen-year-old boy, but Cathy figured the boy was probably a nerd or worse.

The other family, the Jacksons, owned a ski boat. The boy turned out to be Andy, and Cathy found him handsome and easy to talk to. When he took off his shirt to ski, Cathy fell in love. Andy stood tall, muscular, and tan. He combed his sandy blond hair straight back, making his deep blue eyes more noticeable. His ready smile accentuated strong facial features. He was an outstanding water skier, which completed Cathy's infatuation.

They spent the rest of the afternoon with Andy patiently teaching Cathy how to water ski. She learned he had just finished his first year at the U of A school of engineering, and he really liked the campus. On that day she decided she wanted to go the U of A.

Cathy and Andy started going together the following weekend. That was two years ago now. In that time, Cathy had come to love

Andy deeply and passionately. He treated her like a princess, and pledged his life to her. He showed his love for her in so many ways, she sometimes felt she was living inside a romance novel.

Andy put down his pencil, leaned back in his chair, and looked at his girlfriend.

"Hi, beautiful," he said softly.

"Oh, you're back from the world of numbers," Cathy teased.

"Is that a hint that study time is over?"

"It's a hint that I'm hungry and want attention."

"Well, I'm the guy who can take care of both problems."

"I know," Cathy replied, her eyes softening.

Andy leaned forward and spoke in a whisper. "Cathy, you have the sexiest eyes in the world."

"Let's get out of here, Andy. I'm hungry and horny and we can't take care of either one in this place and honey, if you continue to grin like that, the world will know our secrets."

The couple gathered their books and headed out of the library. They walked to the parking lot to Andy's car, a 1964 red Jaguar XKE he had restored. His pride in his car radiated as he treated it with great care. Only Cathy had permission to drive the Jaguar and not very often. They got into the car and Andy started it up. He smiled with satisfaction at the sound of the perfectly tuned engine.

The couple ate dinner at La Indianita restaurant on 4th Avenue. Cathy liked it because they served good vegetarian food. Andy liked it because they served giant portions. As they ate, they engaged in a lively conversation with Mama Gonzales, the owner of the restaurant. She liked Cathy and Andy, and since both spoke fluent Spanish, she felt more comfortable talking with them in her native language.

The couple finished their dinner and said goodbye to Mama. They then headed to Andy's apartment. Andy parked and they both worked to get the car cover on the car. They then walked up the stairs and into the apartment.

Hector Rubio sucked the last smoke he could out of his cigarette as he watched the policemen's children enter the apartment. Juan's information turned out to be correct—the children of policemen often ate at the Indianita. Hector recognized the Jaguar there and watched it. He easily followed them to the apartment. Juan would be pleased with his work.

TEN

Rick Santos bent on one knee and used binoculars to scout the area ahead. A ghillie suit covered the Rhodesian SAS camouflage fatigues he wore. Camouflage paint covered his face. Mike Collins, similarly dressed, knelt three meters away facing the other direction. To the casual observer, they appeared to be two bushes mingled in the mountain landscape.

They were in the Tonto National Forest southeast of Payson and northeast of Rye, in the middle of thick scrub oak sprinkled with ponderosa pine. The clean air bore the pleasant scent of sage and pine. A raven called nearby, and critters scurried in the brush from time to time. Both men's senses were heightened as they scanned the area. Rick had flown over the area the day before in a DPS plane and spotted occasional emerald green patches in the area, an indication of marijuana plants. Now he and Mike were doing a recon to verify Rick's observation.

Rick let the binoculars hang and took out his compass. He laid it on the face of a folded topo map and shot some azimuths. He very slowly leaned back and squeezed Mike's arm. Mike scanned a 180° arc in his field of vision and moved slowly off to Rick's left. He waited until Rick moved a little farther ahead and moved out.

Both men moved ahead ever so slowly, alternately looking ahead, looking up into the trees, and looking down at the ground. They were looking for anything that seemed out of place. A straight line or the outline of part of a human body, a change in the animal sounds, birds taking to flight. human smell—they constantly worked at keeping their minds and senses open to all input.

Rick looked up and started to move his eyes down. When they were looking level and parallel to the ground, his peripheral vision caught a faint line of light crossing the deer path to his right...a straight line across. There are no straight lines in nature. He went to one knee and pushed the transmit button on his radio to break squelch, Mike's signal to stop and go to one knee, which he did.

Mike slowly turned to look at Rick. Rick pointed to his eyes and then drew a straight line in the air, but low and parallel to the ground. He pointed to the line he found. Mike squinted in that direction and a look of recognition crossed his face. He gave thumbs up to Rick. Rick moved forward and Mike fell in behind him, keeping three meters between them.

Rick could feel himself getting tense. He carefully scanned the ground leading up to the line. He moved forward cautiously, taking deep breaths to ease off the building apprehension. He got close enough to see a taut fishing line. Was it a noise warning device or a booby trap?

He got up to the line and looked along to the right. It went to the base of a scrub oak. To the left, though, the line disappeared into a can set in the fork of a branch of another scrub oak. Rick swallowed hard. He slowly turned to Mike and gave the signal for booby trap. Mike's eyes widened. He nodded and assumed 360 security as Rick intently focused on the task at hand.

Rick slowly approached the can. A closer look revealed an M-26 grenade in the can surrounded by nails. The fishing line connected to the pin, and the pin stuck out so it barely held the spoon. Rick knew he had to push in the pin. He also knew Robin just might get pissed off if he did it without waiting for the bomb techs. On the other hand, Robin would probably not want to leave this thing sitting here where anyone could come across it. Rick took out his pocket camera and took pictures of the trap. He put the camera back into his vest. Taking a deep breath, he reached into the can, holding the spoon from the top of the grenade with this left hand, and gently pushed the pin in to the hilt with his right hand. Rick slowly removed the grenade from the can and carefully inspected it to make sure the mechanism looked complete and in good condition. The relative newness of the grenade surprised him. They usually found older ones. Satisfied it all looked safe, he carefully released the pressure on the spoon. The pin held securely in place. Rick spread the end of the pin to make sure it stayed in place and gave Mike the all clear signal. Mike replied with a smile and thumbs up.

Rick placed the grenade in a pouch on his tactical vest and gave the signal to move out again. They resumed their slow movement over the terrain. After fifteen minutes, Rick signaled he saw a marijuana plant ahead of him and slightly to the left. He took a couple of more steps and pointed to other plants around it. The two men were now on high alert. Rick reached the first plant and could smell the odor of marijuana as he watched Mike touch the plant with his glove and see the THC sticking to it. The hybrid plant had many buds on it, all oozing THC. Rick estimated the THC content at well over 20 percent, very expensive stuff. The owners would be serious about guarding it, as the booby trap already demonstrated; time to call Robin and the rest of the Guardians.

ELEVEN

At 2100 hours, Robin and Emmett carefully instructed Eric Newman on what to say to Walton. Robin didn't doubt that if Newman didn't act exactly right during the phone call, Walton would completely shut down the operation, no matter how much money it would cost him. "Loosen up, Eric," Robin said.

"That's easy for you to say. You're not the one staring at twenty-five years in the joint if this plan doesn't work."

"All you gotta do is get him to a place where he can see you have the money, and he will never believe you've been arrested. He will certainly be careful at first, but just work him…like catching the big fish."

Newman raised and lowered his shoulders and stretched his neck side to side. "All right, all right, I can do this."

"I know you can. Otherwise we wouldn't have reached this point."

Newman took a deep breath. Robin nodded his head for Newman to make the call. Emmett started the tape recorder.

"Hello," Walton said over the phone.

"Hey, Carl. How ya doin?'"

A long moment of silence passed. "I'm doing fine, as usual. Haven't heard from you for a while."

"Well, ya know how that goes. Been pretty busy lately. Kinda runnin' around."

"I imagine so. How are the kids?"

"I still have them all with me. They're all fine."

"I'm sorry to hear about your cousin's accident. Were you close to where it happened?"

"Not really. I found out by reading it in the paper."

"Oh, sorry to hear that."

"Thanks. I have some arrangements to make and will be pretty busy for awhile. I wondered if you could take the kids for me."

"Well, I think I can. Call me tomorrow morning at the office. We'll make arrangements then."

"Thanks. I'll call you around ten."

"That's good. I'll talk to you then."

"Adios."

"Bye."

Newman hung up the phone and let out a deep breath.

"What do you think?" Robin asked.

"Well, I think he is sniffin' the hook."

Carl Walton sat at his desk in his home office. He ignored the McClellan's Islay single malt scotch he had poured for himself before Newman called. Walton knew his mind had to remain clear to thoughtfully examine all aspects of the last three days. Ramon's death, Miguel's dangerous anger, and now Eric's call all worked to keep him unbalanced, a mental condition that was foreign to him. Walton did not like it in the least.

The main thrust of Walton's thoughts focused on regaining control. Nothing could be done about Ramon's death. Still, he needed to deal with Miguel's anger by directing the anger at anything but himself. As much as Walton disliked a direct attack on Marlette, at this point he saw no benefit to himself to argue against it. Having Miguel and Juan thinking about revenge on Marlette suited him much better than having them think about Carl Walton. Two out of three problems solved.

Eric presented a different matter. While Walton did not have in-depth knowledge of police operations, Marlette's team had a reputation of being tough, well disciplined, and thorough. It raised the question of how Eric could escape. Had he really been captured and now working for DPS? On the other hand, he said he had the money. There's no way any police agency would let five million dollars be in the custody of an informant. Besides, Eric was his brother-in-law, and Walton knew Eric loved his sister, if he loved anybody in this world. The two were orphaned as small children and had fought to stay together. They took good care of each other.

Eric wouldn't do anything to hurt Ann. Therefore, Walton reasoned, Eric would never do anything to set Walton up.

Still, his nature dictated he remain careful. The meeting with Eric had to be secure from the police. He would make sure Eric brought the money to this meeting. If he didn't, Walton would know Eric didn't have control of the money and all bets would be off.

With this plan, Walton felt like he'd regained some control of the situation. He settled in his chair and sipped his drink. He would have Eric meet him at Superstition State Park, where there were some fairly private open areas. All he needed to do was see the money. He would get there first and would see instantly if anyone followed Eric. It would happen tomorrow evening.

Walton finished his drink and got up. He turned out the light to his office and took his glass to the kitchen. He then went to his bedroom and looked at his wife asleep in their bed. Walton's main feeling about his wife amounted to ambivalence. Beautiful, graceful and articulate, Ann moved comfortably in social circles, which complimented his career. Walton, however, didn't really love her. He reserved that feeling for two things: money and power. He knew she loved him, so Eric would certainly not hurt her by turning informant against him.

Robin and Jim Adams from the U.S. Attorney's office sat in front of Judge Roman's desk. The judge's face turned to stone as he read Robin's application for a wiretap on every type of communication device Walton possessed. The information about Walton's connection to Miguel Rodriquez-Lara and the planned bribes to government officials had to be very unsettling to a man like the good judge.

Jim Adams cleared the state application with the Maricopa County Attorney's Office. The County Attorney had made Jim a Special Deputy County Attorney for this purpose, which allowed him to handle the matter until it transferred to federal court.

Judge Roman finished reading the affidavit, locked eyes with Robin, and put him under oath. Robin accepted the oath and the judge signed the application and the order. He handed the papers to Robin, looking into Robin's eyes again, and in a forceful, hoarse whisper said, "Get these sons of bitches, Rob...get 'em good." Robin nodded his head, saluted the judge, and walked out.

TWELVE

Juan Trinidad had just finished his plan to take revenge on Marlette. Juan's plan called for his men to enter the Marlette house and kill everyone in it. They would wait for Marlette to come home, see his dead family, and then kill him. The men would make sure no one would doubt that Marlette saw his dead family. It would be done in broad daylight. Such an action would send a powerful message to the American pigs.

He also assigned a team of men keeping an eye on Marlette's daughter and her boyfriend. They would kill the boy and then take Marlette's daughter. Before Marlette died, he would know this, too. It would be a message to all American policemen their families were not protected from the organization. The cartel could do whatever they wanted.

He rose up from the desk in his suite in the ranch mansion and headed for Miguel's residence down the hall. He passed two guards, who nodded respectfully to him and entered Miguel's quarters.

"Miguel!" Juan called out.

"Si, amigo, I am in the study."

Juan followed the voice into the study. Miguel sat at a leather card table with borders of inlaid gold, wearing a white linen shirt under a green silk smoking jacket and reading the *Wall Street Journal.*

"What is it, my friend?"

"I have the plan for revenge on Marlette."

"Ah, good, let me hear it."

Juan related his plan to Miguel. He could see Miguel looked pleased. Miguel had wanted to kill Marlette for quite some time. Now he could see it finally happening. As usual, however, Miguel wanted more.

"Before you actually kill Marlette, I want him to *watch* his family die."

"That would make it more difficult, Miguel. My plan is better."

"He and his men killed my brother!" Miguel shouted angrily. "I don't care about difficult."

"Listen to me, Miguel. Before he dies, he will know we also have his daughter."

"Good! But I want him to *see* his family die." Miguel's eyes flashed with a mad fury.

"I will see it is done, Miguel."

"*When* will you do this?" Miguel snapped.

"We will do it within three weeks' time."

"Good. You will also bring me his balls."

"Of course, Patron."

Robin's eyes focused on Newman's blue Chevrolet pickup as it moved along U.S. 60 heading towards the Superstition Mountains to meet Walton at Superstition State Park. Newman had the money and wore a Nagra tape recorder, a very sensitive voice recorder. Robin instructed Newman to wrap the recorder harness around his inner left thigh, right next to his genitals. Walton probably wouldn't search there, if he looked for a wire at all. Robin rejected the use of any transmitting body wires for this contact, just in case Walton knew enough to check for such things.

Robin rode in a U.S. Customs Cessna 192 at five thousand feet. Jack and Oscar were doing the flying as Robin looked through large gyro-stabilized binoculars. Shifting back from Newman's truck, he saw a van about a half mile back, carrying DPS SOU Team Two. Ernie Jackson and his team were set up a half mile from Superstition Park. The money would go to no one but Walton.

Robin's team went to Superstition Park area at 1500 hours, dressed in camouflage and ghillie suits and spread out around the park. They reported Walton had arrived an hour before the meet time. Robin told Burke and Emmett to move in as close as possible without blowing the surveillance. They moved in, but at a painstakingly slow pace.

As Newman got closer to the park, he tried not to be nervous. In truth, he had never liked Walton. He didn't believe Walton loved his sister, Ann, but he gave her a comfortable life, if not happiness. Ann confided this to Newman, and Walton's ruthless pursuit of power worried Newman. The lawyer's cold and calculating mind made him dangerous, and Newman had to be careful about how he pulled off this meeting. Newman turned on to the road leading to the park entrance.

Robin ordered all vehicles to back off. He told Jack to loiter about two miles away from the park. It was up to Newman, Burke, and Emmett now.

Emmet noticed Newman as he went through the park gate and started driving around the outer park road, but he kept an eye on Walton. Newman turned the truck towards Walton. Emmett was close, but not close enough, he thought. As the pickup rolled to Walton, its tires were crunching the gravel and making enough noise to cover Emmett's movements. Emmett saw Walton looking at Newman. He made his move to get closer.

Newman saw a strange figure moving towards Walton. His heart plugged his throat. He had almost slammed on his brakes when the figure dropped out of sight. He suddenly realized the figure was the big black cop. He took a deep breath and drove up to Walton.

"Brother," Walton said.

"Howdy, Brother," Newman replied. The men gave each other a light hug.

"I am happy to see you're okay, Eric."

"Not half as happy as I am, Brother."

"How did you get away?"

"I just jumped in the truck and took off. I thought they would chase me, but they didn't. It may have something to do with them killing Ramon. That big helicopter kicked up a lot of dust and maybe they didn't see me. The moonlight allowed me to keep my headlights off until I got a couple of miles down the road. I feel pretty damned lucky."

"I guess so," Walton replied. He could not detect anything that would lead him to believe Newman was lying.

"How pissed off is Miguel, Carl?"

"Very."

"Is he going to kill me?"

"He mentioned it, but he backed off when I told him you kept the money. You do have it, don't you?"

"It's here." Eric walked to the back of the truck and unlocked the window to the camper shell. He opened it up, and after looking around, Walton reached in and pulled the zipper on a large black duffel bag. He retrieved one of the packages, opened it with a small pocket knife, and thumbed through the stack of one hundred dollar bills.

"Let's get it loaded into your trunk."

"No," Walton said. The statement startled Newman. "I want you to hold on to it. You're going to make the deliveries, as usual. You worried me for a little while, Eric, but I can see by some miracle you got away. The shooting probably did hold them up."

"What worried you?"

"That you might have been caught—that you were working for the cops."

"I would never do that to you and I would certainly never do it to Ann."

"I know, Eric. I know. That's why I only worried a *little*." Walton formed a slight smile on this face. "Go home and call me in two days. I will have instructions for delivery ready for you."

"Okay, Carl. I just don't like being responsible for *all* of this money. If something else goes wrong, I am a dead man."

"Don't worry. Nothing will go wrong. It will just be business as usual, except you won't have to pick up the payoffs from me. Now go home."

"Okay, Carl." The two men embraced again. They went to their respective vehicles and drove out of the park. The last of the day's sun glowed orange and red behind the hills.

When they left the area, six shadowy figures rose from different places around the site of the meeting. Emmett keyed his radio.

"Two Nora Six-Two, Two Nora Six."

"Two Nora Six," Robin replied.

"Meet is complete. No transfer took place. Repeat. No transfer took place."

"Ten-Four, Two Nora Six-One. Two Nora Six to Victor Thirty-Two."

"Victor Thirty-Two, go ahead Two Nora Six," Ernie replied.

"Latch on to our boy and escort him to DPS."

"Ten-Four, Two Nora Six."

Robin leaned back in his seat, surprised Walton did not take the money. *Mr. Walton is indeed a careful man. On the other hand, it shows he still trusts Newman. It will be good to get the wire up.* Robin couldn't wait to talk to Newman and listen to the tape.

THIRTEEN

Chris Fleming gazed out the window. He always enjoyed coming back to Quantico, to the nearby FBI academy. He had many fond memories about the academy from his years working for the Bureau. He was currently standing in an office at the Detention Center at the Quantico Marine Base—not one of his favorite places. He sipped his coffee and heard footsteps coming down the hall. Chris turned around to a knock at the door.

"Come in," he said. The door opened by a young smartly uniformed Marine holding the handcuffed Cuban by the arm. Another Marine stood behind them. Chris knew this man's name wasn't Manuel Garcia-Galbodon—it was Carlos Casconda, and he was indeed a Cuban. The FBI Counterintelligence shop confirmed this, and also confirmed Carlos worked for Cuban intelligence. They knew of his presence in Mexico; they just didn't know what he did there. At this point, they still did not really know, but his contact with the Rodriquez-Lara organization greatly interested them. Counterintelligence agents told Chris they believed Casconda's wife also to be in Mexico.

Although a handsome man, today Carlos looked like hell. His eyes were bloodshot, hair uncombed, and he wore a week's worth of beard. He'd lost weight. Chris learned from the Marines the prisoner barely ate and acted sullen while in the detention center. He didn't speak much to anyone. Chris needed to change that today. He pointed Carlos to a chair.

"Sit down, please, Mr. Casconda," Chris said in Spanish. Carlos' eyes flashed with surprise. He stared at the FBI agent for a few seconds and then sat down.

"That will be all, Marines. Thank you."

"Our orders are to remain outside the door, sir."

"That will be fine." The Marines stepped out of the office and closed the door.

"Would you like a cup of coffee?" Chris asked.

Carlos paused for a second and then said, "Yes" in a hoarse voice.

Chris went over to the coffee pot and poured a cup of coffee. As he stepped back, he moved the office chair from behind the desk and put it at the front left corner, three feet from the Cuban. Chris put the coffee cup on the desk and motioned for the man to raise his hands off of his lap. Carlos gave Chris a dubious look, but raised his hands. Chris removed the handcuffs, sat down, and took another sip of his coffee. He waited for the Cuban to take a sip too.

"You look like hell, Carlos."

The man grunted and looked at Chris. "You know my name."

"It didn't take us long to find out who you really are. We've been aware of your presence in Mexico for some time."

"How?"

Chris smiled. "You know I can't tell you that." Carlos grunted again, but this time Chris detected a slight chuckle to it.

"Are the Marines mistreating you?"

Carlos looked at Chris and smiled. "No. The Marines are professionals. I respect them. Why do you ask?"

"Like I said, you look like hell."

The Cuban turned away for a few seconds. He looked back, but said nothing.

"It's been four days since we found you in the desert. Whatever is bothering you is not getting any better with you sitting here, doing nothing. I am guessing Miguel has you worried. If that is the case, I am the only person who can help you. I do not say this lightly and I am not bullshitting you. I know you are a professional."

Carlos' mouth twitched, his face reddened, and his eyes were like drills into Chris's. The FBI agent immediately knew he had found the right button. Carlos had to be worried about his wife. Chris couldn't think of another reason a seasoned intelligence agent would be so agitated, but he knew to proceed carefully.

"I do not believe you can do anything for me," Carlos said with a sneer.

"Really? Four days ago you were in the custody of the state police in the middle of the desert in Arizona. Today, you are in Quantico, Virginia *in my custody*. I flew you here in a military aircraft. I put you in a military detention center. *I* dictate your custody status." Chris let that sink in. "I have been in this business for a long time, Carlos. I know how to get things done, and I know who to contact to get them done. I can help you right now, but time is running out. It's up to you."

Carlos had his arms folded, his right hand nervously rubbing his left forearm. Perspiration beaded on his forehead. Chris hoped listing straightforward, simple facts of things he accomplished in the last four days would register with the man. Chris also knew he faced stiff competition with the Cuban agent's Soviet training.

Chris stood up. His next movements were carefully choreographed in his mind. He just needed to perform them flawlessly. He turned away from the Cuban and walked to the coffee pot. He picked up the pot and called out, "Marines, enter please." He poured coffee into his cup as the Marines entered. Chris turned around and leaned against the table supporting the coffee pot. He lazily crossed his legs at the ankle and took a long sip of coffee. He nodded towards Carlos and said, "He is *apparently* ready to go."

The Marines stood Carlos up and handcuffed him. They turned towards the door and started out of the office. Chris involuntarily held his breath. They went through the door, and the second Marine reached for the door handle to close the door when Carlos yelled, "Stop! I need to talk to him!" Chris breathed again.

The Marine looked back at Chris, who waved them in. The Marines ushered Carlos back into the room and quietly left, closing the door behind them. The Cuban wearily sat down, his face ashen and his hands trembling.

"My wife. I fear for my wife."

"Why?" Chris said as he poured Carlos another cup of coffee.

"Miguel is a madman and he will be furious about his brother and the money. He expected me to protect the both of them. Miguel told Ramon I'd be in charge, but the idiot never intended to follow

Miguel's orders. My wife and I live on Miguel's compound. She is there and I know she is in danger."

"All right, I'll get to work on that problem, but first tell me what happened the night you were arrested."

Carlos took a deep breath. "No. First you tell me how you will protect my wife."

"We are just starting to talk to each other. I will only tell you there are assets available in Mexico to deal with the problem. Until we know each other better, you will have to just believe that. I think you know I have been straight with you so far."

"You think I am a plant."

Chris shrugged his shoulders. "I have to take necessary precautions." The Cuban looked at the floor, his jaw muscles working. His hands were clasped, and Chris noticed his knuckles were white. He knew Carlos struggled with his training.

"My friend, if you make a mental list of the people you can trust, those you can believe right now...it boils down to just me."

Carlos looked up at Chris for a long moment. He breathed in and leaned back in his chair, unclasping his hands. He let out a long, slow breath. "Ramon and I crossed the border three days before that night. We rented rooms at the Biltmore Resort and Ramon went crazy. He got drunk and used cocaine every night with two or three call girls in his room. On the third night he made so much noise, I went in and threw out the women and told him to go to bed or I would kill him. He was angry with me, but he did it because he knew I *would* kill him."

"Why did he act that way? Didn't he realize he'd draw attention to you guys?"

"Ramon acted like a stupid child. Miguel has taken care of him ever since their parents died and he never allowed Ramon to grow up. He protected him."

"Whores and cocaine sounds like a stupid adult to me. What did you guys do next?"

"I got Ramon up at noon the next day and worked all afternoon getting him sober enough to take care of business. He remained angry and uncooperative with me until I told him to stop acting like an idiot, or I'd call Miguel and tell him to take Ramon off the delivery. He calmed down and apologized. I took him to dinner and gave him a couple of beers. He seemed better. We drove out to southwest Phoenix and rented a cheap motel room and waited until it was time to go to Rainbow Valley. I drove the pickup and he drove the Blazer."

"Which way did you go?"

"We took the road that goes around the north end of the Estrellas."

"Did you see anyone else out there?"

"Dusk had set, but we didn't see anyone."

"What happened next?"

"As usual, Newman landed on time. He really is a good pilot."

"And probably a little crazy to fly the way smugglers do."

Carlos laughed, "He does take chances when he flies a load. Anyway, we started to unload the money when I heard the sound of the Blackhawk. I yelled to Ramon to get into the Blazer. Ramon argued with me and told me he should drive. Even though I knew better, I jumped into the passenger seat. Newman got in the pickup truck. Ramon fumbled with the keys for what seemed like forever.

'The Blackhawk flew overhead when the pickup took off. Ramon finally started the engine of the Blazer and just started to roll when the Blackhawk's light hit us and dust went flying everywhere. I couldn't see anything and the roar of the Blackhawk hurt my ears. It was deafening."

"That big bird is scary at night, that's for sure."

"Yes it is, especially the way those pilots flew it. They are madmen!"

Chris chuckled. "That's been suggested more than once. Go on."

"Well, Ramon floored the accelerator, but the Blackhawk jumped in front of us and we were blinded by the searchlight. Ramon turned sharply to the left, almost rolling the vehicle, but the Blackhawk cut us off again and Ramon slammed on the brakes.

"I knew we had to get out of there, so I grabbed Ramon by the hair and pulled him over to the passenger side. The Blazer still rolled slowly, but I kicked open the passenger door and dragged Ramon out of it. I yelled into his ear for him to hold on to my belt and run with me. Instead, he pushed me away and pulled his AK-47 out of the Blazer. His eyes were crazy and he screamed back at me he wanted to kill American policemen, so Miguel would be proud of him."

"Jesus, he really was crazy!"

"Yes and I decided to leave the idiot and get out of there. I heard gunfire over the sound of the Blackhawk. I ran through the dust and sprinted for as long as I could. My legs hurt because I ran into cholla cactus and the spines set deep in my legs, so I hid under a palo verde tree. I tried to catch my breath and used my knife to remove as many of the cholla spines as I could.

"The Blackhawk started circling in wider arcs. I figured the police officers were tracking me. Then, the Blackhawk's searchlight pointed right at me and did not move. I bolted and ran down a wash with high banks, looking for a hole to duck into. That's when the policeman tackled me. Now, I'm here."

"Thank you, Carlos. I appreciate your honesty. Now, is Miguel the main threat to your wife?"

"Yes. If she is still alive, the one man who is probably keeping her safe is Juan Trinidad."

"Who is he?"

"He is Miguel's enforcer and number two man in the organization. Juan acts like a friend, and I hope he will protect my wife."

"I wonder why we don't know about him."

"He stays low and moves like a ghost. He is extremely dangerous."

"What is your wife's name?"

"Maria."

"You don't seem positive Juan will protect Maria."

"Miguel has made Juan a very rich and powerful man. Juan's first allegiance will always belong to Miguel. Juan is also ruthless."

Chris thought for a minute. "Is there a way to contact Juan?"

"If he's at the ranch, I can call him."

"I think it is best at this point to call Juan. We can accomplish two things by calling him. We can get some information on Maria and we can find out just how upset Miguel is."

"I am not sure what to tell him."

"Tell him the truth...right up to the point where you got arrested. Did he feel the same about Ramon as you did?"

"Yes, he had no use for Ramon."

"Good, then he will understand you did everything you could to get Ramon out of there. You can tell Juan everything you told me, except instead of getting arrested, you kept on going. The helicopter didn't come after you, but stayed over the vehicles."

"What do I say about not calling him?"

"Come on, Carlos, what did they train you to do when you may have been compromised?"

"Go underground until things cool off...Ah, I see."

Chris reached over, picked up the telephone, and put it in front of Carlos. "Now is as good a time as ever, my friend."

Carlos put the headset to his ear and dialed. Chris could hear the phone ringing. It rang five times. Carlos was starting to hang up when Chris heard, "What is it?"

"Juanito."

"Carlos! It is good to know you are alive!"

"Yes, Juan, I am. A little full of cactus spines, but I am alive."

"Where are you?"

"I stayed at a motel in Casa Grande the last couple of nights. I am at a phone booth now and I can probably start working my way back to the ranch."

"That would not be wise, Carlos. Miguel is furious about Ramon. He wants to kill you."

"He is not upset about the money?"

"No, we found out Newman escaped with the money. The police apparently did not chase you because they shot and killed Ramon."

"Yes, I saw on the news they killed Ramon. Juan, I tried to save Ramon, but he would not listen to me. He said he wanted to kill an American policeman so Miguel would be proud of him. I had to leave him and try to escape. I've been lying low until things cooled off."

"Ramon was worthless. You did the right thing, Carlos."

"What about Miguel?"

"I'll handle Miguel. Stay low and call me in three or four days."

"Juan, is Maria safe?"

"Maria is safe for now. Just do as I say and she will stay that way."

"I will. Please tell Maria I am safe."

"I will, Carlos. Adios."

"Adios, Juan."

Carlos put the handset back into the cradle. "Did you hear everything?" Chris smiled and gave Carlos thumbs up.

FOURTEEN

Robin lay on the ground under a piñon tree and peered through an infrared scope at two men ten yards away, watering their marijuana plants. Burke Jameson lay next to him, taping the men's actions with a camcorder equipped with a night vision scope.

They were the third shift into the surveillance. The previous shifts verified a large garden, well cared for and guarded. The Guardians had found two more booby traps. Most of the players were filmed and pictures sent for identification. All the guards were counted and their habits and favorite locations plotted. The two men Robin and Bob watched were the last ones on which the officers needed good film.

Robin slowly used the infrared scope to do a 360 °security check. He saw one coyote and a deer. He looked for the other two lookouts for the group, but didn't see them in the immediate area.

The two officers lay in that position for almost two hours. Robin thought no matter how many times he did this, he could never find a position in which he could stay comfortable. Right now cold seeped into his body, even through the thick ghillie suit. His ribs ached from lying on the ground for so long. His neck hurt from the position he kept to maintain situational awareness. This, in turn, caused a headache.

Burke used the camcorder on a small tripod. He pulled his eye from the lens and turned and looked at Robin. Burke grinned at Robin's obvious discomfort. Robin shook his head and smiled. He wondered why Burke always took such joy in his misery. Burke's white teeth were accentuated by his camouflage-painted face. He signaled to Robin he had shot good tape of the suspects.

A short time later, the two suspects finished watering and moved down a small trail. Robin gave the signal to move out and the two officers silently withdrew from the area.

They made their way back to base camp and Emmett greeted them with freshly cooked hamburgers and cold beer. Before eating, Robin made arrangements by radio to meet the sergeant of Cooperative Enforcement Unit for the Payson area at the Rye store in the morning. He then returned to his meal as he contemplated the men around the campfire.

All of these men were brothers to Robin, as much as a sergeant could feel so. Robin understood when he accepted promotion, he had to maintain a certain distance from his men so he could actually supervise them. He gave them much leeway to handle their assignments, but insisted on regular updates. He was a stickler for reports that were thorough, accurate, and on time. He made it clear to his men if they failed to produce, he would have them transferred quickly—but because of his fairness, the men of his squad grew to trust him. Robin didn't spend much time correcting problems, and never had the occasion to transfer anyone.

Robin finished his meal and started to turn in for the night. He told the men he would take the watch at 0300 with a gentle reminder it would be an early morning. He left them to discuss whatever they wanted, including him, which they did.

"How come he always has to take the tough jobs?" Mark said in a low whisper.

"That's called leadership, Mark," Burke responded. "He knows he'll have to ask us to do tough jobs. He just wants us to know he'll do them too."

"He is a good sergeant, isn't he?" Burke looked at Mark and smiled.

"Puppy dog, there are good sergeants and bad ones. We got us a good one for now. Enjoy it while you can."

Sergeant Ken Orloe was a tall, thin man who was happy with his lot in life. He lived and worked just where he wanted to be. If shit happened out of Gila County, it didn't much interest him. Like most

DPS officers, though, he always enjoyed hearing from Robin and his team because it meant some action different from the type of investigations his detectives did most of the time. The two sergeants greeted each other warmly in front of the Rye store.

Robin and Ken had worked together as patrolmen on the Beeline Highway, so their friendship went back fifteen years. Ken was ten years older than Robin and nearing retirement. He spent his entire career in Payson.

"What's up, Rob?"

"Oh, looks like we got ourselves some pros here, Ken."

"Yeah, we've got ID's on most of them. Some of these guys are very dangerous."

"Let me guess—ex-military?"

"At least one ex-Army Ranger. All of them have rap sheets."

"Fits," replied Robin.

"You got a plan, ol' Hoss?"

"Yeah, give the case to you and your guys to handle and go home!"

"Hey, you're gettin' to be a funny guy."

"Okay, I got a plan. I've got another tactical team coming in. I'll need your guys and some patrol guys to make sure that if someone gets through us, they won't get away."

"So, we watch the back door," observed Ken.

"Yep, and do the follow-up investigation."

"We can do that."

"Okay, we will brief at 1900 hours tonight at the Payson Sheriff's Office. Have the sheriff or his undersheriff there. We will give them command and control. We'll launch the take down at 0600 tomorrow."

"I'll have our end lined up and I know Sheriff Davis will be there."

"Thanks, Ken."

The two men parted company. As he drove back to Payson, Ken thought back to when he and Robin were young patrolmen. Even then he knew Robin Marlette was a man who got things done. Now, he set up a raid on a major marijuana garden to make the sheriff the hero. The man thinks of everything. Ken grinned from ear to ear.

Jose Molina stood at Mary Tatum's desk. Mary, the narcotics division secretary, had just left for the day. Jose looked at the division roster, trying to memorize the addresses for Burke Jameson and Mike Collins. Mary's roster contained addresses and not just phone numbers, unlike the agents' version. The roster lay in Mary's top left desk drawer. Jose already found out Marlette's address for Juan, but as usual, he wanted more.

"Hi, Jose." Mary's voice startled him and his head jerked up. "I left my glasses and had to come back. What are you looking for?"

"I was looking for...for a staple remover," Jose stammered.

Mary pointed to the top of her desk and said, "It's right there, silly. I thought cops were supposed to be trained observers," she said with a smile.

"Oh, I didn't see it. Sorry. I got so many things going, I'm a little scatterbrained lately. Thanks, Mary." Jose's voice was barely audible. He picked up the staple remover and walked around the corner to his squad room.

Mary stared at Molina as he walked away and thought about how strangely he acted. As she picked up her glasses, she thought if Molina had a lot of things going on, they did not have much to do with police work. Neither she nor the other two secretaries typed many reports for him. She saw the open top left drawer. As she closed it, she noticed the roster.

Walking to her car, she couldn't forget how nervous and evasive Jose seemed to be. She also thought of the man who had been calling Jose lately. She did not like the sound of his voice. Mary looked at her watch and let out an involuntary "Oh, my," realizing she was running late.

The crisp mountain air felt good to Robin. Rays of the morning sun began to glow over the hilltops, nibbling at the night gloom blanketing the trees. A slight breeze rustled the forest. He knelt on one knee in a thicket, Burke ten feet away. They watched the suspect guarding the southern edge of the marijuana garden. Well, sort of. The guard was sleeping.

Rick reported another guard on the eastern edge of the garden was causing him and Mike fits because he was constantly moving. Keeping him in sight while remaining concealed took every bit of their field craft abilities. Then, Mike whispered over the radio the suspect had stopped moving.

Robin radioed Sheriff Davis, and they were set. Sheriff Davis asked the other teams if they were ready. He received affirmative replies. The sheriff's voice then came over the radio loud and clear. "EXECUTE, EXECUTE, EXECUTE! I REPEAT. EXECUTE, EXECUTE, EXECUTE!

Burke moved as a shadowy whisper toward the suspect, who started to rise up. Robin fell in behind. A loud bang sounded to the north, and he figured Sergeant Sean Palmer's SOU team had thrown a flash bang into the camp trailer the dopers used at the northern edge of the garden. Robin heard a man yelp to the east. A coyote burst out the thicket in front of Robin, startling him.

In one smooth move, Burke had the suspect face down in an arm lock. In a calm, sinister voice, Burke told the suspect they were the police and he was under arrest and not to move until told to do so. The suspect lay motionless. Robin keyed his radio: "Two Nora Six, one in custody."

Rick's laughing voice came over the radio. "Two Nora Six-Five, one in custody."

"West side clear," Doug announced.

"Trailer clear, two in custody," Sergeant Palmer called.

Sheriff Davis then said, "All take down teams are clear. All teams can stand down."

Robin and Burke handcuffed their suspect, and Burke started searching. He exclaimed, "Damn, man, you pissed your pants!" Robin looked—indeed, the man had lost control of his bladder.

"What the hell do you expect!" the suspect exclaimed. "You scared me to death! Fuck, this is embarrassing!"

Robin felt sorry for the suspect. If he heard Burke's sinister voice in his ear like that, he might have just done the same, he thought. They lifted the suspect to his feet and sized up a thin young man with black bushy hair, very tan with fearful blue eyes.

"Please don't take me to jail like this," the suspect pleaded.

"There's not much we can do unless you have some extra pants around here," Robin said.

"I do, up in the trailer," the man motioned north with his head. Robin looked at Burke, who shrugged his shoulders.

"Okay, I will let you change your pants on one condition. We found a grenade booby trap on the south side of the garden during our surveillance. Are there more?"

The suspect took a deep breath. "Yes. There are three more: one on the east side, one on the west side, and one in the middle of the garden." The team hadn't found the trap in middle of the garden because they hadn't reached there yet.

Robin keyed his radio. "All personnel stay out of the garden until further notice." He looked at the suspect. "Okay, bud, now we know you are a straight shooter. What is your name?"

"My name is Perry Don Jenkins."

"How are old are you?"

"I'm nineteen years old."

"Okay, Perry Don, take us to the booby trap in the middle of the garden. After we disarm the trap, we'll take you up to the trailer and you can change clothes."

"Thank you," Perry Don said.

Perry Don led the way to the trap, winding through barely discernable paths lined with emerald green marijuana plants. He seemed to relax, and chatted with his captors. He stopped near the center of the garden and pointed out gnarled scrub oak.

"The grenade is over there." Robin disarmed the grenade while Burke watched the suspect. After Robin made the grenade safe, they hiked up towards the trailer.

"Don't you want me to show you where the other grenades are?" Perry Don asked.

"We already found them," Robin replied.

Perry Don became quiet. When the three men got close to the trailer, they could see all the officers standing around the west side of the vehicle.

"Burke, take Perry Don around to the east side so the other guys don't seem him."

"I appreciate you letting me change pants, Sergeant."

"No problem, Perry Don. We're not here to hurt or embarrass you." Burke started taking the suspect away and looked at Robin. Robin pointed to Perry Don's back and then made a rolling motion with his hand, telling Burke to "roll" Perry Don as an informant. Burke nodded and gave a lazy salute.

As Robin approached the group of officers, Sheriff Davis walked up to him and held out his hand. Robin took it and the Sheriff gave Robin a warm handshake.

"Sergeant Marlette, thanks for a great job."

"Our pleasure to assist CEU, Sheriff."

"I understand you are going to let CEU do the follow-up investigation."

"Well, sir, this is your county. I didn't "let" CEU do anything. I expected they would do the follow-up. We are just here to help with the tactical side."

The Sheriff laughed. "When are you going to run for office?"

"Never, Sheriff. I'm not a politician."

"Could've have fooled me!"

They joined the group. Robin saw Mike and asked him why he laughed when he reported they had their suspect in custody.

"That guy gave us fits because he moved pretty damn fast. Then all of the sudden he stops and starts looking around and pulls some toilet paper out of his pack. To make a long story short, let's just say when we arrested him we caught him with his pants down," Mike said with a grin.

FIFTEEN

The next morning, Robin worked at his desk at the DPS office when Emmett came in and sat down.

"Hey, Sarge."

"Emmett, my good man," Robin replied.

"We're ready to go up on the Walton wire starting tomorrow at 0800. Doug and Mark have the surveillance up and running. The pens are active and we are getting good activity. Walton is calling Rodriquez. A lot of calls also to government offices and officials homes in at least four states and D.C. In fact, I calmed Norm Walls down. He's getting a little nervous about it."

"Is he going to be okay? You want me to talk to him?" Robin asked.

"Awww, he'll be okay. He says it's just because he has never seen shit like this. I got him straightened out."

"You're a good man, Emmett Franks," Robin said with a smile. Still, Robin wondered what Norm Walls told the big wigs at U.S. West.

Emmett continued. "The FBI and Customs are bringing in additional people from all over the country to man the wire and help with surveillance. IRS is on board with three agents. MCSO is sending two guys over. Ernie's guys are good to go. That's the good news."

Robin's eyebrow went up. "What's the bad news?"

"DEA is going bonkers because they're not included. Jim Adams is on the hot seat. The U.S. Attorney is not happy."

"I figured we couldn't avoid this. I'll deal with it, Emmett."

"Amen, brother. I do *not* want to be near that problem."

"I will call Jim in a little bit."

"Okee dokee, Sarge." Emmett went back to his desk.

Robin went down the hall to see Lieutenant Hammel. Mary told Robin Hammel was in Captain Pearle's office. Robin went to Pearle's office and stood in the door.

"Look what the cat drug in," Tom Pearle joked.

Lieutenant Hammel turned around and waved Robin in. "We were just going to try to find you. Good hit on that garden yesterday."

"Thanks. It got even better. We rolled a young kid up there and turned him over to Ken Orloe and CEU. He gave them two more garden locations and all the names in the group. Ken says they are taking down people who have been on their list for a long time."

"Outstanding!" Hammel exclaimed.

"What else do you have, Robin?" Pearle asked.

"We are ready to go up on the Walton wire tomorrow at 0800. My team will not be available for anything other than maintaining our current informants and SOU calls, and we may not even be able to field a full team for those."

"We will do our best to pass on stuff, Robin, but you know how that goes," Pearle warned. "We all do what we need to do."

"Tom, you guys have got to cut me slack. This case must have priority." Robin went on to relate Emmett's report.

"Wow!" Hammel exclaimed when Robin finished.

Tom Pearle leaned forward in his chair and looked Robin directly in the eye. "Robin, we are well aware of the importance of the case. I have stuck out my professional neck a hundred miles for you and this case. But the world does not come to a standstill just because you are working a major case. Hell, part of your predicament is you! It's you who insisted on training up to be a SOU team on your team's OWN TIME! It's YOU who took on the marijuana eradication program coordination and the Customs Air Support assignment." Pearle took a deep breath. "We will do our best for you. That's all we can do."

"I appreciate it," Robin said as he got up and walked out. Though an old and good friend, Robin was seething with fury at Tom Pearle. Robin did insist his team train up to be a SOU team. This idea came to him three years prior when on two occasions he requested the SOU team for high-risk search warrants and they turned him down because they could not field enough officers in time. Robin asked Glendale PD SWAT team to do the first one and the Maricopa County Sheriff's office team to do the second one. He requested his team be allowed to go to the MCSO one-week eighty-hour SWAT course, but the department turned him down. So, his whole team signed up for vacation for the week of the training.

The SWAT commander, Lieutenant Danny Wilson, came to Robin's office and told him his team could not go to the training. Robin looked directly at the lieutenant and said, "Danny, I am a rolling locomotive. You can either get on board or get out of the way." Lieutenant Wilson looked at Robin for a minute and then left. He came back thirty minutes later and handed Robin written orders assigning his team as Team Six of the DPS Special Operations Unit. After reading the order, Robin looked up and Lieutenant Wilson had left.

As for accepting the eradication coordination and Air Support assignments, Pearle specifically asked Robin to take them because the programs were in disarray. It seemed a tad bit unfair to Robin for Pearle to throw those in his face now.

Robin went into his office and sat down. His irritation was still percolating when Rick Santos came in to his office.

"Hey Sarge, I just got some hot intel from Jorge, that disabled *Federale* working for us out of Nogales."

"What's he got for us?" Robin quickly forgot about being angry with Pearle.

"Like we asked him to do, he got hooked up with some boys working security for Rodriquez-Lara." Robin perked up. "He hit pay dirt, Rob. He has been asked to join the security team at the ranch southeast of Nogales Chris told us about. It has tons of shit stacked up, ready to be smuggled into the U.S. He says he will be heading out there tomorrow, after his new buddies finish partying."

"Damn, Rick! That *is* hot intel. What else did he say about this ranch?"

"That's all he knows right now."

Robin thought for a minute, mulling over what Rick had said. "Jorge is really sticking his neck out. Up his monthly pay another grand. Did you tell him to be very careful?"

"Ooooh yeah, I did. He knows what he is getting into, but I told him if he gets the slightest hint they are on to him, he should beat feet for the border and get a hold of us and we will take care of him."

"Good."

"There is one thing though, Rob."

"What's that?"

"It's his wife and kids. They are in Hermosillo and his new buddies don't know about them. He's worried about getting them here, in case he has to make a run for it."

"Hmm, that's a more complicated problem. I'll talk to Bill Grassley and Chris Fleming and see what contingency we can set up."

Rick laughed.

"What's so funny?" Robin asked.

"I am sure those poor fuckers regret the day they laid eyes on you, Sarge."

"Maybe, but Bill and Chris are good guys and they get things done. Now you get some things done, Santos. We're burning daylight."

"You got it, Sarge."

As Rick walked out of his office, Robin picked up the phone and dialed Jim Adams's number.

"Jim Adams."

"Hey, Jim. It's Robin. How ya doin'?"

"Rob! Boy, I'm glad you called. I'm in a pickle."

"DEA?"

"You got it. They're driving my boss crazy. I'm afraid I am going to have to ask a big favor from you, but before you balk, hear me out."

"Go ahead."

"We met with them yesterday. I reminded them of the problems we've had with them on those two previous OCDETF operations. They agreed there were some problems, but they said you were part of the problem because you were, and I quote, 'undiplomatic.' I agreed you were undiplomatic"

"You did what?! Why did you do that?"

"Because you are, Rob. You are a straightforward, no nonsense, no bullshit guy. You have all the tact of a nuclear device. Exactly the kind of person I want running a task force I'm responsible for. That's what I told them. I didn't agree that you were part of the problem."

"Jesus, Jim, I don't think I'm that bad."

"You are, but I consider it a virtue, not a flaw. I know very few people who approach the world like you do, Rob. Hell, even the guys in your own squad say they just follow behind you and pick up the pieces."

"Aw, what do they know?"

"Since they practically live with you, they know you better than anyone else. But, enough about you. Here's the deal. I need you to happily accept one DEA agent into this task force as a favor to me, so I can calm things down for my boss."

Robin did not answer right away. "All right, Jim, you and your boss have been great to us. I'll take one agent."

"I would like to emphasize the word 'happily.'"

Robin let out a slow breath. "For you, just for you."

"Thanks. I knew I could count on you. I have to get going. Got a hearing to get to."

"Take it easy, Jim."

"You too, Rob."

Robin made it a point to get home a little early that evening. The wire going online meant lots of overtime and less time with his family--the one aspect of his job he hated.

He took some time to sit down with Laurie, who was sixteen and the most serious child in the family. She had already mapped out her career goals. While serious most of time, she went into fits of crazy humor on occasion. Robin figured she maintained a satirical view of life. He gave thanks both of his daughters drew most of their physical qualities from Karen. Laurie looked very much like her mother.

Robin worked the conversation around to Chad Wilson.

"So, who is this Chad person?"

"Just a friend, Dad."

"How much of a friend?"

"Now don't start interrogating me, Sergeant."

"I'm not interrogating you, Laurie. You are my daughter and I love you. It wouldn't be fatherly to ignore a possible boyfriend. It just comes naturally to most fathers, I suppose."

Laurie looked at her father for a moment. "Okay, Dad. We're dating."

"Is he nice to you?"

"Of course he is."

"Well, what I really mean is, does he treat you like a princess?"

"Like a typical Marlette. If he doesn't, I'll punch his lights out."

Robin involuntarily laughed from the bottom of his belly.

Laurie got up and hugged her dad. She looked at him with a warm smile and said, "I love you, Dad."

"I love you, too, honey."

"Don't worry. It's not like I'm looking for the one and only. I have a lot of things I want to do in life before I have a family. Chad is a good friend and fun to be with."

"That's great, Laurie. He sounds like a good guy."

"He is."

Laurie went to wash up for dinner. Robin walked into the kitchen, where Karen was working on dinner. Robin gave her a kiss.

"How long before we eat?"

"It will take the meatloaf about another forty-five minutes."

"Oh, one of my favorites! Would you like to have a glass of wine with me before we eat?"

"That would be lovely."

Robin opened a bottle of Chateau St. Michelle merlot, a new Washington State wine he and Karen enjoyed. He took the glasses of wine out to the living room, handed Karen her glass, and sat down next to her. They toasted each other and said, "I love you" at the same time. They'd done this since the day they were married. They would rather be out on their back porch, but the July heat made the porch out of the question.

"So, the wire starts tomorrow," Karen said.

"It does."

Karen let out a long breath and took a sip of wine. Robin looked at her.

"I know it's tough, Babe. I'm getting a little tired of it myself. I'm missing too much of us and the kids. I'm thinking of going back to patrol after this case is done."

"Are you really, Rob, or are you just trying to make me feel better?"

"Actually, I have been thinking about it for awhile. I would like to go to another rural duty station. Maybe Flagstaff or the White Mountains."

"I thought they were tough spots for a sergeant to get."

"Well, the openings don't come too often because guys just don't want to leave them. But I think I could make a good run at it if one opens up."

"As long as the lieutenant or the captain isn't someone you've pissed off."

"Now you are starting to sound like Jim Adams."

"Why? What did Jim say?"

"He said I have all the tact of a nuclear device."

Karen laughed. "That's an appropriate description."

"Don't get carried away. He claimed it's a virtue, not a flaw."

"That certainly depends on your point of view."

Robin sipped his wine and shook his head. "I would think my wife would have nice things to say about me."

"Your wife tells it like it is. She just does it with diplomacy."

"Well, I guess we make a good pair then. You be the diplomat and I'll be the big stick."

"I always thought you were, honey," Karen said, deepening her voice.

"You are a good woman." They both laughed.

Casey came through the front door. He was carrying Eddie piggyback.

"We're hungry," Casey announced. "Is it time for dinner yet, Mom?"

"It is almost ready. You two get cleaned up."

"What are we having?" Casey asked.

"Meatloaf."

"Aw, I hate meatloaf."

"I like meatloaf," Eddie said.

"So do I, Eddie," Robin replied. "So, we win!"

At dinner, the family discussed getting another dog. Their black lab, Buddy, had died a month ago. Buddy had been in the family for eleven years, after being rescued from the pound. Losing Buddy hit Eddie particularly hard, and he wanted another dog. Robin and Karen decided they should wait a year and see where things were.

After dinner, Robin washed the dishes as the family sat at the kitchen bar and discussed many different things. Eddie asked when they were going camping again. Robin looked at him and felt that guilt building up inside.

"We will probably have to wait until the end of August, Eddie."

"Why, Dad?"

"Work is going to get really busy for awhile." Eddie's face fell. Robin felt terrible. He really needed to get back to patrol.

Later in the evening, Robin and Karen lay in bed after making love. Holding Robin close, Karen fell asleep with his arm under her. Even though it started to hurt, Robin didn't want to move it. Instead, he pulled her closer to him. He wondered why she loved him so much. He knew he was a lucky man and when he finished this case he needed to start looking for a rural duty station. Karen and his children deserved it. He just didn't know how to tell his squad. Robin didn't sleep much that night.

SIXTEEN

At 0515 hours, Robin walked into the Phoenix Police Academy auditorium, a large room half-full of federal, state, and local law enforcement officers assigned to the task force. The purpose of this mandatory briefing was to bring everybody up to speed on the case and to have Jim Adams read the court order along with the wiretap operating rules and procedures.

At 0530 Robin gave an introduction and began a description of the case. He talked for about twenty minutes and concluded by ordering everyone to read an up-to-date report located at the wire room within the week. Then Jim Adams got up and read the court order. He spent the next thirty minutes talking about the wiretap operating rules and procedures. When the briefing concluded, Robin announced the first wire shift and surveillance team should head over to the wire room and meet him there.

Thirty minutes later, Robin arrived at the off-site wire room located in a small, non-descript office building which had been empty for about six months. Situated in a rough neighborhood in central Phoenix, it would be manned twenty-four hours a day by armed law enforcement officers, minimizing any problems posed by the local riffraff.

Emmett Franks and Mike Collins did all of the work in getting the wire room set up. Emmett greeted Robin and took him to a back room set up as a supervisor's office.

"Here's your new digs, Sarge."

"Looks great, Emmett. I'll get settled in. Will you get the listening teams set up?"

"Will do."

As Robin unloaded his briefcase, he heard a knock on his door. He turned around and saw an attractive woman standing at the door. She stood a little shorter than him, and filled her clothes nicely. She appeared to be of Asian descent, but she had the saddest eyes Robin had ever seen.

"Hi," Robin said.

"Good morning, Sergeant. I'm Angie Spurline. I'm with DEA, and I have been assigned to this case."

Robin waved to a chair. "Have a seat, Angie, and you can call me Robin or Rob."

"Thank you." Angie seemed tense. "I will get right to the point. I'm told you're not happy to have me here. I just want you to know I will work hard and follow instructions."

"I appreciate that, Angie, but my beef is with DEA as an agency, not with you personally. I approved an agent to be assigned here. So, don't think you're not welcome."

Angie seemed to relax a little bit at hearing this. She didn't say anything in reply and Robin felt a little awkward.

"How long have you been assigned to the Phoenix office?" he asked.

"I just arrived here yesterday."

"Damn, they didn't even give you time to get settled? What about your family?"

"I don't have a family, so it is not that much of a problem. I'll get settled when my things get here."

"Well, let us know if you need help moving furniture. We'll be glad to help."

"Why, thank you!" Angie seemed surprised by the offer.

"No problem. All you need is a case of beer and you will have all the help you need," Robin said, grinning.

"I'll do that," Angie replied with a smile.

"Well, Angie, if you get with Emmett or Mike out there, they will get you set up on a listening team."

"Thank you, Sergeant...er, Robin."

"No problem, Angie."

What the hell is going on? Robin thought. It seemed terribly unfair to assign Angie to this case when she just transferred into the

Phoenix office. Either the Phoenix DEA SAC Paul Krause had really gone around the bend, or there was something Angie wasn't telling him. Robin certainly had his differences with Krause, but he didn't think Krause was that bad a supervisor. Robin shook his head. Once again, DEA presented a problem to him.

SEVENTEEN

Robin knocked on the door to room seventeen at the Luke Air Force Base BOQ two days later. Chris Fleming opened the door and Robin walked in. He and Carlos nodded to each other, but said nothing. Robin told Chris since Carlos had talked and told the truth as verified by Jorge, Robin's attitude had changed about Carlos as long as he did not insult his men.

Robin knew Carlos didn't tell Chris everything, but what information he did provide turned out to be valuable.

Chris spoke first. "I know this isn't exactly a joyful reunion, but we are at the point where we all have to work together."

"Good morning, Carlos. You're looking much better than the night we met," Robin said.

"Yes...a bad night for me."

"We all have them from time to time."

"Your men were very good that night, very professional."

Robin looked at Chris, who just shrugged. "Thank you, Carlos. They are all good men. I am glad you didn't judge them by my bad temper."

"I should not have insulted your men."

With that statement, Robin stood up and held out his right hand to Carlos. Carlos stood up and warmly shook Robin's hand. Chris looked at them and thought about how, in the end, all true warriors are alike.

"Okay, gentlemen. Let's get down to business. First of all, Carlos, Robin has some news for you."

"Carlos, we have an informant at Miguel's ranch. He has verified Maria is safe and that no one bothers her. The only one who visits her is Juan Trinidad, and she does not let him stay long. I have instructed the informant to let us know immediately if there is any threat to her. He said he would watch out for her."

Carlos seemed somewhat relieved. "How can he do anything against so many men if Miguel tries to hurt her?"

"Let's just say he has the training and capability to take care of business, if he has to. He's certainly better than nothing."

"We are also working on an extraction plan with assets we have in Mexico," Chris said. We have to proceed cautiously because of the corruption factor."

"Yes, I am aware of that problem. I helped cause it." Carlos looked down at the floor. "There are other Cuban intelligence assets in Mexico." Chris' eyes widened. "There are also Soviet assets there," Carlos continued. "The network is heavy around Mexico City and the border."

Chris looked at Carlos. "Why are you telling us this?"

"I have been thinking. If I were an American intelligence agent captured by the Cubans or the Soviets and told them about my wife, they wouldn't care. I have also been thinking about how you both are fighting drugs and I am smuggling them. I sit here and talk to you two and I find myself liking you. At the ranch I am surrounded by scum, not warriors. I am getting confused about which side I want to be on."

Robin sat down. "Carlos, the side you need to be on is the one that doesn't kill your soul at night. Our side certainly isn't perfect. We have our own problems, but the principles our founding fathers settled on are magnificent. We just need to keep guiding ourselves back to them."

"I have read your Constitution. I like it very much, but your government has done some very bad things."

"True, but we manage to do a lot more good than bad. There are a lot of Americans buried around the world who helped free the oppressed."

"Look what you are doing to my country."

"You'll have to decide who is hurting your country. I think you're smart enough to see the truth."

"Carlos, I really appreciate you telling us more about the intelligence operations in Mexico," Chris said. "You need to think about what you want to do. As Robin said, you have to be true to your own soul. We have to check in with Juan right now. You can tell more about the Cuban and Soviet intelligence network later, if you want to. Right now we need to make the call." Carlos picked up the phone and called Juan. Chris and Robin leaned close to listen.

"Hola."

"Juan, it is Carlos."

"Ahh, good. How are you?"

"I am fine, Juan. How is Maria?"

"She is fine, Carlos. Do not worry. Miguel is not as set on killing you as before, but it is still not time for you to come back. I told Miguel I have you doing other things across the border."

"Juan, I *can* do other things for you."

"You are going to. I want you to contact Newman. I want you to be security for the money. He has it. Do you still have his number?"

"Yes, I do."

"Call Newman at four o'clock this afternoon. He is expecting your call."

"I will take care of it, Juan."

"I know you will, Carlos. Adios."

"Adios, Juan."

Robin got up to leave. He reached in his briefcase and then handed Carlos a small paperback copy of the United States Constitution. He shook hands with Carlos and said, "We're much alike, Carlos. We fight hard for principles we believe in. Read the United States Constitution again--the whole thing, including the Declaration of Independence. Then think about where your soul would be most comfortable. I believe I know the answer, but it is your soul and your search. Good luck, my friend. I'll be in touch."

"Thank you, Robin."

When Robin left, Carlos said to Chris, "He is a good man."

"Some people hate him, some love him, but he's one of the best in my book."

The wire progressed into the second week. This early morning Robin and the administrative team sat down for a daily review in the small conference room at the off-site.

Robin leaned forward in his chair. "I don't know about you guys, but it seems like the days are flashing by."

"Well, that's what happens when you put in twelve, sixteen, and sometimes eighteen hour days," John Lucheck answered. "You've taken one day off since the taps went up. You need to slow down, Rob."

"These taps have proven to be more successful than I ever dreamed. We are finally hitting the corrupt government officials and businessmen who make drug trafficking possible. We've been working very long hours, and it won't let up until we are done. Our commanders have stuck their collective necks out for us, and we're not going to let them down. I appreciate your concern for me, and I appreciate the hard work you have been doing," Robin said.

Lucheck looked down at the table. "I didn't mean to upset you, Rob."

"You didn't, John. I'm just telling you how it is. Now, what did Walton do yesterday?"

Lucheck smiled at Robin. "Walton's been busy contacting those who get payoffs and arranging deliveries. We all know he has contacted law enforcement officials at every level--a prosecutor, local politicians, local and state administrative officials, state legislators, five members of congress, and two senators--but we really hit pay dirt yesterday evening. He contacted Robert Mickerson, the President's Chief of Staff."

Robin gave Lucheck a hard look. "Any indication the President is involved?"

"Not so far, Rob."

"Did we get any incriminating statements?"

"Definitely. They talked about payoffs for information about FBI and DEA investigations Mickerson gave in the past. He wants a raise."

Robin could feel his jaw tighten. He knew Mickerson's actions in the past had most likely caused the deaths of informants and maybe even law enforcement officers. Although impossible, Robin wanted to be there for the arrest of the son of a bitch. "Go on."

"The progress of the case has built enough evidence to finish Walton and send him to prison for the rest of his life. He speaks very carefully on the telephone when arranging the payoffs. He uses a well-entrenched code. His main downfall is that Eric Newman and Carlos Casconda were making the deliveries. They are both wearing Nagra recorders during the deliveries, and code isn't used during those discussions. We also have a lot good surveillance photographs and videotapes of many of the meetings. Walton is in regular contact with Miguel Rodriquez-Lara. While they are both careful about what they say, the code is not sophisticated and we've been able to interpret the conversation."

"What is the surveillance on Walton telling us, Ernie?"

"Walton's most confidential communications with Rodriquez are through meetings Walton has with a man identified as Juan Trinidad-Nunez. The teams assigned to conduct the surveillance on these meetings report that Trinidad is very observant and has his head on a constant swivel. Surveillance is difficult for any length of time. Moving surveillance is virtually impossible without an aircraft, and even that's difficult."

"Do we have any idea at all what they talk about?"

"The surveillance teams reported that on the last two of these meetings, the two men seemed agitated with each other, but we don't know why."

"Damn, I wish we could get a tap on Rodriquez's phone!"

"Why don't we?" Angie asked.

"There's no way we could get a court order in Mexico, let alone keep it secret." Robin took a deep breath. "Angie, how are we doing on the follow-up taps?"

"We now have seven more wiretaps in five states and Washington D.C. because of the activity on Walton's phones. We have the evidence for more taps, but there's just not enough people or money to do them."

"What are the other agencies reporting as far as evidence from the current taps?"

"Same as ours, Rob. A lot of government officials and businessmen, particularly bankers, are going down."

"Does that go for the taps DEA is running for us?"

"Yes it does, Rob."

Robin leaned back in his chair and smiled at Angie. "Well, Angie, it looks like DEA and I have finally been able to work together. I credit you with helping out on that score." Angie smiled but did not reply.

"Okay, folks, thanks for the update. Let's get back to doing something productive."

Angie hung back as the others left the conference room. "Rob, I really haven't been able to thank you for going to bat for me with DEA."

"Hell, Angie, it's stupid of them to want to replace you just because the case got so large that we needed get them fully involved. They were just trying to put their favorite boys in. Besides, I really didn't do it. They would never listen to me about something like that. Jim Adams held them off."

"You led the fight, Rob."

"Look, Angie, you've done an outstanding job these last couple of weeks. You jumped right in to replace Chris in the admin function when he got tied up with Carlos on counterintelligence leads. You carry your load without bitching, and don't hesitate to help the other guys out. That's why I fought to keep you."

"Thanks, Rob. I've learned so much from working with you and your team. I appreciate everything."

"We appreciate you, Angie." Angie waved and left.

The next morning Robin sat at his desk, after hanging up from one of his endless phone calls, Robin leaning on his elbows and rubbing his temples. Emmett's deep voice interrupted him from the doorway.

"You okay, Boss?"

Robin lifted his head. "Yeah, Emmett, I'm fine."

Emmett came in and dropped his large frame into the chair next to Robin's desk. "Rob, do you know from five in the morning to noon, I counted that you handled one hundred and thirty-seven calls? I can't even begin to count how many people you talked to or how many questions you answered. I don't know how you can switch gears so fast and keep so much in your head. I swear we are going to have to start following you and pick up the information falling out of your ears."

"I'm dictating. I've got it covered."

Emmett leaned towards Robin. "Rob, you're doing too much. You need to give more admin stuff to John and Angie."

Robin took a deep breath. "Maybe you're right. I will try to do that."

"Promise me, boss, or I may have to get violent."

"Okay, okay, I promise."

"All right, see you later."

"Thanks."

Robin got home at midnight to a dark and quiet house. He felt lonely and guilty. His stomach growled, but he didn't have the energy to do anything about it. As he walked back to the bedroom, he stopped to look in at each of his children. When he got to his room, he dropped is clothes and put his pistol up in the closet. Putting on his sleeping shorts, he laid his exhausted body down and snuggled up to Karen. She was awake, as usual, and put her hand into his. He fell asleep.

Robin opened his eyes to see Eddie's eyes looking intently at him. Robin sighed, as this happened almost every night. Robin put his arm around Eddie's waist and pulled him into bed between him and Karen. Robin's heart ached.

EIGHTEEN

At eight the next evening, Robin had just finished a federal wiretap affidavit to convert a state order in Texas into a federal order. He needed to get a federal agent to co-sign the affidavit application and deliver it to FBI and DEA headquarters first thing the next morning. It needed to go through the federal administrative approval process before being submitted to a federal judge. Chris was in D.C. again, so Robin called Angie at home, since she had assumed Chris' admin duties and since DEA was jointly running the tap with Texas DPS.

"Hello," Angie answered the phone in a soft, melancholy voice.

"Hey, Angie. It's Rob."

"Oh hi, Rob!" Angie's voice brightened.

"Hey, I finished this affidavit application. All it needs now is your signature."

"Oh, okay, I'll come over to the wire room."

"No, you don't have to do that. Just tell me where your new apartment is and I will bring it over."

"Oh...oh...I, well, okay." Angie seemed frazzled.

"Angie, are you all right?"

"Yes, yes. I'm okay, Rob. Just come over. Do you know the apartments south of the FBI office?"

"The ones where one of the FBI's safe houses is?"

"Yes, that's it. Chris found this place for me. I am in number 212."

"I'll be there in about fifteen minutes."

"Okay, bye."

Robin gathered his papers and put them in his briefcase. He said goodbye to the night listening teams and walked out into the warm

Phoenix air. The summer sun, in its last stages, mercifully started to allow the earth to cool. Another glowing orange Arizona sunset grew against the dark blue, cloudless sky.

Robin scanned the area as he walked towards his van. He looked for anything out of the ordinary. He climbed into the van, started the engine, and put the air conditioner on full-blast. The van now sounded like a wind tunnel. He turned up his police radio.

As he drove he thought about his conservation with Angie. Over the last week, they had worked closely together. Robin liked Angie, and he found it kind of nice to work with an attractive woman, but Angie guarded her private life. Robin knew virtually nothing about her outside of their common work. Even though she seemed to be comfortable around everyone, she still had those sad eyes.

Robin steered his van through traffic. He regularly checked his rear view mirrors and the cars around him at stoplights. He drove past the FBI office and turned right on the next street, then turning left into the parking lot of the apartment complex. Robin could see Angie looking through the security eyehole in the door. When she opened the door, Robin walked in, stunned by an almost bare two-room apartment. Personal items were strewn around the floor. A card table and a lone chair stood in one corner, near the kitchenette. An empty McDonald's bag was crumpled on the table. A small T.V. sat in the opposite corner. The door to the bedroom was closed.

"Please, sit down, Robin." Angie pointed to the chair.

Robin opened his briefcase and handed the affidavit application to Angie. "You're going to need the chair to read this."

Angie promptly dropped to a sitting position on the floor. "I prefer the floor. Sit in the chair." Robin could tell she was trying to sound authoritative. Robin mentally shrugged as he pulled the chair out and sat down. He looked at Angie, who was reading the affidavit. He noticed her shoulders were shaking and her hands were trembling. She was crying.

"Angie" Robin stopped midsentence. He didn't know what to say. Angie put the papers aside, put her hands to her face, and silently cried. Robin knelt down beside her and touched her shoulder. She put her arms around his neck and clung tightly to him, burying her face in his chest. Robin put his arms around her and gently held her, letting her cry.

After a short while, Angie seemed to calm down.

Robin lifted her face. "Do you want to talk about it?"

She got up and went into the bedroom and came out with a tissue box. Wiping the tears from her eyes, she sat down on the floor next to Robin.

"Did you hear about the incident in New York where a female DEA agent was accidentally shot and killed by other agents?" Angie asked.

"Yeah, a while back...about six months ago."

"I came here from the New York office."

"Was the woman agent a friend of yours?"

"Yes." Angie began crying again. Robin waited for her to calm down.

"What a horrible tragedy. My heart goes out to you, Angie."

Angie looked at him and then put her head on Robin's chest. "That's only half of it, Rob. One of the agents who shot her is my husband."

"Oh God, Angie, I don't know what to say. What an unthinkable situation!" He held her as the sobs continued.

"How did it happen?" Robin asked softly.

"They were trying to arrest armed and dangerous narcotics suspects in an apartment complex--a man and a woman. My husband and another agent were covering a walkway. They were on surveillance there for hours and didn't attend the briefing."

"That's not good. Did they use a tactical team?"

"No. The senior agent in charge of the operation doesn't like the tactical guys, and said his team would handle it without tactical."

"Angie, that borders on criminal conduct. It certainly is incompetent supervision. What actually happened?"

"It just turned dark. Some agents saw the male walking down the walkway further up. They started shouting. My husband saw a female coming around the corner with a gun. He didn't know that a female agent came with the arrest team. He and his partner yelled, "DEA!" She turned toward them and they opened fire and killed her."

"Damn, that's as bad as it can get."

"Ever since the shooting, they won't let me see or talk to my husband. I tried and tried, but they wouldn't let me see him. They have him and the other agent in administrative quarantine."

"I don't think they can do that."

"They have us over a barrel because they are still paying his salary."

"Ahh, I see. Have you considered hiring an attorney?"

"They have not charged my husband with anything, so I am waiting. I raised so much hell, they transferred me here and told me if I didn't take the transfer, they would fire me for insubordination." Angie took a deep breath. "Rob, I have been so torn up inside, and so lonely. I love my husband--I miss him terribly."

Robin looked into Angie's eyes. He felt engulfed by their sadness. He gently stroked Angie's forehead. "Angie, there is nothing I can say or do to take this pain away from you," Robin said softly. "But I want you to know I am here for you. If you need to talk or just need a hug, I'm here."

Angie rose to her knees and looked at Robin. Her brown eyes were still so sad, but so beautiful. She leaned over and gave him a soft kiss. She hesitated there, and Robin felt her mouth begin to open. He very gently pushed her back as a searing flash of desire shot through his body. He slowly got up and then helped Angie to her feet.

"Angie, you're a beautiful woman and I have become fond of you since we have been working together, but you love your husband, and I certainly love my wife. As much as I am tempted, it simply isn't in me to turn our relationship into a romantic one. I don't think it is really in you, either."

Angie looked at Robin. She then kissed him gently again. "You're a good man, Robin Marlette. Thank you for your understanding tonight."

"I'm here for you, Angie. You know I'll keep our conversations to myself."

"I know. Thank you."

"I'd better get going. Call me in the morning if there is a problem with the application."

Robin walked out the door to his van. Conflicting thoughts, guilt, and jumbled emotions cascaded through his mind and heart. He took a very deep breath. Emotionally drained, he needed to go home and hold Karen.

NINETEEN

The next afternoon, Mark Warren watched Walton and the guy named Trinidad through the periscope in the surveillance van. The suspects were sitting in Walton's car in the parking lot of the Central Plaza Shopping Center. He snapped pictures through the scope.

"I hope these guys move soon. We're running out of ice for the auxiliary cooler," Doug Auriel observed.

"We may just have to get hot. We're not turning the engine on around these assholes. Come look at these two guys who came with Trinidad. This is the first time he has brought anyone with him," Mark said. The agents changed positions.

"Damn! Those are some hard-looking hombres," Doug commented.

"You got that right." Mark thought for a moment. "Doug, do you think we ought to take these guys down now? We're getting warrants for Walton and Trinidad. It's not like we don't have probable cause—and these two guys with Trinidad concern me."

"I don't know, Mark. You know Robin. He has a plan."

"I know, I know, but he also always tells us to use initiative when we feel we should take action."

"Well just look at it from a tactical point of view. You know Trinidad and his boys are armed. Walton may be, too. There are only two other guys besides us out here today. That's even odds. Tactical principles say we should get the odds in our favor and have a plan. I say we hold off for now. We'll be taking these guys down soon enough."

"I guess you're right, partner."

Doug swung the periscope back to Walton's car just in time to see Walton slam his hand against his steering wheel. "Walton is pissed again."

"That guy is crazy. From the looks of Trinidad, Walton won't be around long if he keeps that up."

"Mr. T is leaving now. Think we should follow him and his two goons?"

"As much as I would like to, we don't have air assets today. Mr. T would probably burn us, especially with four more eyes in the car. Robin wouldn't like that—especially when we're so close to busting these guys. Let's just stick with Walton. He always provides us with an interesting day."

"Roger that, partner. Let's get rolling."

With his usual calm and calculating composure completely gone, Walton shook with rage. *I can't believe Miguel is not only going to kill Marlette, but is actually serious about killing his family. Why doesn't that idiot see he would cause law enforcement to pull out all of the stops to get the people behind it and send the public into a frenzy? This is not good. All of my contacts will panic and he thinks it will only make them more afraid of him and make him more powerful. What an idiot. What a crazy fool.*

Walton pulled into his slot in the parking garage of his office building. He put the car in park and turned off the ignition. His head slowly sank to his chest. *It's over. Everything I've worked for will be gone.* He sat still. Then his head shot up. *I must disappear. I need to get as much money as I can out of my accounts and holdings and leave the country. I'll have to transfer what cash I get to my secret Swiss accounts. I must get started now.*

On foot in Walton's parking garage, Mark watched Walton from behind a concrete pillar. He saw Walton quickly get out of his Mercedes and walk to the elevator. Walton's behavior was totally foreign when compared to the Walton Mark had watched for almost a month now. Something new had changed him, and he definitely did not like it. Mark needed to brief Robin as soon as possible.

TWENTY

Robin sat in his office at the wire room early the next morning, on the phone with Jim Adams.

"Rob, all of the arrest warrants are ready."

"Good. The follow-up search warrants would be signed today, but coordinating the numerous arrests and raids across four states and D.C. is a definite pain in the ass. I'm just grateful for how everyone is working and cooperating, even DEA."

"That *is* outstanding!"

"Yes it is. I'm excited about bringing this investigation to the next level."

"Let's do it!"

"We're on it. Talk to you later."

Robin hung the phone and leaned back in his chair. Mark Warren came in to his office.

"Did you see my report on Walton's activities yesterday?" Mark said.

"I did. Something is definitely up—I don't like the looks of it. As a precautionary measure, I put out a memo to all members of the task force advising them to be extra careful when out and about. I told the wire room staff to keep a lookout and be careful when coming or going. We asked Phoenix PD to increase their frequent patrols of the area. I don't know if they are going to get violent, but there's no sense in taking chances."

"Well, Sarge, we've had intelligence about hit contracts on one or more members of the squad on a regular basis."

"Many police officers go through it, but a hit rarely ever occurs. But it does happen. So, that's why we aren't taking any chances."

"I'm with you, Sarge." Mark waved and went back to working on search warrants.

Robin spent the next five hours with Angie tying up loose ends on the arrest plan. Their relationship remained friendly.

Angie looked at Rob and spoke in a low whisper. "Thanks again for being a good man, Rob. I appreciate your restraint and recognizing I'm in a very vulnerable state."

Robin smiled, "I'm just glad we can be friends, Angie. You've been a very valuable team player in this operation. I appreciate all of your hard work and I'm still here for you."

Angie reached over and touched Robin's hand. "Thank you."

Emmett stuck his head in the office doorway. "Hey, boss, Mike, John and I finished the follow-up search warrant affidavit and the accompanying warrants. We're heading over to federal court to get them signed. "

"Good work. We'll see you when you get back." Emmett saluted and left.

"The next few days are going to be non-stop. I have a few more things to do, but I'm going home for the afternoon to spend time with the family. I'll be back in the evening."

"Okay."

Robin gathered up some papers when the phone rang. He looked at it with a thought of not answering it for a moment, but sighed and picked it up.

"Sergeant Marlette."

"Hi Rob, it's Mary. I have a call for you. I think it's Chucky."

"Oh, great, okay, Mary, put him through."

"Here it comes."

Robin heard a click. "Sergeant Marlette."

"Robin, ol' boy, it's Chucky."

"What's up, Chucky?"

"Hey, I've stumbled on some serious shit, man. I got info that will make me your favorite informant!"

"You already are, Chucky. Whaddya got."

"Military explosives."

"What did you say?!"

"I bought some military explosives off some soldiers from the Flagstaff Army Depot. They stole them from there."

"Where are you?"

"I'm down at 24th Street and Camelback."

"Can you meet me at the parking lot of the shopping center in Ahwatukee on Elliot Road in about thirty minutes?"

"I can."

"See you there."

Robin picked up his briefcase, jumped in his van, and drove to Ahwatukee. He parked his van in an empty corner of the lot and watched for Chucky's clunker. He noticed a new Mercedes cruising the parking lot. It meandered for a minute and then headed towards Robin's van. His head cocked with surprise and suspicion when he saw Chucky driving it. Chucky parked next to Robin and got into the passenger seat of Robin's van.

"Chucky, tell me you didn't steal the Mercedes."

"C'mon, Rob, I haven't done anything like since I got out of prison."

"Okay, where did you get the money for a Mercedes?"

"I've made amends with my family."

"Oh, so you've been accepted back into Long Island society?"

"Not quite, but my family finally believes I'm not a career criminal."

"Just how did you convince them of that?"

"I told them I worked with law enforcement."

Robin gave Chucky a hard look. "Exactly what did you tell them, Chucky? And don't bullshit me, because I know what a con man you are."

"I told them you and I were friends and I decided to spend my time helping you fight crime." Robin gave Chucky a dubious look. "Don't worry, I told them I wasn't a cop."

"If you're really going straight, why don't you just get a real job and become a productive member of society?"

Chucky looked out the window. "Rob, I can't do that. It's too boring. I need excitement in my life. In my younger and stupid days I thought I needed to pull scams and get away with it to put excitement in my life. Then you came along and put me in prison, thank you very much. I had plenty of time to think there. I knew you were an honest cop, so I decided to help you get bad guys. Besides, I don't need to work. Daddy is giving me stipend."

"I hope it's enough to live on."

Chucky laughed. "Rob, you really don't know much about rich people, do you?"

"Never been one."

"Well, let's just say my stipend is about triple your salary."

"Must be nice."

"It isn't bad."

"Okay, let's get down to business. Who are these guys you bought the ordinance from?"

Chucky handed Robin a slip of paper. "Those are the names of the guys. I only got the last name of one of them. The other two only gave me their first names. They're all pretty young, and one of them is definitely a gang banger."

"Yeah, military recruiting is going to hell lately. You got the stuff?"

"It's in my trunk."

"What did they charge you?"

"A hundred bucks an item."

"Let's take a look." The men climbed out of the van and went to the back of the Mercedes. Chucky popped the trunk and opened a large duffel. Robin counted six satchel charges and eight grenades.

Robin zipped up the bag, carried it to the van, and put it in the back. He reached into his briefcase and pulled out an envelope containing confidential investigation funds. He took out twenty-four one hundred dollar bills and handed them to Chucky.

"What's the extra thousand for?"

"Just because you've rejoined the wealthy doesn't mean I'm not going to pay you for your work. This is a good haul, Chucky. We need to get these guys."

"When do you want me to set up the next meet?"

"We're tied up all next week, so call me in about ten days."

"Why so long?"

"Read the paper in about two days."

"Okay, Rob. See ya in about ten days."

"Adios, Chucky."

Andy Jackson had talked Cathy into going to the Pima Air Museum. While Cathy did like to go to the museum, she didn't particularly want to go in the summer time. Many of the aircraft were outside, and she didn't like standing in the heat just to look at airplanes. She would rather be spending this Saturday morning swimming or hiking up on Mt. Lemmon. Andy even insisted on riding with the top down in his Jaguar on I-10.

"Andy, slow down, honey."

"Aw come on, Cathy. This is a Jaguar. It's born to go fast."

"If we get stopped by one of my Dad's friends again, I will never talk to you...*again.*"

Andy slowed down. "That's a little drastic, isn't it?"

"Probably." Cathy smiled at him.

Andy took the Valencia Road exit and stopped at the light. Two cars, each filled with several Hispanic men, stopped behind them. Another car pulled up next to the Jaguar on the right side. They gave the Jaguar a hard look. Cathy saw them.

"Andy, don't look now, but the guys next to us don't look very nice."

"There's a bunch behind us who don't look so nice either."

The light turned green. Andy thought about his .357 S&W revolver in the console. As he started to turn left, he opened the console. Suddenly, the car on the right accelerated ahead of the Jaguar and cut in front of it, under the overpass.

"GO! GO! GO! ANDY!" Cathy screamed.

Andy jerked the wheel to the left and jammed his foot onto the accelerator. The Jaguar surged, but one of the cars behind them slammed into the front left side. The Jaguar crashed into the car that cut in front, wedging the Jaguar between the two cars and blocking it from the rear by the third.

Fury and fear surged through Andy. He grabbed the .357. The man in the front passenger seat in the car on the left tried to put a weapon through the shattered window. Andy recognized it as an Uzi. He raised his gun and fired at the man, but missed. The Uzi was now pointed at Andy at point-blank range. Andy fired again, and the man's head exploded into a chunky red mist. Cathy screamed. Andy whirled around and saw men trying to drag her out of the car. She was a blur of arms and legs, kicking, punching, and clawing. Andy shot the man trying to grab her left arm. A heavy blow to his upper right chest slammed him back in his seat. A man in front pointed a gun at him and fired.

Airmen Sam Cowen and Jerry Parker had just finished the night shift with the Air Police at Davis-Monthan Air Force Base and were heading to the apartment they shared near the U of A. They were on Valencia Road approaching I-10 when an accident took place right in front of them. A car had rammed into a Jaguar involved in the first accident. Hispanic men swarmed all over the Jaguar, some of them trying to pull a young woman out. Then gunfire erupted.

Sam yelled, "Jerry, get the gun out of the glove compartment!" He accelerated his Chevy pickup toward the men and the girl. Another man came around the car that had rammed the Jaguar. Sam aimed the pickup at the man and skidded into him. The man went flying. Sam jumped out as Jerry jumped out the other side, a Beretta 9mm in hand.

Sam pulled one of the men from the girl and grabbed him in a choke hold. He squeezed his forearm and biceps, wrenched the man's neck, and threw him to the ground. Then he headed toward another man, when Sam crumpled to the ground, shot in the back.

Jerry Parker saw his best friend go down. Jerry had just shot the man near the front of the Jaguar. He turned to shoot the man who shot Sam. Another man popped up from the other side of the first car and fired at Jerry. The round hit him in left shoulder and spun him around. He slumped against the pickup. As the man came around the back of the car, Jerry shot him. He struggled to get up, but what felt like a sledgehammer slammed him in the head. He went down again. Barely conscious, he tried with all of his might, but nothing moved. He became sleepy.

Cathy fought for her life. Her fear turned to pure fury when she realized Andy had been shot. Years of karate training her father had insisted she go to jumped into high gear. She used fists, feet, knees, elbows, forehead, and teeth, but too many arms and hands held on to her. A face appeared in front of her. She jerked her right hand free from whoever held it and jammed her fingers into the eyes of the face. The face erupted into a screams of agony. Cloth covered her face from behind. A chemical smell engulfed her. A balloon suffocated her. She struggled with all her strength, but consciousness slipped and slipped away. Echoes of screaming and curses faded into nothing.

A shaken Hector Rubio tried to stay calm and control his driving. He drove west on Valencia and then south on Alvernon Way. What should have been an easy kidnap had gone very wrong. Out of ten men, only Hector and three other men were left. He himself had had to shoot Jesus after he shot the big man in a uniform. He shuddered as he thought of those mangled eyes.

The other men in the car were all cursing and describing what they were going to do to Cathy Marlette when they got back to the ranch. They all had various injuries caused by her vicious struggle. Hector let them talk. No one would touch her until Miguel gave the go-ahead. He had specifically told Hector not to hurt the girl—he had plans for her.

Hector worried about her. He held the cloth full of ether over her face longer than he wanted. When they put her unconscious body in the trunk, her skin looked like porcelain and her breaths were short and shallow. He needed to check on her when they got to La Posada. He turned onto the Old Nogales Highway and headed south.

Highway Patrol Officer Jim Albright drove westbound on I-10 approaching the Valencia Road exit. He was following a speeder, signaling the driver to stop with emergency lights. The speeder pulled over to the right on the overpass. Officer Albright exited his patrol car and walked up to the driver. Just then dispatch called him on his portable.

"Tucson, Three Paul Forty-Three."

"Three Paul Forty-Three."

"We have a report of a multiple-vehicle accident under the overpass at Valencia Road."

"Standby." Officer Albright walked over to the edge of the overpass and looked down. "Holy shit!" he uttered involuntarily. "Get out of here!" he yelled to the speeder. Albright ran to his car and turned on the siren. He drove a short way on the freeway and then turned onto the on ramp going the wrong way.

"Paul Forty-Three, send me back up and multiple ambulances." He pulled up to the scene. Several people were standing off. He saw a dead man. He had been shot. There were other bodies. "Paul Forty-Three, roll CI and the SO. This is a multiple homicide," he said into his portable. Albright saw a body in the Jaguar. He recognized the Jaguar and his stomach twisted. He had stopped it before. Moving quickly to the car, he barely recognized Andy as the boyfriend of Sergeant Marlette's daughter. The lower left portion of his face was mangled flesh and bone. Albright checked his pulse. The kid's heart was still beating.

Albright saw Deputy Craig Jenkins pull into the junction of I-10 and Valencia. Jenkins trotted towards Albright at the Jaguar. Albright was working to stop the bleeding from the boy's neck when he suddenly heard, "Sheriff's Department! Don't move!" Jenkins pulled out his gun and pointed at someone on the ground. Albright moved quickly over to Jenkins, who covered a man in a U.S.A.F. uniform on the ground with a gun in his hand. The man raised his head and tried to speak. Albright knelt down next to the man and moved the gun.

The man looked at the officer and spoke with a weak and hoarse voice. "They...they took" The man's head went down for a moment.

Albright got closer to him. "They took what?"

The man raised his head again. "They took the girl." The man passed out. Albright bolted up and immediately radioed dispatch.

As he drove, Robin rehearsed in his mind how to tell Karen to take the kids to go stay with her parents for awhile. She wouldn't react well to the suggestion. Turning onto his street, he saw a car occupied by four Hispanic males coming down Sequoia Trail.

Robin had trained many officers in his career. He often talked about the "little voice in your gut." He told officers to trust that little voice, the subconscious mind telling you, "We have been here before. Watch out!" The hair on the back of Robin's neck tingled, and his little voice screamed.

Robin picked up the microphone to his police radio. At the same time he saw a car with several Hispanic males coming around the corner from Modoc Drive. He keyed the mic, and, with the calmest voice he could muster, said, "Two Nora Six, Nine-Nine-Eight, Nine-Nine-Nine, Ten Forty-Two," the emergency codes for an officer needing immediate help. Shots fired at his home. Robin's years of training, experience, and physical conditioning all came together in the next four minutes and thirty-eight seconds.

Robin accelerated towards his house, ran the van over the curb, and bounced onto his front lawn. He turned the wheel hard left and braked, skidding the van broadside up to his double front doors in a cloud of granite rocks and dust. He jammed the gear shift into park and stepped in between the seats. Reaching over and unlatching the sliding side doors, he unhooked the detachable corner gun locker, grabbed his bug out bag, and jumped out the door. His mind repeated: *Think- slow is fast.*

Robin could hear automatic gunfire and the thud of bullets hitting the van. He could also hear them smacking against the stucco siding of his house. Holding the gun locker close to his right side, he lowered his left shoulder and smashed into the left door. The door exploded open, and Robin tripped and skidded across the tile floor, slamming into the wall opposite the door. He hit it so hard, the dry wall partly caved in. He yelled, "GET DOWN, GET DOWN!" *Think - slow is fast. Need a 360 defense.*

Bullets hit everywhere. Pieces of furniture, glass, and drywall flew through the air. Robin saw Casey on the floor and slid the gun locker over to him. "Get the rifles out!" he ordered. Robin drew his Colt .45. A man with an Uzi appeared at the front door. Robin shot him twice in the chest. The man fell back, spewing bullets into the ceiling. Casey slid the Galil over to Robin. Casey grabbed the MP5 and charged it.

"Cover the back door!" Robin yelled. A man appeared at the front window on the left. Robin fired two rounds and the man went down, leaving Robin unsure if he had hit the suspect. The deafening noise thundered and reverberated in the house. Robin noticed Eddie lying down in the hallway. Eddie looked at him with wide, terrified eyes. Robin fired the last four rounds in the .45's magazine: one through the left window, two out the door, and one out the right window. He dropped the magazine out of the .45 and slammed a fresh one in and charged the weapon. *Think - slow is fast. Need a 360 defense.* He slid the gun over to Eddie. "Cover the back hallway, Eddie!" Robin did not have time to see what Eddie did, as he could see movement in the front yard. Several rounds hit the dining room table, sending wooden shrapnel into Robin's right shoulder, neck, and head. He heard Casey cry out in pain as Robin fired the Galil at the corner of the window on the right. He saw the reflection of a man in the van window and fired at the wall, approximating where the man was standing on the other side. The Galil's 7.62 rounds easily penetrated the wall, and blood spattered on his van. Robin heard his wife and daughter screaming behind him. He went prone and saw ankles and feet on the other side of the van. He fired at one leg and missed. He fired again, and a man screamed and fell on his side. Robin shot him in the torso. The other pair of legs started running away. He could hear sirens.

Casey yelled because wood and metal shrapnel had hit him in the buttocks and leg. He didn't have time to look, because a man appeared on the patio. Casey aimed the MP5 and pulled the trigger. A stream of 9mm bullets smashed the glass doors and tore into the man. The burst surprised Casey. He thought he had put the selector switch on semi-auto, like his dad taught him. He stripped the magazine from the gun, reached over and pulled a fresh magazine out of his dad's bag, and jammed it into the gun. He charged the weapon and thumbed the selector switch.

Sergeant Gabe Martinez, with siren blaring, drove like a man possessed. He barked orders over the radio to his men and the other units responding to the triple nine call from Robin. He directed units to enter the neighborhood from all directions. As he approached the back of Robin's house, Gabe drove his car over the curb and stopped right next to the wall. Grabbing his 12-gauge shotgun as he jumped out of the car, he ran to the back and bounded onto the trunk, then the roof and onto the wall. As he did, a man with an Uzi came through the side gate. The man saw Gabe, but Gabe snapped the shotgun to his shoulder and shot the man with a 00 buck round.

Another man stood at a back window to the left. He raised his weapon toward Gabe just as the window shattered and the man went down. Gabe could see the patio doors were broken; a dead man was sprawled on the patio. He jumped down and took cover behind the pool filter. Another man came through the gate. Gabe rose and shot him. The round knocked the man back through the gate opening.

Robin heard sirens coming from all over and gunfire outside. He could discern the comforting sound of 12-gauge shotguns. Rounds were no longer coming into the house. The gunfire died down. He looked at Casey and could see blood coming from his leg. He started toward him, but Casey said, "I'm okay, Dad."

Robin put a fresh magazine into the Galil and carefully moved to the front door, his rifle up against his cheek. The man he shot at the door lay face up and appeared to be dead. Robin stepped over the dead man and moved to the left of the entry alcove. He carefully moved to look down the right side of the house by "slicing the pie" and saw the man he shot through the wall, crumpled against the right front tire of the van in a large pool of blood. Robin stepped over the dead man in the alcove again to the right side and pied down the left side of the house. He saw the man who had dropped at the window. He sat upright, holding his shoulder. Suddenly Robin heard," Police! DON'T MOVE!" The wounded man looked to his left.

Robin called out, "DPS to the suspect's right! I have him covered!"

"Is that you, Sergeant Marlette?" Robin recognized the voice of Gene Blumen, one of Gabe's men.

"It's me, Gene. You can move in and cuff him." Gene appeared at the corner of the van and saw Robin. He put his shotgun against the van and grabbed the suspect and rolled him on his stomach. The man yelled out in pain. "Shut up, asshole," Gene said as he put handcuffs on him. Two other officers appeared. More sirens were coming. Bullet holes riddled the van. Robin realized the van had stopped or slowed a lot of rounds. Gene looked at Robin with anger and anguish in his eyes. "They killed Johnny Gardner."

Robin stepped past Gene and looked a patrol car with officers all around it. Through the shattered windshield he saw Johnny Gardner's head slumped on the steering wheel. Robin's heart sank.

He went back into his house and stared at the wreckage. Shredded pieces of furniture and drywall were scattered all over the living room and dining room. A thick cloud of dust hovered, and broken glass was everywhere. Bile crawled into Robin's throat. Karen cried and shook as she put towels on Casey's wounds. She looked up at Robin with frightened and angry eyes.

Laurie cried out, "Dad! You're hurt!"

"I'll be all right, honey." Robin took her in his arms.

"Rob! It's Gabe Martinez! The back is clear. I'm coming in!"

"It's clear Gabe. Come in." Gabe stepped through the broken glass from the patio door. Eddie came around the corner from the hallway, the .45 down at his side. He was trembling. Robin took the .45 and holstered it, then held his daughter and son. Gabe walked up to them.

"I have Fire coming. We have units everywhere now. Thanks for taking that guy out, Rob. I thought he had me."

"What guy?"

"The guy by the back bedroom window."

"I didn't shoot anybody out back." Robin looked down at Eddie.

"I...I...shot him," Eddie said, his voice shaking.

"Well, I'll be damned," Gabe replied in a low voice. He reached down and picked Eddie up into his giant arms. "Eddie, you're my hero!" Eddie managed a little smile.

"Gabe, they got Johnny Gardner." Gabe put Eddie down and walked outside.

Robin walked over to Karen and Casey. He knelt down. "You okay, son?"

"I think so, Dad."

Karen would not look at Robin. Her movements were rigid. "Are you all right, Karen?"

She didn't answer. She just worked on Casey's wound, but Robin could see the bleeding had stopped.

Police officers from the Phoenix Police, Chandler Police, Tempe Police, DPS, and the Maricopa County Sheriff's office were all around the house and the neighborhood. Portable radios crackled with calls of a foot chase and one vehicle pursuit of suspects in the shooting. Robin heard the sound of helicopters overhead.

Paramedics from the Phoenix Fire Department came and started working on Casey and Robin. Karen held Casey; he had an arm around Laurie. Eddie buried his face in Robin's chest.

Jack Moore screamed obscenities into the intercom as he flew the Blackhawk over Robin's house.

"Dammit, Jack," Oscar said. "If you don't calm down, I'm taking over!"

"How can I calm down? Our buddy's family gets attacked while we were sitting on our asses only five minutes away with this machine and two Miniguns!"

"From what I can tell, it was just about over in five minutes anyway. We wouldn't have been much help."

Jack seemed to deflate. He breathed deeply and the Blackhawk smoothed out.

"Lima Two-One, Control." Customs dispatch called the Blackhawk.

"Lima Two-One," Oscar responded.

"Lima-Two-One, can you see a school near the scene?"

"Roger."

"Officers are clearing a landing site there for you. Land and stand by for further."

"Roger, Lima Two-One."

Juan Trinidad drove eastbound on I-10. Marlette's appearance at his house had taken them by surprise. Trinidad actually remembered with admiration how Marlette had maneuvered his van to provide cover for his movements. It had also blocked his teams' attack plan. He fought to stay calm as he left Marlette's house. Several police cars sped by him before he made it to I-10. Juan drove off I-10 at Riggs Road. He would take the old highway to Tucson.

As Robin let the paramedics clean up his wounds, the Director, Tom Pearle, and Lieutenant Hammel came in the front door, their faces grim. The Director walked up to Robin.

"You all right, Robin?"

"I'll be all right, Colonel."

Pearle then came closer. Hammel hung back.

"Rob, we are making arrangements to get your family to a safe place, but first, we need to talk to you and Karen."

"What's going on?"

"You need to get Karen over here."

Robin took Eddie to Karen and the other two children. "Eddie, stay here. Honey, you need to come with me."

"Why?" Karen asked, her voice full of anger.

"Please, Karen. Tom says he needs to talk to us." Robin helped Karen up and they walked over to Pearle.

"Okay, Tom. What's going on?"

"You two need to brace yourselves. This is not going to be easy to hear."

"What in the hell are you talking about?" Robin's voice got louder. Pearle took a deep breath.

"Andy and Cathy were attacked about an hour ago." Karen sank to her knees. Robin stood like a statue, his fists clenched. Pearle took another deep breath.

"Andy's been shot and seriously wounded. He's in critical condition." Karen started sobbing. Robin tried to hold back the tears, but they began rolling down his cheeks.

Pearle took his deepest breath yet. He looked Robin in the eye. "Rob, they kidnapped Cathy. They have Cathy."

Karen screamed. Robin knelt down beside her. She looked at him with fear and fury. She slapped him and started beating his chest with her fist.

"I hate you! Look what you have done to my family!" Karen collapsed.

TWENTY ONE

Robin sat alone in a BOQ at Luke AFB. The last twelve hours had been a blur, a horrific blur.

After paramedics treated Karen at the scene, the whole family flew in the Blackhawk to Luke. Karen and Casey were checked out at the hospital and released. She would not even look at Robin while doctors treated him.

The rest of the Guardians and their families were gathered up and flown to Luke. Jim Adams, Chris Fleming, and Bill Grassley all called in markers and got permission to move the families to Fort Bragg in North Carolina. The Air Force ordered a C-5 cargo plane diverted to Luke. The families were gone in six hours. None of the Guardians went.

Robin had been told Ernie Jackson and his family were being housed temporarily at Davis-Monthan. When Andy stabilized, a medical transport collected him and his family and took them to Walter Reed Hospital. Ernie and his family would also be housed at Fort Bragg.

Robin also received word Jim Adams had decided to immediately execute all warrants. While the Guardians were participating, the Director prohibited Robin from doing so. He didn't want to anyway. His mind flooded with thoughts of Cathy, painful bursts of reliving Karen's anger and her shunning of him, and the fearful, worried faces of his other children. Robin knew their survival resulted from a matter of luck as much as their willingness to fight back.

A knock sounded at the door. Robin's watch showed almost midnight. "Who could that be?" he wondered out loud.

He opened the door. There stood Ernie Jackson.

"Ernie! What in the hell are you doing here?" Ernie looked haggard, his eyes red and empty. He walked in and Robin closed the door.

"I came here to see you."

"You should be with Andy and your family."

"Maybe, but I know you and I know what you're going to do." Ernie gave Robin a hard look. "You're not going without me."

"Sit down, Ernie. You want a drink?"

"I would love a drink." Robin opened the stocked minibar in the room. He took two small bottles of Jack Daniels and made drinks.

"Ernie, you need to be with Andy."

"I know you're going to that ranch. You seem to forget my son loves your daughter. He would want me to go with you to get her back. We'll save a lot of time if you don't try to bullshit me into not going. I *am* going."

"All right, we'll do it together. Where are you staying?"

"They gave me a BOQ here. It's a couple of doors down."

"What do you have for wheels?"

"I brought my Bronco. I thought it would come in handy. I also have all of my gear."

"Well, let's get some sleep and we'll get our shit together in the morning."

"Okay, I could use some sleep. I'm exhausted."

"Me too, brother."

Ernie held up his drink. "I'll take this with me if you don't mind."

"Absolutely." The men hugged each other and Ernie left.

Robin sat and slowly sipped his drink. His thoughts returned to his family. His heart ached, and his brain pounded into his skull. He put his drink down and dropped his face into his hands. His family swirled in his mind. He could not contain it any longer, and started sobbing. Tears streamed into his hands.

"What have I done?" he said in an anguished voice. He felt utterly empty and alone. Time stopped.

Slowly, he became aware of soft knocking at the door. He walked to the door and opened it. Angie stood there. "Oh, Rob," she said, her voice full of anguish. She stepped in and put her hand on his cheek. He closed the door and Angie put her arms around him. They embraced as Robin cried into her neck.

"It's all right, Rob. Let it out. It has been a horrible day." After a while, he raised his head and looked at her with a weak smile.

"Seems like we have reversed roles." He turned and walked back to the couch.

"It seems to me we are playing the same unfortunate role—alone and hurting terribly. I heard about Karen's anger."

"She has a right to be angry."

"Yes, but not at you."

"Yes she does, Angie. Despite the red flags, I fell behind the curve putting it together. I let my family down."

"Twenty-twenty hindsight is a bad thing to judge yourself by."

"Karen is the best thing that ever happened to me. Now I'm afraid I have lost her and maybe my family. I feel so powerless right now. I have to fix this, but I don't know how."

"Rob, Grassley and Chris are working on getting Cathy back."

"They will never get the federal government moving fast enough to get to her in time."

Angie put her hand on Robin's arm. "Rob, you can't do everything yourself. We all want to help you. I want to help you." Angie put her hands on Robin's cheeks and gently pulled him closer to her. Looking into her eyes, he felt himself falling into those beautiful brown pools.

"Sometimes, Robin Marlette, we have to care for our own souls before we can care for others." She put her soft lips on his. As her mouth started to part, Robin could not resist. The kiss felt warm, tender, and giving. As they kissed, she took his hand and put it over her left breast.

"Come," she said as she led him to the bedroom. She kissed him more and started undoing his shirt. He started to do the same. The clothes came off slowly, both of them gently touching and caressing each other. When they were naked, Robin picked her up and laid her on the bed. He looked at her body. Her long dark hair curled over her shoulders and the top of her breasts that curved upward, like an artist's finest brush stroke, to dark pink tips. Her body flowed down, curving in inviting symmetry.

"You are beautiful, Angie."

"You are too, Robin." He kissed her lips and then her neck and more. They each explored the other's body with lingering kisses. When Robin entered Angie, real passion flowed between them, but it was restrained. They both knew this solace could only be a solitary, soul-soothing moment in time.

TWENTY TWO

Cathy Marlette struggled for consciousness. The echoes in her head faded and she tried to open her eyes. She had a fog-laden memory of being in an enclosure that opened up. A man shook her and tried to wake her, but she couldn't. The enclosure shut again, but felt much cooler. She faded out again.

Cathy was laid out on some kind of bed. She felt for the edge. She moved to it and put her head over and retched. Cathy's stomach seemed to be coming up into her throat in painful contractions. It surged into her esophagus over and over.

The retching finally subsided, and Cathy lay back on her side. She never felt so terrible in her life. Her head felt like it was splitting open. Every muscle hurt. A painful thirst raked her raw throat.

She heard voices. The door to the room opened and a fuzzy image of a man entered and then closed the door. He carried a pitcher and a glass and walked with a limp. He stopped ten feet from Cathy.

"I am told you are a vicious young woman." Cathy looked at the man with a blank stare. "I am not here to hurt you. I have water and I can get food. If you fight, you will get nothing."

"I won't fight. I can't fight." Cathy said with a hoarse and exhausted whisper. "I *need* water." The man walked to the bed and knelt down beside Cathy. He poured water into the glass and held it to her lips. She sipped a little. When she tried to gulp a mouthful, the man gently pushed her hand back.

"Easy, Senorita, it would not be good to drink too fast." The man helped her to sit up. He again held the glass to her lips. "Drink in small sips for now."

Cathy knew she should follow his advice. She sipped the delicious liquid. She stopped for a moment and looked at the man. He had kind eyes. He cleaned up the vomit on the floor.

"Thank you for the water, sir. What is your name?"

"I am Jorge." The man leaned closer to Cathy. In a low whisper he said, "Do not talk. Do not react." Jorge looked directly into Cathy's eyes and continued. "I work for your father. Always do as I say. I will protect you." Jorge backed away and stood up. In a normal voice he said, "Drink slowly. I will be back with food." Jorge left the room.

Cathy's heart pounded. *Jorge said he worked for Dad!* Her mind raced. *Is that possible? Should I trust him?* Her mind settled on her father. *Of course it's possible. Dad is the best. The Guardians are the best. Jorge's eyes were true. Yes, he told the truth.*

Then, the searing hot knife of her last sight of Andy ripped through her mind and heart. She collapsed back on the bed in despair.

Jorge waited in the kitchen as Leona, the ranch chef, prepared a small breakfast for Sergeant Marlette's daughter. Jorge worried. He now had two charges to protect in separate places on the ranch.

He watched out for Maria on the sly. No one knew, not even Maria. Maria remained relatively safe because of Juan Trinidad, but if Juan lost interest, things could get difficult. On the other hand, Miguel gave him the job of watching the "Senorita," as he called her. Miguel did not trust anyone else because of the injuries she inflicted on some of the men. The others also attributed the deaths of their friends to her. They reasoned if she had not fought, the operation would have ended quickly and they all would have escaped. Many of the men wanted revenge, vicious revenge.

Jorge thought he would have to devise an escape plan for all of them. He did not know how long Miguel would keep the senorita here. Obviously he had plans for her. Jorge needed to contact Rick.

Cathy was crying quietly when the door to the room opened again. Instead of Jorge, another man entered the room—the most evil looking man Cathy had ever seen. She struggled to a sitting position. The man stopped five feet from her. His face formed a hideous sneer.

"I am Miguel Rodriquez-Lara. Your father killed my brother. By now, your entire family is dead. You are going to be a further example to the American police not to trifle with me. When the time is right, you will feel me on you, over you, and in every part of you. Then I will let my men have you. We will film it and send to the American police. They will know none of them are safe." A chilling laugh spilled from his throat. Cathy spat at him. Miguel lunged forward and reared back to smash her face, but checked himself.

"No, no, I am not going to damage you yet. When the time is right, the world will see you violated over and over, and then torn apart." He gave her an evil grin and walked out.

Cathy was stunned. *Her entire family dead? It can't be, it just can't be!* She collapsed back onto the bed and drew herself into a fetal position and cried until she had no tears left.

TWENTY THREE

Mary Tatum anxiously waited for Captain Pearle to come to work. He greeted her as he walked by her desk to his office. Trembling, she got up and followed him.

As Tom Pearle opened his office door, he saw Mary coming after him.

"You need to talk to me, Mary?"

"Yes, Sir."

Pearle saw her trembling. "Are you all right?"

"I really need to talk to you in private, Captain."

"Certainly. Come in and close the door."

Mary walked in and closed the door behind her. She stood there, looking at Pearle. "Oh, Captain, I hate doing this." She started to cry. Pearle put his arm around her and gently placed her in a chair.

"Mary, you have worked for me a long time. You know you can trust me with anything." Mary took a deep breath.

"Captain, I think Jose Molina is giving information to the bad guys. I think he told them where Sergeant Marlette lives."

"Why do you think this?"

Mary explained what she had seen and how nervous Molina seemed. She pointed out she had noticed the open drawer and the division roster when she saw Jose at her desk. She also told Pearle about the man with the evil voice.

After she finished, Pearle first called the Director. This made Mary even more frightened. Next, Pearle called Lieutenant Johnson in the Communications Section. He told Johnson to pull the tapes on the Street Narcotics Section phone numbers since the takedown in the desert. Pearle told Johnson to get them to him immediately, and not to tell anybody by order of the Director. He turned to Mary.

"Thank you for telling me this. You did the absolute right thing. We'll get to the bottom of Jose's conduct. Please tell Lieutenant Hammel to come to my office. "

"Yes, sir." Mary still trembled.

"It will be all right."

"Thank you, Captain."

Captain Tom Pearle hadn't felt anger like this in a long time. He directed part of the anger at himself and the top brass of the department. They always said the tapes on the phone system should be reviewed, but they never were. Everyone knew they weren't. If these tapes showed any evidence Molina was a bad cop, that would certainly change. Hammel walked into Pearle's office.

"Les, we may have a serious problem with one of our officers." He filled Hammel in on the situation. "Block off your afternoon and get Molina's sergeant in here. We are going to be very busy listening to tapes."

When Robin woke up in the morning, he felt calmer. Angie left after they lay together and talked. He had never dreamed things would turn out this way when they first met. Robin hoped she and her husband could make things work as much as he wanted things to get better with Karen.

Robin and Ernie met and worked up the first part of their plan. Later they ate breakfast with Emmett, Mike, Chris, John Lucheck...and Angie. They all filled Robin in on the progress of the case. He learned about the arrest of Walton at the airport. He was carrying millions in cash in his luggage. Emmett laughed as he told Robin that Walton had tried to bluff and bluster Mark and Doug. Emmett broadly grinned as he related Mark and Doug listened politely for about two seconds—then they spun Walton around, laid him over the hood of his car, and handcuffed him. In a loud voice in front of a growing crowd, Mark enumerated the charges against Walton, including felony murder. Walton now sat in jail with no bond.

Across the country, all the other hits went well. Much more evidence implicating more people was found during the execution of the search warrants. Phones rang off the hook at all of the task force offices.

Chris spoke to Robin. "We're working to get permission to go in and get Cathy. HRT is gearing up, but we can't go until the State Department gives the green light." Robin looked at Chris. "Rob, you have to let me get this done. We all know you. You cannot try self-help. You will end up in prison if not dead."

"I appreciate your efforts."

"Rob, promise me you won't go south. Give me the time to work it out."

"What time? They have my daughter."

"Don't be foolish. I know you are planning something, or else Ernie wouldn't be here."

"Ernie and I are going to Tucson to see Jerry Parker, the Airman who fought for our children. We're also going to meet his family and the family of Sam Cowen, the Airman who died. Work the time you have."

"Don't be bullshitting me, Rob."

"I'm not. Have an agent go to the hospital this afternoon. We'll buy him lunch."

They all finished their breakfasts and started to leave. Angie walked up to Robin and looked into his eyes.

"Be careful, my good friend."

"Keep the case running Special Agent Spurline. I mean *very* special agent. You are my very good friend. Thank you, again."

Angie gave him a polite hug and walked away.

Ernie and Robin climbed into Ernie's Bronco. They covered their gear under tarps in the back. They headed for Tucson.

Emmett called Burke Jameson. "They're headed south. They say they're going to see the wounded Airman and his family. Do you think that's what they're really going to do?"

"Of course they are. I'm sure they want to pay their respects. Robin also set it up so the Feds can't stop them from going south. Then they will head for the border. Get everyone mounted up and headed south. We will meet near the hospital no later than 1400."

"You got it, Brother. See ya there."

Emmett hung up the telephone and heard a knock at his BOQ door. He opened it to see Carlos standing there. He and Newman were brought back to Luke when the raids started going down.

"Good morning, Carlos. What's up?"

"I wondered where Sergeant Marlette went?"

"He went to Tucson." Emmett spoke as he put his MP5 into a duffel.

"Yes, and I know why. You know my wife is at that ranch. I know every inch of it and the layout of the buildings, including the main house."

Emmett stopped his packing and looked at Carlos, trying to figure out what to say. Without conviction Emmett said, "Carlos, you're in federal custody. I can't take you with us."

Carlos laughed. "You are worried about that when I know you are about to violate just about every international law there is?"

Emmett lowered his head and chuckled. "You're right, Carlos. Hell, we might as well make this a complete clusterfuck. Besides, we sure can use your information. Get what stuff you need and meet me back here."

TWENTY FOUR

Miguel Rodriquez-Lara's brain filled with rage, confusion, and fear. In one day he had lost over fifteen men. Juan Trinidad, of all people, had failed in his mission. Marlette and his family were probably still alive.

"Patron, I do not believe all of Marlette's family could have survived our attack. We riddled the house," Juan offered.

Miguel screamed in reply. "But there is no fucking way to know for sure, is there, Juan?! There's no fucking news coverage about the condition of Marlette or his family! There's no news coverage about Marlette's daughter, who is now captive in this house! There's only news about a multiple murder in Tucson and about a massive gunfight with many people shot at Marlette's house! The press said at least two fucking police officers were shot! The fucking government would not release any more information until the certain facts were known AND THAT IS ALL WE FUCKING KNOW, ISN'T IT, JUAN?!"

"Miguel, I saw one police officer die. Maybe the other one is Marlette, but I cannot be sure."

"What we can be sure of, Juan, is that everything I have worked for is in jeopardy! Our control in the States is being eroded! All I hear on the fucking news is Walton and everyone else we own is under arrest! My bank accounts are frozen and everything I own there is being seized! THIS IS MY FUCKING WORLD! I OWN IT AND I RUN IT. THIS IS NOT SUPPOSED TO BE HAPPENING IN MY FUCKING WORLD!" Miguel's fury roiled for a few moments longer. He looked at the faces of Juan and Hector Rubio and could see in their eyes they did not have the same respect they normally did. He unclenched his fists and took several deep breaths.

"Hector, even though you lost men, you *did* get the girl. That is good. What I want you to do now is make sure the men stay away from her. Only Jorge will deal with her."

"I will see to it, Patron." Miguel went to his desk. He opened a drawer and reached into it. Juan moved his hand to the gun under his shirt. Miguel pulled out a stack of cash and Juan moved his hand away from his gun. Miguel walked over to Hector and handed him the cash.

"This is for bringing the girl to me. Go now." Hector rose and walked out of the room.

"Well, Juan, what do you think about all of this?"

"With respect, mi Jefe, I think we need to take a few days to gather intelligence on what the Americans are doing. If we take any action now, we are doing it blindly."

"It appears we did it with our eyes closed yesterday!"

"Again, with respect, Patron, we had a run of bad luck yesterday. That and I admit I underestimated Marlette. He is not just an ordinary policeman."

"All right," Miguel said with exasperation. "Get in touch with our people in Mexico City. Find out if the Americans are trying to get them to act and what the Americans are telling them."

"I have already done so, Patron. They assured me they would not allow the Americans to come into Mexico. We should also be hearing from Carlos. It does not appear that he or Newman was arrested. They've been working together for the last two weeks. I am sure Carlos has them lying low. He will probably be moving to get them here soon."

"Why is that important?"

"Patron, Newman is the only one who has been to this ranch who I worry about giving information to the Americans. If any of our other people were arrested, they wouldn't talk. They know we will get them out of jail as soon as we find out where they are. They also know what will happen to their families if they do talk."

"It is good you are thinking about these things, Juan. Have you thought about anything else?"

"Yes, mi Jefe. We have Marlette's daughter. At the right time, she could be our most important asset."

"Yes, we are thinking alike about that. At first, I wanted to let the men have her and film it. Then send it to the Americans for Marlette to see if he is still alive. But now we will wait. We may have to negotiate. With her, we can still negotiate from a position of power."

"Si, Patron." Juan rose from his chair. "If you will excuse me, I have urgent work to do."

"Yes you do, Juan. Yes you do."

After Juan left, Miguel brooded. He was losing faith in Juan. He knew Juan remained loyal to him, mainly because Miguel made Juan rich beyond his dreams. Juan, however, had proved many times to be the most dangerous man Miguel knew. His own men greatly respected Juan. Getting rid of him would be a very difficult task. Miguel hoped Juan would regain the full faith Miguel once felt. He hated it when he had to do the difficult tasks.

TWENTY FIVE

Robin and Ernie stood at either side of Jerry Parker's bed. Jerry looked at them with conscious, groggy eyes. Jerry's parents were also in the room. Jerry tried to apologize to the two fathers for not doing a better job of defending their children.

"I fought as hard I as I could, but just not hard enough."

"You fought hard enough," Robin replied. "Real fights are not like television fights. They aren't scripted. You thrust yourself into a chaotic fight already in progress and you managed to kill two of the men attacking our kids. Your action, along with Sam's, threw their plan off."

"But they got your daughter!" The anguish in Jerry's voice wrenched Robin's heart.

Ernie spoke in a low, reverent tone. "My son is alive because of you. He is going to pull through, although he has a rough road ahead. If you didn't fight like you did, I'm sure they would have killed him." Jerry lay back in his bed, weak from his wounds. The two sergeants each took one of Jerry's hands. Robin spoke.

"We came here to thank you for what you did. We want you to know that whatever you or your family need, just let us know. We will see it gets taken care of."

"Sergeant Marlette, just get your daughter back. That's all I want."

Robin leaned close to Jerry's ear and whispered, "Mission accepted." He squeezed Jerry's hand.

Jerry squeezed both men's hands, "Godspeed."

Robin and Ernie walked out with Jerry's parents. Sam Cowen's father stood in the hallway.

"I heard what you told my son," Mr. Parker whispered. "When you go to get your daughter, you kill as many of those sons of bitches you can," he hissed.

"Kill all of them," Cowen said in a low growl. "They shot my son in the back, the low-life cowards." Robin looked at Mr. Cowen.

"Your son gave his life protecting our children. We'll take care of business." The four men shook hands, and Robin and Ernie headed for the Blazer.

When they were walking in the parking lot, Ernie spoke. "I don't know how you plan to kill everyone at the ranch. There are only two of us."

"Ernie, there's no problem that can't be solved with the application of the proper amount of explosives."

"What in hell are you talking about?"

"Just be careful going over bumps," Robin joked.

"Are you telling me there are explosives in my truck?!"

"Just get in and drive. You'll see when we get to where we are going."

Burke Jameson and Rick Santos watched as Robin and Ernie drove out of the hospital parking lot.

"They're on the move," Burke said into his mic.

"Ten-Four," Emmett replied.

"Ditto," Doug said.

The Guardians were in three vehicles. Ernie's team and Carlos were also there, for a total of twelve men. They followed their sergeants out to I-10. Robin and Ernie went eastbound. They exited at U.S. 83.

"They are headed to where we expected," Burke said into the radio. "Just hang back until we get closer." The men settled in for the drive.

Captain Pearle's telephone rang. "He's here," Hammel said. Pearle looked at Lieutenant Morrison from Internal Affairs, "Game time." The two men walked down to the Street Narcotics Section office. Pearle seethed inside. The tapes were more than damaging to

Molina. They were sickening. They met Hammel just outside the door.

The Captain whispered to Hammel, "You place him under arrest. I am sure he will invoke. Mike will take it from there."

"Yes, sir."

The men walked in. Molina sat at his desk, holding his head in his hands. He looked up and saw the three men and focused on Lieutenant Morrison. He jumped up and backed against the wall. Molina's eyes had the look of a cornered animal. His hand went for his gun.

"Don't do it, Jose!" Hammel screamed. The three command officers drew their guns and moved in different directions. Molina put his gun to his head and cried out, "I am so, so sorry." He pulled the trigger.

Pearle rose from his crouch and approached Molina's body with his gun drawn. He took the gun out of Molina's hand. Pearle felt cheated. He'd wanted to kill the son of a bitch himself.

Angie sat writing a report when John Lucheck walked into the wire room supervisor's office.

"Hey, Angie, where are Rob and Ernie's guys?"

"Oh, I am sure they have a lot to do about their families' security and everything."

"Well, I wish they would have told me at breakfast. I needed to talk to Emmett about shutting down this place." John walked out. Angie took a deep breath and went back to writing. The phone rang.

"Agent Spurline."

"Angie, its Mary Tatum. I have a phone call Rick Santos said I should give to you."

"Yes, Mary. Put the call through."

"Here it comes." Angie heard a click and then a man say, "Hello?"

"This is Agent Spurline with DEA. Is this Jorge?"

There was a pause. "I don't know if I should be talking to you."

"Then don't. Just listen. The Guardians are coming tomorrow morning an hour before dawn. Do you understand?"

"Yes."

"Are Cathy and Maria safe?"

"Yes."

"Can you get them together about an hour before dawn?"

"I don't know. Let me think." Jorge paused. "Tell them I will have both of them in the small guest room in the main house. I'm sorry, I must go." He hung up.

Angie hung up the telephone and sat back. Now she would wait until the Guardians called. She had felt much better about all of this since Rick told her both squads were joining their sergeants, and she was relieved to hear Cathy was safe for now. Rob would feel better with that news.

Frustration made it impossible for Chris to sit in his office chair. He talked to Hank Rawls, the Chief of Staff for the Deputy Director of the FBI, about the rescue. Rawls kept on saying, "State is still negotiating with Mexico."

They only had a small window of time to get this rescue done. Chris knew Cathy, which fueled his frustration. She was a great kid.

The FBI Hostage Rescue Team sat staged at Fort Huachuca in Sierra Vista, Arizona. Their team leader debriefed Carlos at Luke AFB early in the morning. HRT had the layout of the ranch and all of the buildings. Their manpower had been supplemented with a team from Delta Force. The Mexican government just needed to give approval. The telephone rang.

"Agent Fleming."

"Chris, it's Hank."

"Give me the good news, Hank." Chris heard a deep breath on the other end.

"State says no go, Chris. I'm sorry."

"What! This is insane!" Chris yelled.

"Calm down, Chris. State says the Mexican government is going to handle the situation. They are going to put the word out that they want to negotiate with Rodriquez-Lara." Anger flooded through Chris and he knew he shouldn't say anything else.

"Thanks for trying, Hank." Chris hung up and called the wire room.

"Agent Spurline."

"Angie it's Chris. Is Robin back from Tucson yet?"

"No, he isn't."

"Okay, put Emmett on the phone."

"He isn't here either."

Chris thought about this. "Is there anybody from Rob or Ernie's squad there?"

"No."

"Angie, please don't lie to me. Did they all go south?"

After a moment, Angie said, "Yes they did."

"Damn! Angie, meet me at the Air Support office."

"I can't leave here."

"Yes, you can. Forward the phone to Air Support."

"I can't. I'm waiting for a call from the guys. I have important information for them."

"Angie, please trust me. I'm not going to try to stop Robin from going after his daughter. State shut down the HRT op. All I want to do is help them. Now please, meet me at Air Support."

"Okay, Chris." Twenty minutes later, Chris opened the door to Air Support as Angie drove up. He waited for her, and they walked in together. Jack Moore and Oscar Leighton greeted them. Bill Grassley and Russ Martin walked out of Martin's office.

"What are you guys up to?" Grassley asked.

"Bill, State said no go on the HRT op."

The book Jack Moore was holding went flying across the room. "Those goddamn motherfuckers," he yelled.

"And Rob and Ernie's squads are headed for the border."

"And Carlos," Angie interjected.

"Oh, that's just fucking great!" Chris threw his hands up into the air.

"Angie, what else do you know?" Bill asked in a calm voice.

"According to Rick Santos, they are planning to hit the ranch an hour before dawn. Rob and Ernie were going to do it alone. They don't know about their squads, and Carlos coming after them."

"Why are you here, Chris?"

"We have to help them...the Blackhawk!"

"That's a bit fanciful at this point, don't you think?"

"But Bill" Grassley held his hand up to quiet Chris.

"Everybody sit down. I'm going into Russ's office to make a telephone call. Do nothing, say nothing outside of this room until I am done. Don't look at me like that, Chris. You have no idea what I'm about to do." Grassley turned and went into Russ Martin's office.

"I can't believe Rob would do this without us," Jack said.

"Hell, Jack, he and Ernie were going to do it alone!" Chris said.

"I know. That's crazy!"

Oscar Leighton spoke up. "You know Rob has a plan. He is a master tactician. He isn't crazy. He wouldn't endanger his daughter for nothing. He has something up his sleeve."

Thirty minutes went by without Grassley emerging from the office. They heard him laugh intermittently. Finally, he came out.

"Jack, fire up the 'Hawk. I want you and your crew to go to Davis-Monthan, refuel, and wait for my directions. Monitor the TAC frequencies. I am sure that's what the Guardians are using. Let me know if you hear anything."

"I'm going with them," Chris said.

"No you're not, Chris. You are staying with me and Angie. We may be calling in every marker we have tonight. You are more valuable here. In fact, I need you to find out when HRT is leaving Fort Huachuca. If they are planning leave before tomorrow, I am going to need you to stall them. Russ, you go with Jack. If we take action, you will be in tactical command. Everybody got it?"

Jack, already headed out the door, yelled, "Yes, sir!"

Jordan Yates, the CIA Deputy Director for Operations, thought about the conversation with his old friend Bill Grassley as he walked to the Director's office. Many years before, he and Grassley were young CIA agents working all over the Middle Eastern part of the world. They were a highly respected covert team. They went through many tight spots together, and became close.

Then Bill Grassley fell madly in love with a beautiful Lebanese woman and got married. He decided he wanted to be home with his wife instead of traipsing all over the world. He left the CIA and joined U.S. Customs. Yates and Grassley were still good friends.

As Yates approached the door to the Director's office, he glanced at this watch. It read 7:00 pm. The Director started work at five every morning, something you don't always see in a political appointee. The hours he kept necessarily meant the other members of top staff also worked long hours. Yates stood at the Director's door. The Director motioned him in, and Jordan walked in and sat in a chair with a parlor set in the corner of the Director's office. The Director left his desk and sat in a chair next to Jordan.

"Tell me more about this Arizona issue."

"Well, sir, we have what appear to be two rogue police squads about to violate one hell of a lot of international law to try to rescue their leader's daughter."

"This is all related to the attacks in Arizona we were briefed on last night, right?"

"Yes, sir."

"I thought we were going to send the FBI HRT and Delta in to get her out."

"State just said 'no go.' Mexico says they will handle it."

The Director grunted. "What is your friend Grassley's suggestion?"

"Bill is a very astute man. He sees a political liability here that can be turned into a political asset. The way he sees it, we have a highly trained and experienced team about to go into Mexico to rescue an American citizen whether we like it or not. He thinks the chances are good they are going to succeed. If they do succeed, it will be a publicity event that will eclipse anything going on right now. It will be *the* headline—and the headline will be how the federal government failed to act." Yates paused to let that sink in.

"On the other hand, if the team that makes the rescue is a CIA covert ops team, the headlines will be much different. Mexico is going to raise holy hell no matter who does it. If we are in control, we can do the 'we cannot confirm *or deny* U.S. involvement' dance in such a way everyone knows we did it, but we will never openly admit it."

"You have me a little confused. Where is our covert ops team?"

"Those police officers poised to go into Mexico."

The Director sat back in his chair. "How are we going to make *this* work?"

"Grassley suggests we designate them a CIA asset now. This will give us the latitude to give them support, if they need it. When we get them back on this side of the border, Grassley guarantees me he will be able to keep them quiet. There will be no leaks. We will control the reaction to Mexico's objections."

"What would be the officers' motivation for not going to the press?"

"They won't be prosecuted."

"The political aspects of this would be the President's motivation. What is mine for starting all of this?"

"If you want it, you get a highly trained and experienced covert action team we could keep a secret for a very long time."

The Director sat deep in thought for a good five minutes. Jordan knew the Director worked all of the angles in his head, examining the potential of a covert team nobody knew about, the political disadvantages and advantages, and the impact on his future career plans. The Director reached for the telephone on the coffee table.

"Hi, Sally. Tell Walt to get the chopper ready to go to the White House. Call the White House and tell them we are coming and need to see the President ASAP. Thank you."

Thirty-two minutes later, the two CIA officers sat in the Oval Office with the President. The Director briefed the President on the proposal and all the ramifications he could determine. When the Director finished, the President rose from his desk and looked out the window into the faint glow of the beginning summer night.

"These are the officers leading the investigation that found Bob Mickerson was on the take, aren't they?"

"Yes, sir," Yates answered.

The President turned around. "These officers sound like good men—with balls. They certainly did me a favor by uncovering Mickerson. We can use men like them. Go with the plan. Get with my press secretary and make sure he knows enough to not screw up the publicity side of this. Now, if you will excuse me, I am going to get back to having a cocktail with my wife. Thank you, Gentlemen."

TWENTY SIX

Pull over and stop, Ernie. Time to check our back trail."

Ernie checked his mirrors again. "There's no one following us, Rob."

"Just pull over. I've got a feeling."

Ernie rolled his eyes and brought the Bronco to a halt on the left side of Duquesne Road. Robin got out of the truck with binoculars and climbed a small hill. He glassed back along the road. A minute later, he came back to Bronco.

"We have company."

"We do?!"

"Yes. Just sit tight."

"Who do you think it is?"

"It's Burke and probably everyone else."

"How do you know?"

"I saw two vehicles. I just know it's Jameson."

"Because you have a feeling."

"That's it."

"Sometimes you worry me, Rob."

They sat for about five minutes. Then Burke's truck came around the corner. It skidded to a halt. Robin got out of the Bronco. Burke drove slowly up to him. Doug's truck came around the corner.

Burke stopped and rolled down his window. "Hi, Sarge." He had a big grin on his face.

"I guess I don't have to ask what you're doing here."

"Probably a waste of time." Burke still grinned.

"Where's Emmett and Rick?"

"Oh, they're coming. They stopped in Patagonia to make some phone calls." Ernie got out of the Bronco and stood next to Robin. He saw Rocky and Marv in the back of the crew cab.

"Goddammit, you two! Get your asses back to Phoenix!"

"Now, Ernie, don't get pissed," Rocky replied. "You know damn good and well we have just as much right to be here as you two do. Andy and Cathy are family to us too and the rest of the guys."

"Whaddya mean 'the rest of guys?'"

"Everyone is here. Both squads." Marv nudged Rocky. "Oh yeah, Carlos too."

"Carlos!" Robin exclaimed.

"Yep. He talked Emmett into it," Burke said. Emmett's truck came speeding around the corner and skidded to a halt. It drove up to the group. Rick got out and walked up to Robin.

"Cathy is okay for now, Rob. I got word from Jorge."

Robin steadied himself on Burke's truck. He held back the tears of immense relief. "I wish I could get word to Karen."

"Chris took care of that."

"Save it," Robin replied. "We have to get to our campsite. We'll sort all this out then. Drivers, come over to Ernie's Bronco." Robin pulled out a map and showed them a campsite he had chosen. "Start looking to your left when you get about two miles from the border. It will be the largest stand of trees in the area. We will go first and set up a CHEMLITE. Space yourselves out from here. Try to keep the dust down. Any questions?" Nobody spoke up. "All right, mount up, we're burning daylight."

As everyone headed for their respective vehicles, Emmett cracked, "Hey, Sarge, do you know you say that whether it's day *or* night?"

"Glad you're paying attention, Emmett."

Robin and Ernie drove for another twenty-two miles before they arrived at the campsite as darkness was closing in. They stretched out two large camouflage tarps over the campsite, hooking them to the trees with bungee cords. Robin hung the CHEMLITE just inside the trees. Only someone looking for it would spot it.

Eventually, the rest of the team vehicles came in, one by one. After everyone arrived, other tarps were added to form a loose enclosure around the cold, dry camp. No fire. No water nearby; this was strictly business. The men busied themselves laying gear out and checking weapons. Some ate MRE's, beef jerky, or other snacks. They only used CHEMLITEs or small flashlights with red lenses.

Rick took Robin aside. "Rob, Chris wanted me to relay a message from Karen." Robin stiffened. "Karen says, and I quote, 'I love you. Bring our daughter home.'"

Robin deflated. *God, I love that woman!*

"Thanks, Rick. I appreciate that."

A little later, Robin noticed Carlos off by himself, really not busy with anything. Robin retrieved his MP5 from its case along with five loaded magazines and pulled out an old tactical vest. He walked over to Carlos and handed him the gear. Rick came up and handed Carlos a duty rig with a .357 Smith & Wesson revolver. "We can't have you just sitting around. We don't believe in free rides. You'll have to earn this E-ticket."

Carlos showed a relieved smile. "Thank you, Robin." Robin nodded.

After the men started to settle down, Robin stood before them for the mission brief. Emmett brought an easel with a diagram of the ranch and the immediate area Carlos had drawn.

"Gentlemen," Robin announced, "we need to be relatively quiet now. The smugglers will start coming across soon. Keep your voices down to a whisper and the lights to a minimum. I want to first say you're all nuts. You're not only risking your lives; you're also throwing your careers down the drain. Make no mistake about it, when we get back, we'll all be arrested because we're about to commit a multitude of federal and international crimes. I won't have any hard feelings if any or all of you just pack up and go home. In fact, I wish that's what you would do."

"Is he always this full of shit?" a loud whisper came out of the group.

"Well, he's a lawyer, whaddya expect?" Burke whispered back.

Gary Perkins, the oldest man in the group with twenty-five years on Phoenix PD, had asked the question.

"Why are *you* here, Gary?" Robin asked. "I know we've worked together for about five years now and we're friends, but you have your own family. Why are you willing to chuck your career and possible prison for me?"

Gary thought for a minute. He looked over at Jamie Slater and Willy Young, the rest of Ernie's team. "Well, Sarge, I guess because I wasn't doing very well before Ernie, Rocky, and Marv showed up. In fact, I fucked up enough to be close to getting fired. I had a real bad attitude. They kind a perked me up. Perked us all up," he said, waving to Jamie and Willy. "Then you guys came along and we all started working together, I really started feeling like a good cop again. Hell, I would've retired at twenty, if I hadn't been doing this. I figure if you guys are gonna go, I'm going too. At least I'll be going out in style!" Gary looked around at everyone. "The other thing, Sarge, is that deep inside of me I know this is the right thing to do. I like doing the right thing." A murmur of approval went through the group.

"And payback for Andy," Jamie threw in, to more approval.

"Damn, Gary!" Rocky exclaimed in a hoarse whisper. "I didn't know you were such an orator!"

"Blow it out your ass, Rock." Everyone suppressed laughs.

"Okay, Sarge, get on with it," Emmett said. "We're burning daylight." The laughter renewed.

Robin looked at everyone and simply said, "Thanks." He had no other words. He turned to the easel. "This is Rodriquez's ranch. We have a number of buildings. This is the main ranch house."

Rick spoke up. "Jorge says he will bring Maria to Cathy's location. That would be the small guest room. Carlos has marked it with the "C" there. Jorge knew that's where we'll head first. Plus, it is easier to move Maria than it is to move Cathy."

"Carlos, what can we expect in terms of security?"

"The main house is well guarded, Robin. There will be at least four men walking the outside and at least four on the inside, two on each floor. Since Jorge has been assigned to guard Cathy, there may be only three inside hostiles now."

"What about electronic security?"

"There is an alarm system in the house. It is functional and will be armed. There is also a perimeter alarm system, but it has been down off and on for months. It didn't work when I left and no one seemed to be too interested in fixing it."

"Jeez, they sound just like a government agency!" Doug joked.

"Do you know where we might be able to disable the alarm?"

"Yes, I do. I know the code."

"I figured you did. Who else can we expect in the house?"

"There will be Miguel, and he will have a woman with him."

"Who is the woman?"

"I don't know. He brings in different ones. They are stripped naked and brought to him. He is very paranoid. His quarters are here."

"And a real romantic, "Ernie chimed in.

"There will also be Leona, the chef."

"What can we expect from her?"

"She is very loyal to Miguel. He has made her rich. She keeps an Uzi in her quarters and I think she will fight. Her quarters are here on the second floor. And of course, there will be Juan Trinidad. His quarters are here, also on the second floor."

Robin passed a picture around. "That's Trinidad. Don't mess with him. Kill him on sight. He is extremely dangerous." Robin passed around another picture. "I'm sure you recognize this picture. That's Rodriquez. Same for him." Robin passed a third picture. "This is Jorge, our inside man. He is a good guy. He should be with Cathy and Maria." Robin turned to the easel. "These large structures to the east of the main house are barracks-type buildings. Our goal is to contain the people there. Don't make entry. It would be suicide. So, I need Doug and Rick to set up to pick them off at the doors and windows."

"There is only one door," Carlos observed.

"Only one door? Well, I guess Miguel doesn't have to build to code. That should make your job easier, guys. This small house just north of the barracks is where Carlos and Maria live. It should be empty. These two large barn-like buildings along the northeast wall are loaded with tons of dope. Mark, you, Jamie, and Willy set up on those buildings. Shoot anything that comes out. After taking care of the primary mission, we are going to blow those buildings up. I have a load of C4 charges and eight grenades. Split them up between the two teams."

"Where the hell did you get that, Rob?" Ernie asked.

"Probably that little weasel Chucky," Burke said.

"Yep, Chucky came through."

"Jesus, is there anything he can't steal?"

"He didn't steal it, Burke. He bought it off of some military guys who stole it from the Army. We'll deal with them when we get back." Robin reached back into the Bronco and retrieved two large pistol cases. He gave one to Burke and one to Rocky. "Burke, your partner is Mike; Rocky, you and Marv, of course. You guys are going over the wall first. I want you to hunt and take out any sentries you can find. Those hush puppies should make it easier." Burke opened up his case to look at the silenced Smith & Wesson M39 9mm pistol.

"Where did you get two? I thought SOU only had one, "Burke asked.

"Our team owns this one," Rocky offered.

Carlos spoke up. "You can only get over the wall at one place. The rest is covered in glass, spikes, and concertina." He walked over to the easel. "Because of this small gate here, the wall above it is clear."

"How come?" Burke asked.

"They stopped there while they were putting in the gate. They never went back and finished it." The group laughed.

"Okay, what about the gate? Can it be opened from the inside?" Burke asked.

"Yes, it can."

"Good. I'll go over the wall and get the gate open."

"The other barracks building may or may not be a problem," Carlos pointed to the barracks-type building furthest to the north in the compound. "This building may be empty, or it may contain a number of Arabs. There have been up to thirty Arabs there."

"Arabs? What Arabs?" Robin asked.

"I told Chris about this. Several times a year, Arabs, sometimes from Saudi Arabia, Pakistan, or Syria and sometimes from Iran, come to be smuggled into the United States."

"Why?"

"They are coming to destroy your country."

Robin looked at Carlos. The words Carlos spoke seared into Robin's brain, bringing up a silent rage.

"How many come at one time?"

"It varies. Sometimes many, sometimes few."

"Are they armed?"

"Yes. You can expect them to be heavily armed."

"Well, that certainly is important safety information. All right, let's finish this up," Robin ordered. "Carlos, I want you to go with Burke and point out sentries. You guys taking out the sentries work your way to the main house. The rest of the team will stage at the small gate. When you are ready, let us know and we will all enter and head to our assignments. Ernie, you, Emmett, and I will join Burke and the rest of the sentry team to form the entry team. We will stack up at the front door. The stack will be Burke, Emmett, Mike, Carlos, Rocky, Marv, and then Ernie and me. I have an entry charge ready to go if we need it. Ernie, Carlos and Mike are the extraction team. Here are some drawings of the layout of the house. Any questions?" Robin looked over the barely visible faces. "Okay, we will operate on TAC 2."

"Make that TAC 6, Rob," Rick whispered. "The 'Hawk will be monitoring us."

"What's that all about?"

"All I know is that Chris told me Grassley has ordered the 'Hawk to be airborne, and if we need help, he may authorize Jack to do it."

"That's interesting," Robin mused. The sound of a vehicle on the dirt road echoed in the night. "Sounds like the evening runs are starting. We will roll down there at a good clip. Carlos says that will make anyone in Santa Cruz who is awake think we are Rodriquez's men. Drivers use night vision. We will stop around two-tenths of a mile from the ranch and go the rest of the way on foot. Gary, you will stay with the vehicles. When the extraction team calls, you get your ass in there and pick them up. Drop Mike and Carlos off at the trucks, and then you, Ernie, and Jorge head for Tucson and don't stop. Mike and Carlos, we would appreciate it if you would come back and pick us up. Finally, remember, the minute we cross the border, the plan can go to shit. In that case, improvise, adapt, and overcome. Now, everybody quiet down and do what you need to do, including packing a double ammo load. We will launch in about three hours."

The men moved to finish their preparations. Without being told, some of them took up positions to cover their camp. The vehicle and foot traffic steadily increased. Robin thought about how the traffic made the border inconsequential, as this activity occurred all over the border between Mexico and the U.S. Robin's jaws clamped tight. He had long complained to the DPS brass that DPS should be on the border in force—at least to interdict drugs and contraband—but the response was, "It's a federal problem." Robin pointed out Arizona citizens living along the border were being affected by the rampant illegal activity. It didn't seem to matter to the brass. Robin knew this national security problem would only get worse.

Robin looked at the men around him, in private knots of two or three. Burke and Rocky were briefing men on the explosives. Burke checked the crimps on the charges and made sure the M-60 detonators were operational. Robin felt comfortable here. Being around tough, courageous men preparing to take care of business was completely in tune with his nature. There is an aura around highly trained and experienced fighting men. Men you can count on to do what is needed no matter how tough the situation may get.

Being supremely confident the mission would be successful, Robin felt intense pride in himself and the men around him. He had a growing realization that warriors who fight those who prey on the defenseless can never really be at peace with themselves. The fight never ends. His underlying uneasiness over the impact his addiction had on his family lingered.

TWENTY SEVEN

When Jack Moore landed at Davis-Monthan Air Force Base, he immediately asked for the armament chief. A staff sergeant on the flight line gave Jack a ride to the end of the tarmac, stopping at a large building surrounded by half-buried hanger-shaped concrete buildings. They went inside and the sergeant introduced Jack to one of crustiest non-coms he had ever seen. A giant of a man, Chief Master Sergeant Burl Williams wore more stripes than most uniforms could fit. The lines on his face formed a formidable pattern of canyons and crevices, which were only interrupted by his ready smile. The hand he held out in greeting was attached to a thick muscular forearm, and Jack felt at any moment Chief Williams could crush his hand without a second thought.

"What can I do for you, Customs Pilot Jack?"

"Well, Chief, I am going to be loitering at the border very early in the morning on a highly classified mission. I may be ordered south to assist a special ops team. All I have are two Miniguns. I wondered if I might borrow a couple of 2.75 pods." Chief Williams' smile left his face and his eyes narrowed.

"Son, that isn't going to happen," he said in a deep, stern voice.

"The targets are the guys who shot the two airmen just outside the base here." Chief Williams' expression changed immediately. His smile did not come back, but a fire ignited in his eyes.

"You on the level?"

"I am, Chief."

"I knew young Sam Cowen, a damned good man. I'm not sure what happened that day. Nobody is saying much."

"Sam and Jerry Parker jumped into the middle of a drug cartel kidnapping a DPS officer's daughter. Sam and Jerry tried to stop it. They shot Sam in the back."

"Those sons of bitches!" Chief Williams spat. "Did they kidnap the girl?"

"They did, Chief. The mission of the special ops team is to get her back."

Chief Williams immediately spun on this heel. As he marched back to the office bay, he started calling out names and barking orders. Two hours later, the Blackhawk sported four 2.75 rocket pods slung under two stubby wings, all courtesy of the United States Air Force. The installation also included a rudimentary sighting system.

Jack heard footsteps behind him, and an arm went around his shoulders. Chief Williams stood next to Jack, dressed in flight suit, helmet, and air crew vest, complete with a Smith and Wesson .38special. He also carried a M-16 rifle.

"I'm going with you." Jack was going to object when the Chief gave him a hard look. "I decided to retire tonight. The ol' lady has been trying to get me to do it for a while now. I'm gonna go out dishin' some payback. Besides, you need me along to make sure this jerry rig works when you need it to."

Because of all Chief Williams did for him, Jack simply said, "Welcome aboard, Chief. Let's get airborne."

Robin looked over the men. He could barely make out their facial features because of the darkness and the camouflage paint they were wearing. The smuggler traffic tapered off, the tarps taken down and the gear stowed in the trucks. A light breeze made the desert cooler. The stars shone thick and sparkling above them while the hills and trees were only dark shadows. The final details of the mission were hashed and rehashed. All of the men were prepared.

"All right gentlemen, let's get rolling."

The three-truck caravan rolled over the border and raced toward Santa Cruz, going between fifty-five and sixty miles per hour on the well-traveled dirt road. They hit an occasional rut or hole that would jar the trucks and briefly fling the men around in their seat belts. They saw no one. They came to Santa Cruz in sixteen minutes, and they went by it in less than one. Robin only saw two lights in the little dark town.

The hills on either side of the road grew higher as they drove on. Robin knew they were close. After two more minutes, he told Ernie to slow down. After one more, he instructed him to stop one-tenth of a mile from the ranch.

The caravan pulled into a ravine and parked. Robin got out and motioned for Burke and Carlos to join him. They climbed a small hill overlooking the ranch, where they could see inside the fortress fairly well. Security lights lit the area, but the lights cast shadows in many places. Robin counted a number of men in the area.

"Burke, do you have enough shadow to work with? There are at least ten men moving around down there."

"I guess it will have to be enough. We're not going back now."

Robin thought for a minute. "We're going to forget blowing up the dope. We're facing long odds in numbers and we can use the guys who were going after the dope to work with the bunkhouse security team to hold back any counterattack. We'll use the explosives to whittle down the odds and move both teams closer to the main house so they can cover all of those buildings. Let's move."

Back at the trucks, Robin briefed the men on the changes.

"As we move in, perimeter defense teams set two of those charges as close to the bunkhouses as you can. You'll have to light them then. The fuses are three minutes. Save the other two satchels for tactical use. Okay, sentry team, get moving. As soon as you have cleared enough space for us to come in and maneuver, let us know. We'll move in."

"We're gone," Burke said.

"Mark and Rick, come with me back up the hill, so you can get a look-see." From the vantage point on the hill, Robin, Mark, and Rick watched as Burke's team moved along the wall. When they got to the small gate, the team formed a human ladder. Burke went over the wall. Robin didn't see the gate open, but he saw the rest of the team go through it. He and his men went back to the trucks.

"Form up. We'll move to the wall and wait for the word. Hang tough, Gary. We'll be calling soon."

"I'm ready, Rob."

Jorge had a difficult time convincing Maria that Carlos had changed sides and was working with the Americans. The explanation was not made any easier by the fact that Jorge could not explain why Carlos had done this. Jorge had no idea. He fell back on common sense.

"Señora, do you like the men here?"

"I despise them."

"I am sure your husband has come to the same conclusion. I have not talked to your husband. I just know he wants you to come to him and I am instructed to help get you to him. I am also supposed to help another young woman escape. We must leave now!"

That was enough. Maria went with him, although reluctantly. As they made their way across the compound, Jorge heard Maria gasp. He looked over and saw an American lowering the body of a sentry slowly and quietly to the ground. He could see darkness flowing from the sentry's throat. Tugging at Maria's hand, he swiftly and quietly brought her to the back door of the main house. Jorge punched the code into the alarm keypad and opened the door. As they entered the house, Jorge heard a door open and close and footsteps coming down the back stairs. He pushed Maria into an alcove. Juan came striding by, heading for the back door. He punched the code into a keypad and uttered a curse about incompetent security. He went through the door. Jorge literally flung Maria up the hall and into the Señorita's room.

The Señorita's eyes were wide. "I thought you weren't coming! You told me you were coming at three!"

"Carlos works for your father?" Maria asked Cathy in Spanish.

Cathy replied in Spanish, "I do not know what you are talking about."

"She does not know," Jorge said. "This is not business for a child."

"I am not a child," Cathy retorted. Jorge groaned and rolled his eyes to the heavens for guidance. His relationship with women was going downhill.

Jorge, in order to redeem himself, turned to Cathy. "I am told you know how to shoot a pistol."

"My father taught me."

Jorge handed her a Browning High Power 9mm pistol, his personal and favorite weapon. "We may need you to help."

"My father has one just like this. I know how to use it."

"I would like a gun," Maria insisted. Jorge sighed, reached into an ankle holster, and handed her a Walther PPKS .380. The women looked at each other.

"Jorge, are we getting out of here alive?" Cathy asked.

Jorge did not answer.

Burke, Mike, and Carlos moved deliberately in the shadows created by the lights in the compound. So far, so good. They had taken out three sentries, all knife work. Burke was relieved when Mike took out number three. Mike had never killed anyone with a knife before, but he met the ugly necessity. Burke saw a man and woman heading for the house. He also saw Rocky taking care of business on the other side of the compound. He realized the man and woman had to be Jorge and Maria. Carlos started for Maria, but Burke grabbed him and put his finger to his lips. He called in Robin and his team.

As Burke and Mike closed on the house, they saw two men toward the front by a car. Nearing the rear of the house, they heard a door close. Burke handed the Hush Puppy to Mike and nudged him and Carlos toward the two men in front of them. Burke glided silently to the rear of the house as he heard the muffled thumps of Mike's shots.

Juan Trinidad walked out of the back door and stood on the porch. He wanted Maria, and he wanted her tonight. He did not care about Carlos. He did not care about Miguel. He stepped off the porch and stopped mid-step. He heard a familiar sound…a silenced pistol.

A flicker of a shadow caught the corner of his eye. He turned, reaching for his gun.. The shadow loomed large. It struck Juan in the gut with a flash of steel. He felt the cold blade penetrate him, then again and again. Surging with fury, he twisted his hand to point his pistol up and fire. He and the shadow fell to the ground in unison, side by side. He saw Burke's face. Burke jerked his shoulders with a grunt of pain, and the blade sliced up Juan's gut. Juan's breath left him. He could not feel his gun. His arms were pinned. He kneed Burke in the groin and lunged with his face, biting into Burke's right cheek and ripping off a chunk of flesh. Burke growled and brought the blade up to Juan's sternum. He raised his knee and rolled on top of Juan, his knees on Juan's shoulders. Weakening, Juan tried to twist and kick, but Burke stayed unmovable. He raised his blade,a razor sharp, double-edged Ka-Bar knife. Juan stared at it as it came down on his face. He didn't flinch. His eyes met Burke's with cold resignation. Burke's eyes drilled Juan with flaming revenge and then death as the blade plowed into his brain and sent him to oblivion.

When Burke made the call for the rest of the team, they entered through the gate and moved to the ranch house. Ernie and Emmett were behind Robin. The rest of the team started ghosting towards the house to form a perimeter. It seemed to be going well, Robin thought...then a shot. Robin's thoughts changed immediately. The shot compromised the team. He keyed his mic.

"Nora Six-One, Ten-Twenty." Burke didn't answer.

"Victor Three Twenty-Four, we're headed for the front door," Rocky said.

"Nora Six-Three we're close," Mike called.

"We are almost there," Robin said. Suddenly a dark figure appeared at the northwest corner of the front of the house. He shouted in Spanish and fired a burst towards a car. Robin fired two shots at the man, but he had disappeared. More shouts in Spanish. The front door slammed. A crescendo of small arms fire built in the compound. Mike came out from behind the car and crossed in front of Robin.

Robin reached the northwest corner of the house and quickly peeked around. He thought he recognized Rocky.

"Nora Six!" Robin shouted.

"Victor Three Twenty-Four!" Rocky shouted back. They both moved to the large double doors. Other team members followed.

Robin tried the doors, but they were locked. The doors were ornate and too heavy to kick in.

"Ernie, the charge!" Ernie brought up a door-sized piece of cardboard. A double pattern of detonation cord covered the front of the cardboard and strips of folded duct tape were attached to the back. Robin and Ernie stuck the back of the board to the doors.

"Stack up!" Robin ordered. He pulled the igniter and moved to the rear of the stack. It dawned on him Burke wasn't in the stack. He thought of the first shot and swallowed a lump in this throat.

The charge blew sharp and loud. A blast of debris, smoke, and dust engulfed the stack and the front porch. The team moved in, throwing stun grenades in every direction. Emmett and Mike moved right into a large room. They immediately engaged two men who were struggling to get up and killed them with bursts of 9mm rounds from their MP5s. Carlos and Rocky dumped left into a smaller room, and Carlos killed one man there.

Robin saw a man at the top of the stairs and his Galil roared. The man fell back against the railing and his limp body crumpled down the stairs like a ragdoll. Marv posted at the stairs as Ernie and Robin moved down the hall. Heavy explosions rocked the compound as the charges went off.

Ernie and Robin were joined by Emmet and Mike as they moved further down the hall to the room where Cathy was supposed to be.

"Jorge!" Robin called.

"Dad!" Cathy called. Jorge opened the door, and Cathy rushed out to her Dad. Robin put his left arm around her and hugged her tight. He kissed her on the cheek and pushed her to Ernie. The firefight outside briefly stopped after the explosions, but it was starting up again.

"You, all of you, have to go…now!" Robin ordered.

Maria exited the room and saw Carlos. She ran to him. Carlos grabbed her and pulled her to him. He gave a thankful glance to Robin.

Robin nodded. "Get going! Everyone!"

"Dad!" Cathy cried.

Ernie pulled her down the hall. "C'mon, Cathy, your Dad has some killing to do." Ernie keyed his mic. "Victor Three Twenty-One, move in!"

"I'm here," Gary's voice came over the radio.

"Up the stairs!" Robin ordered. The rest of the stack went up the stairs, with Marv in the lead. They reached the top and started down the hall. Marv fired a burst at a man at the end of the hall, blowing his head in half. The man pitched forward, his head hitting the floor and sounding like a broken watermelon. A woman in a nightgown stepped into the hall and fired at them. Marv fired back as he went down. The woman collapsed, her head bouncing off the tile.

Rocky hesitated, looking at Marv, who bled from a bullet wound to right side of his torso not covered by his vest. "Go!" Marv yelled. A man Robin recognized as Rodriquez fired one shot with a pistol from a doorway on the right. The bullet hit the opposite wall just inches from Robin. He fired four rounds at Rodriquez, who moved back and slammed the door. Robin did a tactical reload.

Rocky bent down and grabbed the rescue pull ring on Marv's vest.

"You guys get Marv outta here and to the cars!"

"Sarge—" Emmett started to say.

"Don't argue with me, Emmett. Get going!" He keyed his mic, "All units move to the extraction point!" The rest of the men moved down the stairs, Emmett looking back at Robin. Robin turned his attention to Rodriquez's door. He prepared a stun grenade. Suddenly, the upstairs back door opened and Burke stumbled through.

"Burke!" Robin said, alarmed.

Rick and Doug were barely in position behind a long concrete planter when shots and yelling brought men coming out of the bunkhouses in a rush. The two officers opened up, Rick with his MacMillan Sniper Rifle and Doug with his Galil, and started dropping those men. Then more men burst out of the windows; others came running from the back.

"If there isn't a back door, there must be windows," Rick yelled. He switched to the MP-5 he brought as a back up. There were just too many bad guys coming at them to be using a bolt action rifle. Bullets whizzed overhead and smacked into the concrete scattering chips everywhere. Doug's Galil roared reply.

Rick glanced to his left. Mark and his team seemed to be holding their own. He could see Willy Young helping with the south bunkhouse men. The south bunkhouse charge went off. The concussion stunned Rick, and debris started raining down on them. Seconds later, the north bunkhouse charge went off. A thick cloud of dust glowed and swirled in the security lights, covering the compound. More debris flew through the air. The gunfight slowed down to a few scattered shots.

"Two Nora Six-Five to Two Nora Six-Six," Rick called Mark.

"Go, Rick."

"We're going to move to your position to get ready for extract."

"Ten-Four. We'll be watching for you."

"Let's go, Doug." Rick and Doug headed for Mark's team near the northeast corner of the ranch house. The gunfire picked up again. Doug moved in front of Rick. Rick heard the sickening slap of a bullet hitting flesh, and Doug went down in front of him. Doug uttered a curse, his voice filled with pain.

"Mark! Doug's hit!" Suddenly, Mark emerged from the dust and helped Rick pick up Doug and his rifle. Doug tried to walk, but he couldn't move fast enough. The other two men dragged him. They reached the other team's position and laid Doug down. Rick saw Doug had been shot in the buttocks. Rick turned his head and gasped as he saw Jamie lying on the grass with a wound to his head.

"He's still alive," Mark said. They helped Doug get into a position to help with the fight. More men were coming at them, and the gunfight heated back up. These men were not yelling Spanish, but a different language.

"Arabs," Mark yelled. "There are a helluva lot of them!"

Rick pulled out a grenade, pulled the pin, and tossed it at men trying to rush his position. It bounced to the left and went off. All the men went down, but a few seconds later half of them were shooting and starting to move again. Mark threw a grenade at another group. His grenade seemed to have more of an impact on them. Only one rose. Still it seemed an unending stream of men were coming out of both barracks.

"Come on, Rob. Call the extraction," Rick muttered through the din. "This fight's going south." Several seconds later, he heard Robin's voice call for extraction.

"I'm all right, Rob."

Robin could see differently. Burke had an ugly wound on the right side of his face. His missing left sleeve revealed a bloody bandage on the shoulder, and the front of his camo fatigues looked dark with blood.

"Trinidad was a tough motherfucker," he said, as if stating a simple fact. "I'm *all right*, Rob," Burke said again, in response to Robin's concerned look.

Robin pointed to the door. "Rodriquez." Burke nodded and seemed to rejuvenate somewhat. The gunfire continued outside. Rounds zinged through the house intermittently. Shouts of men in combat came from all directions. Explosions punctuated the gunfire. Robin tried the door handle. It turned.

"I'm going in, low and right. You cover me high from here," Robin whispered. He held up a stun grenade. "On three." Burke nodded. Robin pulled the pin on the grenade. He opened the door, and two rounds flew at them. Robin tossed the grenade, counted two, and went in. Burke fired a burst. The grenade went off. Robin made it to the corner of the entry to the master bedroom and dropped prone. Rodriquez fired five more rounds. A woman screamed words in Spanish...three more shots. The woman stopped screaming. So far, Robin counted eleven rounds fired by Rodriquez. There could be at least eight more.

Robin could hear muttering in Spanish, then in English. It kept alternating and getting louder. He pinpointed where Rodriquez was hiding in the large room. Robin hunkered behind an oversized oak rolltop desk in the corner of the room to the left and in front of Robin. He knew his Galil would punch through the wood of the desk, but for some perverse reason, Robin prepared another grenade. He pulled the pin and tossed it. It hit the floor and bounced to the exact spot where Rodriquez was hiding.

Rodriquez yelled. The grenade exploded with a bright flash and dense smoke. Robin moved to the corner of the bed and went to one knee. He saw a nude woman dead on the floor next to the bed. Rodriquez screamed as he staggered towards Robin, aimlessly firing his pistol in different directions. Robin rose like a ghost in the thick smoke and drove his rifle butt into Rodriquez's face, knocking him down. Burke came up next to Robin as Robin stepped over to Rodriquez and kicked the pistol away from him. Rodriquez was lying face up, blood pouring from his nose and mouth. His eyes met Robin's.

"I'm Robin Marlette."

Rodriquez's eyes widened. His breath came faster. "You are a policeman. You...you cannot hurt me. It is the rule!"

Unrelenting ice gripped Robin's soul, creating a conflict so deep in his nature, he shuddered—but only for a moment. "When you try to kill me, the rules apply. But you tried to kill my family. You kidnapped my daughter. When you do such things, there are no rules." Robin raised his Galil and pointed it at Rodriquez. He said, "GOTU." Rodriquez screamed and crawled backwards, his bloody, contorted face a stark display of raw fear and hatred. Robin fired two rounds into Rodriquez's face, obliterating any recognizable feature.

Burke put his hand on Robin's shoulder. "There *is* a time to kill."

"Let's get out of here."

The two men hurried out of the room and into the hall. They went down the stairs. Through the front door, they could see dawn glowing behind the hills. Gunfire reverberated outside. A satchel charge went off to the left. Dust and debris flew everywhere.

"Extraction vehicles are here! Rocky! Marv! Robin! Burke! C'mon, let's go! We've got wounded! We gotta get out of here!" Mike screamed into the radio.

A voice came over the radio along with loud gunfire. "Get out of here, Mike. We can't make it. Marv's too badly hit...and I'm hit," Rocky said.

Once at the door, Robin saw the two extraction vehicles were taking heavy fire as the perimeter teams got in them. "Burke, get to the vehicles."

"I'm staying with you." Robin looked into Burke's resolute eyes.

"Goddamn stubborn Indian." Mike frantically motioned for Robin and Burke to come to the vehicles.

Robin keyed his radio. "Mike, go! We'll catch up. That *is* an order!" Robin looked to his left and saw Rocky and Marv crouched behind a small concrete building against the perimeter wall. They were shooting down the side of the ranch house. He and Burke moved to the corner of the house and saw the source of fire: five to six men with Uzis and AK-47s stationed near the car Robin had seen earlier.

"Let's light 'em up, Burke." They opened fire, and immediately two of the men dropped. A third stood up, and Rocky shot him. The other men turned and ran to the back of the ranch house, shooting as they ran. Robin shot another one and he crashed into the ground.

"Burke! Go to Rocky!" Robin sprinted toward the vehicle. Bullets kicked up turf and dust as they ricocheted all around him. His left foot flew out from underneath him, and he went sprawling onto the grass. He jumped back up and ran another ten yards. Then a blow to his hip spun him around and onto the paved driveway. Robin crawled the rest of the way to the car, which immediately began taking fire. He opened the driver's door, and was relieved to find the keys in the ignition. He painfully climbed into the driver's seat and started the car, a BMW, and accelerated to Burke, Rocky, and Marv. Bullets thumped into the car, causing glass and metal to slice into and all over Robin. He hunched down and protected his eyes, screaming, "FUCK! FUCK! FUCK!" at no one in particular. He skidded up to the concrete building and all three men tumbled into the back seat, Marv cursing in pain.

"GO, ROB, GO!" Burke yelled. Robin floored the accelerator, and the car fishtailed forward. He straightened it out and made it through the gate. He felt relief for a half a minute until he saw headlights come out of the gate behind them, then more headlights.

"I guess it ain't over until the fat lady farts!" Robin muttered. He turned the headlights on to see better in the dawn's gloom. He looked down at the instrument panel. "Shit!" he said.

"What's up, Rob?" Burke asked.

"We're overheating. They probably nailed the engine."

"Keep going!"

"No shit!" They careened through Santa Cruz, almost hitting an old pickup and a mule pulling a cart. They went another two miles.

"They're gaining on us, Rob!" Burke yelled. They could smell the hot engine. Smoke started to filter into the passenger compartment.

"We're losing power. We gotta stop and set up a defensive position soon. Start looking for a good spot."

Burke leaned forward to Robin's ear and recoiled, shocked to see the right side of Robin's head and neck bleeding heavily. Burke swallowed hard. "Rob, Marv's in a bad way. We got to get him to a hospital."

"I figured that, Burke, but I'm not a magician. This beamer's done."

"That looks good up there, Sarge! To the left!" Rocky yelled.

Robin angled the car over and skidded to a halt. They all climbed out of the car. Robin saw Rocky dragging his left leg, his pants covered in blood. Robin's hip throbbed with pain, but he could still move. He pushed Rocky aside and lifted Marv out of the car, putting him over his shoulder in a fireman's carry. Marv screamed in pain.

"Rob, you're hit!" Rocky yelled. "There's blood everywhere."

"We're all hit. Get moving." Rocky hesitated. "Let's go, Rocky! Up the hill!"

Over his headset, Jack could hear the calls of men, his friends, wounded friends. He couldn't take it anymore. Without permission from Grassley, he jerked the stick right with hard right pedal and flew across the border, headed for Santa Cruz, slightly amazed Russ and Oscar made no objection. Jack looked over at Oscar, who scanned the area with his night vision. Jack's headset crackled.

"Super Four-Nine, Lima Two-One."

"Go, Four-Nine." Jack wondered who could be calling him.

"We are coming up on your left." Jack looked over and saw a black HH-53 helicopter with no markings coming up into his view.

"Identify."

"Heavy backup. You have two Angels behind you and coming up on your right." Oscar strained to look to his rear right.

"I've got two U.S.A.F. Air Rescue 'Hawks."

"Happy to have the company," Jack said with relief. "Stand by while I get a Situation Report. Two Nora Six, where are the hostages?"

"Victor Thirty-Two, Lima Two-One, we are approximately six miles north of Santa Cruz." Ernie's voice sounded tense. With his night vision goggles, Oscar saw a vehicle speeding towards the border. He hit the spotlight switch and aimed the light at the vehicle. It stopped.

"That you, Ernie?'

"Yep."

"Stand by, we're going to pick you up."

Lima Two-One, Romeo Zero-Three we will be landing with you. Have your striper transfer to this helicopter tell him *it is an order*."

"Roger, Zero-Three."

Mike Collins came up on the radio. "Lima Two-One, Nora Six-Three, we are just now passing through Santa Cruz with many wounded, at least one critical."

"Romeo Zero-Two, Nora Six-Three, are you dark?"

"Ten-Four...err, roger, sir."

"Turn your lights on...okay, Nora Six-Three, we have you. Stop and stand by for pickup, we have what you need."

"Roger."

While the pickups were being made, the HH-53, with FBI HRT and a Delta team aboard, used onboard sensors to see into the night. The operator saw a vehicle careen out of the compound, followed by several others. He could see occasional muzzle flashes from the following vehicles.

"Super Four-Nine, Lima Two-One, are all of our people accounted for?"

"Negative, Four-Nine. We think we are missing four, including the team leader. We've been trying to make contact, but we're not getting an answer."

"Romeo Zero-Two, our new passengers confirm four team members still in the compound, last seen under heavy fire."

Jack flew over the compound, looking for Robin and the others. He followed Ernie's suggestion to use the rockets on the buildings storing all of the dope.

"Lima Two-One, Two Nora Six, are you in the compound?"

"Negative, Two-One. We are in deep shit a couple of miles north of Santa Cruz. We need help!"

"Stand by."

"Super Four-Nine, we have their position and we are moving in. Romeo Zero-Three, follow us in."

"Zero-Three, roger."

"Nora Six, we have you in sight and are moving in."

Robin and the others struggled up the hill. They found a small depression in the ground and jumped into it. Robin laid Marv down. Marv looked at Rob with a weak smile. "I always wanted a sergeant to be my valet."

"I assume since you can still be a smartass, you can still fight."

"Yes, sir." Robin handed Marv back his MP5.

"You got north."

"I'll take care of it, Rob." Marv's words were slurred.

"I got east," Burke volunteered.

"Rock, take west. I got south."

"Roger, Sarge."

Robin saw the other vehicles had stopped, but he could not see any men.

Loud whooshing sounds echoed across the desert, and the early dawn sky lit up in the direction of the compound. Robin heard the roar of a Minigun. A shadow moved in front of him and then dropped. It rose again, and Robin fired. The shadow yelped, and it sounded like a man rolled down the hill. Radio traffic constantly streamed between Jack and several others. Burke and Rocky continued firing. Gunfire erupted from Robin's side, and bullets kicked up rocks and dust around him. He ducked, and then rose back up. He fired at another figure moving to his right.

What felt like a mule kicked Robin in the back. At the same time, he heard a burst from a submachine gun. He heard Burke yell, then a scream and a shot. Robin couldn't breathe. He tried to suck in air, but pain gripped his chest and back. He braced himself on all fours, gasping. *Can't breathe!*

"Lie down on your side, Sarge," Rocky yelled. Seconds later, Rocky's voice screamed, "Three Twenty-Four, Nora Six is down hard! We are all wounded!"

Robin turned and saw a man lying at the bottom of the depression with Burke's knife in his chest. Burke was lying on the north side, holding his bleeding left side. Robin shook off Rocky. He struggled to his position. Having dropped his Galil, he drew his .45. He kept gasping for air. His vision blurred. A man appeared in front of him, screaming "Allah Akbar!" Robin fired two quick rounds into the man's chest by sheer muscle memory. He tried to stand up, to keep fighting, but his legs were rubber and he fell to the ground again. He just could not breathe. The air around him roared and dust swirled.

Gunfire increased, and men shouted in English. Strong hands grabbed him. He struggled. A gruff, gentle voice said, "It's all right. We're going home." Karen's face appeared in a swirling mist. Her face rose into the air and he reached for her. *I have always loved you!* The swirl carried him up as he strained to touch her, and then her face melted way in a blinding light.

The words "Nora Six is down hard; we are all wounded," put a hard lump in Jack's throat. Enraged, he made repeated runs on the compound, spewing fiery death and destruction all over. The gunners fired until they were out of ammunition and their barrels glowed red hot. The Blackhawk departed, leaving the compound in flames with nothing left standing.

Robin struggled for consciousness. He gulped refreshing cool air. As he started to rise, a gentle, firm hand held him down.

"Try not to move, sir. You have multiple wounds—I think you have some broken ribs. You've lost a lot of blood." Robin opened his eyes and saw an Air Force Pararescue Jumper. "I gave you some morphine to help with the pain. You have an oxygen mask on your face. We will be at Davis-Monthan shortly."

Robin worked at focusing his eyes, realizing he was lying on a stretcher in a Blackhawk helicopter. Burke lay on a stretcher across from him. Robin hoped Burke was only sleeping. On a lower stretcher, two people worked on Marv. Robin moved his head and saw Rocky in a seat, his leg being splinted and bandaged. Their eyes met, and Rocky raised his hand to his forehead in a solemn salute. For some reason, Robin knew the salute meant they were all going to make it. He slipped off into sleep as Karen's lovely vision beckoned him.

TWENTY EIGHT

Robin only had brief moments of consciousness, at times aware of being moved. He saw Bill Grassley's fleeting face and heard Grassley gasp, "My God!" He could feel medical personnel working on him from time to time and heard them talking with concerned voices. There were vehicles, then an aircraft. He tried to wake up, but a soothing female voice said, "Night, night." Echoing voices seemed to go on and on.

Robin felt like he could wake up. His eyes opened, but they would not focus. He felt dull pain all over his body and with each breath. His throat ached with thirst. He heard Karen's voice calling for a nurse, and then her warm hand on his.

"Rob, it's me, Karen." Robin squeezed her hand. "It's okay, now. You're safe." Her voice cracked. "Oh, Rob, I love you. I love you so very much." He squeezed her hand again.

"I love you, Karen," Robin said in a croaking whisper. Then he felt less gentle hands on him. The hands probed and moved his body. He grunted with pain.

"Sorry, Sergeant. I have to inspect your wounds. Your body has taken a real beating and you will be hurting for while."

Robin started to get focus. He saw Karen and smiled at her. She leaned over and kissed his cheek. He realized he was lying braced up on his right side. A woman in a military nurse's uniform appeared in front of him. She had the bars of an Army Captain on her collar.

"We want you to be awake now. You have to start working with us to heal your wounds. You are on your right side because you have three cracked ribs in your back. That's why it hurts to breathe.

You also have damage to your back muscles. You were hit by three bullets there, but your ballistic vest stopped them from penetrating too far—although the last one did get close to your lung. We have you in a new type of torso cast to minimize movement of those ribs." The nurse looked for understanding from him.

Robin nodded his head.

"You also have a wound to your left hip. The tissue damage is significant, but no bones were hit. It's a good thing, because it looks like an AK round hit you. You had a slight wound to your left heel. The paperwork that came with you said your left boot had a bullet hole in it."

Robin nodded again.

"The most serious wounds are to the right side of your neck and head. You had a lot of glass and metal shrapnel there. Your prior wounds made the penetration of the shrapnel easier this time. Some of the shrapnel came very close to some vital areas. You had extensive surgery in that area, including taking out shrapnel that went through your skull. That's why you have been out so long. Luckily, you apparently have a hard head and the shrapnel didn't penetrate too far. "

Robin cleared his throat. "Water."

"Oh, honey," Karen cried. She reached over and poured water from a pitcher into a glass. She took a straw off of a tray and put it in the glass. Karen held the glass so Robin could sip water. After a few sips, his throat felt better.

"Cathy?"

"She's fine, Rob. She has been alternating between you and Andy."

"Where am I?"

The nurse spoke. "You are at Walter Reed Hospital, in the custody of the United States Army Military Police. As soon as we can, we will be moving you to Fort Bragg."

That's interesting.

"I'll be back in a while," the nurse continued. "We're going to have to get you as close to a sitting position as we can. We need to get you well enough to move." Without further comment, the nurse left.

"How are the rest of the kids handling all of this?" Robin asked.

"The first couple of days were rough for them, but the Marine guards took Casey and Eddie under their wings and they keep them busy. Laurie is doing okay. She's been moody. She is doing much better since Cathy came."

"How about you?"

"I've been miserable. Rob, I am so sor..." Robin gently put his fingers on her mouth.

"No apologies. I screwed up. We need to just think ahead and love each other." Karen leaned over and kissed him.

"How are the guys? I know some were badly hurt."

"Everyone got back, but almost everyone was wounded except for Ernie and Gary. Marv and Jamie are still here with you. Both will recover, but I guess Jamie will take a while. They have everyone else at Quantico."

"How are the other families?"

"They're doing better now that you guys are here." Karen looked pensive.

"What's up, Babe?" Robin could feel sleep starting to come over him again.

"Rob, we've been forbidden to talk to anyone. They tell us if we do, you will all go to prison. Bill Grassley has told us to be patient—that all of this will be worked out, but we need to be quiet. The press is going crazy with stories of an official complaint by the Mexican government about a military incursion by the U.S. that resulted in the death of over sixty Mexican citizens. Our government is denying any knowledge of it, but everyone believes the U.S. did it."

"Don't worry, honey. The most important thing is that we got Cathy back." Sleep overtook Robin. "I'll deal with it as soon as I can stay awake."

For the next seven days, Robin fought pain, minimizing the pain medicine the doctor ordered him to take. He pushed the limits, trying to get back on his feet. Karen stayed with him day and night; Robin noticed she looked haggard. On the morning of the fourth day, the doctor came in to the room.

"How are you doing today?"

"Doc, I want to stop the pain medicine."

"I don't advise that. You still have a lot of pain."

"I don't care about the pain. I want to get my brain out of this fog. All the pain medicine is doing is interfering with my brain trying to heal me. As long as I know why I am hurting, I'll be fine. I also want to get out of here. I need to see my kids and my men."

The doctor looked at Robin, sizing him up. He turned to Karen. "Well, Mrs. Marlette, you certainly know your husband." Robin looked at Karen.

"What's that supposed to mean?"

Karen smiled. "I told the good doctor that as soon as you started feeling a little better you would start giving orders."

Robin sighed. "Sorry, Doc, I'm not trying to be demanding. I am just stating my preferences."

"Well, Sergeant, if you think you're ready, I won't stand in your way. There is some basis to your assessment about the pain medicine and environment being better at Fort Bragg. You will have to continue your physical therapy there. If you can stand the pain, I will release you with a prescription for pain medicine you can take at night so you can sleep."

"I'm ready to go, Doc, as soon as I visit my men who are still here."

TWENTY NINE

B y the time the plane ride to Fort Bragg ended, Robin's pain medicine had worn off. Robin hid his agony as the children greeted him and Karen, but they could see the bandages and the torso cast. He saw the concern in their eyes.

Eddie held on to Robin's hand and would not let go. He put Robin's arm across his shoulder. "Here, Dad, lean on me. I'll help you." Robin hesitated, but looking into his son's eyes, he couldn't say no. "Thanks, Eddie, I could use the help."

Two MPs helped Robin into the back seat of a van and drove the family to their quarters, located in a section of Randolf Pointe, cordoned off by MPs. All of the men and their families were housed here. As they walked through the makeshift entry, two MPs came to attention. One of them winked at Eddie.

"I'm not a military officer, gentlemen. No need to come to attention for me."

"On the contrary, sir," said a sergeant whose name tag read "McManus." "We don't know all the details, but we have general idea of what you and your men did and why security is needed. We are honored to be here, sir."

"Thank you, Sergeant."

As they passed through the gate, Robin saw Burke Jameson standing with the help of a crutch near a door that turned out to be the entrance to Robin's family quarters. Robin walked up to Burke. They painfully embraced in a bear hug.

"We made it, Boss," Burke said, the mischievous sparkle in his eyes brighter than ever. "According to the news, we caused a helluva lot of trouble." Burke's face broke out in a broad grin, cut short as he reached to hold the bandage on his right cheek.

"Well, I think that fits our style just fine," Robin replied. He stepped into the quarters and saw almost the entire team and their families were there. Two things he saw gave him pause. First, all of them, save Ernie Jackson and Gary Perkins, were bandaged in various places. Second, Marv Allen and Jamie Slater were not there at all. Pain filled his heart. Each one of these men had done this for Cathy, for him.

Robin looked about him for a minute. "As you all know, I'm not a man of few words on most occasions." Knowing chuckles rippled through the group. "Today is different. I simply cannot tell you how thankful Karen and I are for the sacrifice all of you gave to get Cathy back. I thought I could go it alone. I had a plan." More chuckles; Robin smiled. "I guess I always have a plan. It's just sometimes they don't work out too well. As our various wounds testify, I probably would not have made it, which means Cathy would not have made it." Robin's head bowed.

"Hey, Rob, do you know how long I have been waiting for a free fire zone?" Emmett piped up. "In 'Nam, we had fucked up rules of engagement that wouldn't let us kill the bad guys. When we hit that compound, I felt liberated. We knew these were righteous bad guys; we knew they were out-and-out dangerous, and most importantly, you taught us that we were more dangerous than them—and by God, we proved it. We love you and Karen and the kids. So shut up. We're burning daylight."

A roar of laughter erupted from the group. Robin stiffly walked amongst the team and their families, thanking them and answering their questions about the future as best he could. During the reunion, Bill Grassley called Robin.

"Rob, two vehicles will be by to pick up the team at 1300 tomorrow to take you to another location on the Fort. We'll settle the team's situation then."

"Okay, we'll be ready."

"No questions?"

"Not now. We trust you, Bill."

"I'm glad to hear that. Both our futures depend on it. We'll see you tomorrow."

"Okay, bye." Robin rejoined Karen and went back to talking with his men and their families.

Soon just the team remained, and Robin sat down with his men. Pain and exhaustion were haunting him, but he needed to find out some things.

"I'd like to get filled in on what happened to everybody during the raid. Rick and Mark, how did the perimeter fight go?"

"Actually, Sarge, if the original intelligence had been good, our plan would have worked," Rick said. "The Arabs threw us off. There had to be thirty to fifty of them."

"That's a fact," Mark chimed in. Those charges and grenades you gave us were the reason we all got out alive. They took care of a lot of assholes, but there were still a lot of them left."

"How did you two get wounded?"

"We both got wounded getting everyone into the extraction vehicles, as did Mr. Young over there," Rick explained.

"Having those two vehicles in the same place was a mistake," Rick continued. They became the targets of most of the enemy firepower."

"I agree," Mike said. "That's also where Carlos and I were both wounded."

"Me too," Emmett said.

"There is a lesson learned. Where is Carlos?"

"The Feds have him and Jorge under wraps more than us," Burke said. "And, by the way, the Feds got Jorge's family out of Mexico. They are here with him now."

"I'm glad to hear that, since we promised him."

"Well, Mr. Santos over there jumped on ol' Grassley's back and wouldn't get off until he took care of it."

"Who got us out?"

"The Air Force got us out," Mark said. "Another one of their choppers got you out too."

"Jesus, how many choppers were down there?"

"I counted four," Mark replied.

"That's about right," Rick agreed. "HRT and Delta were there. They are the ones who got the Arabs off your back when you got cornered...even captured two of them alive."

"Amen, brother," Rocky chimed in. "I was never so happy to see the FBI in my whole life. I take back every bad thing I ever said about them. Those guys fast roped in there and started taking care of business. Then the Air Force PJs came in and started getting us out."

"I tell you, Rob, I didn't think we were going to get out of there." Burke's bandaged face bore a solemn look. "I thought we reached the end of the trail in that dirty little hole."

"We didn't give up, did we? We kept on fighting."

"I don't know how you did, after taking that burst in the back. You did make me feel a little better when you blew the Arab away with your .45."

"They really pissed me off!" The group laughed. "I'm just happy I wore my ballistic vest. I wouldn't be here." Robin took a long, painful breath. "Tomorrow at 1300, we're going to be taken to somewhere on the Fort. Grassley says our situation will be worked out then. It is probably going to be both good and bad. We're facing federal prosecution for a lot of crimes. I know you all have been told to keep quiet or you will go to prison. That tells me they don't want to do that, but assuming they don't, it won't be for free. They are going to want something from us. The only way we can get through this with a minimum amount of further damage to us and our families is by sticking together."

"Are we screwed, Rob?" Ernie asked.

They have taken a public position that gives us some bargaining power. We can only make the most of that power by staying united. I talked to Marv and Jamie before I left Walter Reed and they are in. Is there anyone who wants out?"

"Our families are scared, Rob," Gary observed. "My wife and I are so close to retirement" Gary's voice trailed off.

"That's my point, Gary. All of our families want and need security. We need to stick together and make sure we take care of each other."

Gary nodded his head. "I'm in."

"Anybody else with questions or concerns?"

"We assume you have a plan, Rob," Ernie observed.

"I do, but in this skirmish, we are strictly tactical. We're primarily dealing with Bill Grassley. He is somebody we all trust. I don't believe Bill is working for Customs anymore. It seems to me he is in the intelligence business now. We'll have to see." Robin looked around for more comments. "All right, let's hit the sack. We'll see everyone out front at 1245 hours."

After everyone left, Robin painfully made his way to Karen's bedroom. When he approached the door, it opened. Karen stood there, her lovely image filling Robin's heart and soul with warmth and questioning anxiety.

"Welcome to *our* bedroom, Sergeant." Tears began streaming from Robin's eyes. Karen gently put her arms around his neck. "Robin, you have to know I will always love you." Her mouth met his, soft and moist. Karen's tongue told Robin of the passion waiting for him to heal.

THIRTY

Jack Moore, Oscar Leighton, and the rest of the Lima Two-One crew stood at attention as Chief Williams formally retired from the United States Air Force. The Chief stood ramrod straight in his dress blues. Jack thought if Mrs. Williams smiled any broader, the expression would become permanent.

It had been a close thing. The transfer of Chief Williams to the Air Force Rescue chopper saved him from disciplinary action. He now stood proud in his retirement ceremony with full honors. The Air Force awarded Chief Williams the Silver Star and a life saving award for his actions in pulling Robin off of the hill in the clandestine operation. Jack wore a contented smile.

Two black Chevrolet Suburbans picked up the team at 1300 hours. At 1332 hours, they sat in a large conference room inside the Delta Force Command Center. The conference room did not look like a typical government room. There were no windows, and large monitors and high-end electronics and computers lined the walls. It contained quality wood furniture and a collection of original military action paintings hung on the beige walls. The room maintained a sense of urgent formality. Bill Grassley came in with another man. They were followed by a Major General.

"Good afternoon, gentlemen. I'd like to introduce you to Major General Dave Buchanan, the commander of Delta Force. This is Mr. Jordan Yates, CIA Deputy Director of Operations. He's now my boss." Several members of the team looked at Robin and smiled. "When I told Robin about this meeting, he surprised me when he had no questions. He told me all of you trust me. I hope I will live up to your trust.

"As you all are very well aware, you violated many United States and Mexican laws. The Mexican government wants your heads. They have filed a formal protest and are threatening to go to the International Criminal Court. We have, of course, denied everything, with appropriate slips to the media."

Robin spoke up. "Can't we shut the Mexican government up by threatening to tell the world about the Arab terrorists they harbored?"

"That issue has been secretly discussed, which is why this incident won't go any further than a formal complaint to the U.S. government. That doesn't mean you're out of the woods. There are special interest groups in this country and others who want to know the whole story, who are claiming that this whole operation amounted to genocide."

"That's all bullshit, as you know," Robin said. The men made comments of approval.

"We know and will protect you from all of this, but there is a price." Grassley saw no surprise in their faces.

"I see Robin has figured this out also." The men laughed. "All of you are finished as law enforcement officers in Arizona. Your records at DPS and the Phoenix Police have been confiscated. To them, you no longer exist." Grassley looked around the room again. "We have hinted, but not confirmed, that you were all killed."

"We are going to move you to the Northwest. We have substantial military assets there that can get you to where we need you, when we need you. You will work for us, the CIA. We will not want you full time. Just when we need a team no one knows about."

Robin stood up. "First things first. We need money to live on. How can we survive if you are not going to need us full time?"

Grassley looked at Yates, who nodded and stepped forward. "We are going to set you up in business. We are proposing a worldwide export/import business. You will be fully capitalized, including transportation assets and a generous five-year operating budget. We want the business to be located in the Seattle area."

"Do we get to run the business?"

"Yes."

"Okay, what will be our status when we work for you?"

Bill Grassley stepped forward again. "When you deploy you will be absolutely covert. You will have nothing with you that connects you with us. If you are captured by anyone unfriendly to us, you will be on your own. If you are killed, your families will receive the benefits of the rank we will give you in the Army."

"You're confusing me, Bill."

"We will provide you with all the support we can for a mission, whatever it takes. But if we are using you guys, it is because we cannot be connected with the operation. Our basic plan is to give you the mission. You plan it. You tell me what you need in support and money. When we agree, that will be the deal. But make no mistake— if you get captured by unfriendlies, you're on your own. It may be that way even with friendlies.

"The reason we are giving you all a rank in the Army is because, as a team, you will have to have access to military facilities for training and such. You will all be given a rank that befits your experience, education, and training. We can negotiate the ranks if necessary."

"How much do we get paid?"

"As I said, you will be giving me a budget for each mission. Once we agree, that's it."

"Can you give us about fifteen minutes?"

"Absolutely." Grassley, the general, and Yates left the room.

"Okay, guys, you heard it all. Any comments or questions?"

Gary looked around. "Rob, at some point can I opt out of the missions? I'm asking because I am not getting any younger."

"I'm afraid not, Gary."

"I'm not sure I can physically do what we have been doing for much longer."

"Can you do what you did on the raid?"

"Oh, yeah, I can do that!"

"Well, we will always need extraction and a 'wheel man,' so to speak. That will be your job. You plan it, you arrange it. You make sure we all get out."

"I can definitely do that."

"Anybody else?"

Ernie spoke up. "I don't like the idea that we are on our own if we get captured."

"You have to look at it another way, Ernie. I take it they won't get in the way of our own rescue mission to get one of us out."

Ernie smiled and shook his head. "Rob, you just might be the most dangerous man I know. I don't think Grassley fully comprehends what he is about to loose upon the world."

"Oh, I think Bill Grassley knows exactly what he is doing. Think about it. He gave up a promising career in U.S. Customs to get us out of this jam. He would've been the head of Customs eventually. I think his main job is to pick missions for us and to keep us under control."

"Why do we need control?" Emmett asked with a touch of irritation. Robin just looked at him. "Oh, you mean that going into a foreign country and killing a bunch of assholes on our own type of thing."

"The thought crossed my mind." Emmett's face broke out in a sheepish grin.

"Are we all in? The emphasis is on the 'all.' There is no shame in saying no. This deal definitely has good *and* bad points. Speak up or forever hold your peace." Robin waited for a good minute. Nobody said anything. "Okay, we are all really Guardians of the Universe now. Hold on to your asses, because here we go. Burke, bring our new bosses in."

Burke opened the door. "We're ready, Bill...I mean, Boss."

"Nothing like keeping the suspense, Burke," Robin said with light-hearted reproach. The rest of the team laughed as Burke hung his head with a sly smile. As Grassley and the rest came in, Robin stood up.

"We're in."

Yates spoke next. "Actually, you were in the minute you stepped across the border. I didn't say this at first, because I didn't want you to think I was blowing smoke up your butts. This impromptu op you guys pulled amazed us. I know you got shot up, but all the same you accomplished the mission against overwhelming odds. You didn't give up and kept on fighting. That's the kind of team we want. We will give you training which will make you even better than you are now. We will give you the best equipment. You will have the assets to make your missions work. You have my word on it."

"And mine," Bill agreed.

"Robin, please come forward," General Buchanan said. Robin walked up to him and came to attention. "Robin, by order of the President of the United States, with the advice and consent of the Senate of the United States, you and your men are hereby commissioned into the United States Army Reserve with the rank of colonel. Ernest Jackson will have the rank of major; Rockwell Barnett and Burke Jameson, lieutenant. Colonel Marlette and Major Jackson, you are hereby authorized to assign non-commissioned rank amongst your command as you see fit. Your immediate superior will be the Commander, Special Operations Command, MacDill Air Force Base, Florida, which will be the only place any record of you will exist." General Buchanan handed Robin his orders. "Congratulations and welcome to SOCOM."

Robin accepted his orders. "Thank you, General. We will strive to make the Army proud of us."

"I am sure you will, Colonel. It's just nobody will know, will they?"

"I guess not, sir."

"Now, if you will all please stand and repeat after me."

The men all stood, raised their right hands, and repeated the oath of office.

Bill Grassley walked up to Robin after they were done. "Rob, we're going to give your team three months to heal up, and then we will start training. I know Jamie may need more time to heal and that's fine. We'll go with your recommendations concerning him. We're going to move your families to more permanent quarters here. The children can register for school on the Fort. We are starting here because Delta will be your primary trainers."

"What about our kids in college and about to start college?"

"They have their choice: Georgetown University or West Point."

"But"

"That's the best I can do, Rob. I think it's pretty damn good."

Unless your kid wants to play baseball. "I'm not complaining. We'll adjust."

"Any other considerations?" No one spoke up. "All right, gentlemen, some folks would like to meet you."

The door to the room opened up and a group of men walked in.

"Guardians, these are the men from FBI HRT, Delta, and the Air Force who pulled your butts out of the fire."

"Gentlemen, we are very pleased to meet you!" Robin exclaimed.

The two groups stepped toward each other and merged into handshakes, thank you's, and congratulations.

"Did I ever tell you guys how much I love the FBI?" Rocky loudly proclaimed to a couple of HRT operators.

Robin talked to the HRT and Delta team leaders and thanked them on behalf of the whole team. "If you guys weren't there for us, many of us wouldn't have made it, including me."

"We were glad to be there," the Delta leader said. "It's always fun to whack drug smugglers and terrorists."

"Same goes for us," the HRT leader agreed. "We train and train, but don't deploy as often as we like. This operation was a kick!"

After a half hour of discussion, Grassley announced a barbeque was being served in the courtyard of the building. Everyone moved there and enjoyed more conversation, steak, and beer. The Guardians met their future trainers, and the Delta operators guaranteed the Guardians their skills would be greatly enhanced by the time the training finished. The Delta guys told the Guardians they would go through training evolutions with the SEALs and Air Force PJs, in addition to Delta. The Guardians were getting excited about their new job.

Later, Karen talked to Robin in their quarters. Robin finished telling Karen about the CIA's plan. "It's not like we have a lot of choices. I know all of this has been tough on you and the kids, and moving to a whole new part of the country won't make things any easier."

"We are a tough family, Robin Marlette. Will you be gone all of the time again like when you worked narcotics?"

"That may be a good side to this. I will be away from you when we are on CIA missions, but I won't be doing that all of the time. I will be a businessman in Seattle. When I travel for this business, I can take you and the kids with me."

"That sounds like it might be fun."

"Overall, honey, I should be with you a whole lot more than before."

"That's all I ever wanted, Rob."

"Believe it or not, Karen, that's what I want too." Robin kissed his wife.

An hour later, Robin worked on plans for the team when Karen came into the room.

"Honey, you need to talk to Cathy."

"What's up?"

"She just came back from the hospital. She and Andy are having trouble. Cathy is very upset."

"What is the trouble?"

"I think she should tell you." Robin went upstairs to the unit where Cathy and Laurie were staying. He knocked, and Laurie opened the door.

"Hi honey, how are you doing?"

"I'm doing fine, Dad, but Cathy sure isn't. She's in her room." Robin walked over to the door and knocked.

"Cathy, it's Dad. Can I come in?" Cathy didn't respond. Then after a short time, she opened the door.

"Want to talk?"

Cathy sat on her bed and started crying.

"What's up, Cathy?"

Cathy slowly looked up to her father. "Andy says I should go away and leave him. He says his face is horrible and he doesn't want to be with me anymore. He wants me to find someone else." Cathy fell on her bed, sobbing.

"Did you tell your mom about this?"

"Yes."

"How do you feel about it?"

Cathy shot upright, giving her father a fierce look. "I love Andy with all my heart. I want to be his wife. I love him for his heart, not his face!"

"Well, are you a Marlette or a mouse?"

"What do you mean?" Cathy asked with a quizzical look.

"Are you going to give up, or are you going to take matters into your own hands?"

"I love Andy. I'll do what it takes! I just don't know what to do. Will you help me, Dad?"

"I'll take care of the technicalities. Let's go see Mom."

Robin and Cathy went downstairs and Robin called to Karen. "Honey, are you here?"

Karen came out of the bedroom and put her arm around Cathy. "Have you decided what you're going to do?"

"Dad says I should act like a Marlette and take control of the situation."

Karen glanced over at Robin. "That would be your dad. What do *you* want to do?"

"I love Andy and I want to be his wife."

"Any idea when you want to do this?"

"I wanted to marry Andy two days after our first date." Cathy began to cry, and buried her face in Karen's shoulder.

"Oh, my dear first-born child, you are so much like your father." Karen gently pushed Cathy from her shoulder and looked lovingly at her. "I know that no matter what Andy says, he loves you with all of this heart. Let's you and I go see Uncle Ernie and Aunt Sally." Karen turned to Robin. "Colonel, will you please handle the technicalities while we go see the Jacksons and get ready for a hospital wedding?"

Robin saluted Karen. "Can do, General!"

Robin called Andy's doctor and told him of the situation. The doctor knew about the argument between Andy and Cathy. He told Robin Andy had sunk into a deep depression and he would be happy to take care of the blood tests. Cathy had received a complete physical at Walter Reed after the rescue, so the hospital records contained both her and Andy's blood analysis. That made the marriage license easy.

Three days later, both families were flown to Walter Reed and met the Walter Reed Chaplain.

As they were walking to Andy's room, Ernie stopped her. "Cathy, are you sure you want to do this? Andy is going to be going through a rough time. Even when he is through reconstructive surgery, he is not going to look the same." Ernie's last words were strained with a tight throat, and tears welled in his eyes.

Cathy's eyes shot fire. "I know exactly what I am doing, Uncle Ernie. I love Andy, I want to be his wife, and that's it!"

"Cathy, we love you"

"Ernie," Robin interjected. "If you don't want my shy and retiring daughter to kick your dumb balls into your throat, I suggest you shut up and let's get on with the wedding."

Sally Jackson grabbed her husband's arm and with an exasperated look pulled him to Andy's door.

Robin looked at his daughter. "You're on, kid. Make him believe."

Cathy kissed her father, hugged her mother, took a deep breath, and walked into the room. She wore a simple white dress with white daisies hand-picked by Karen in her hair. She held a small bouquet of other flowers. Her bright blue eyes sparkled with a fierce passion. Andy appeared confused and dazzled by her beauty.

"Andrew Jackson, do you love me?" Andy did not answer right away. Eventually, he spoke, trying to make his jaw work.

"Yessh." He turned his face away.

"Andy, look at me." Andy turned his head back. "I love you with all my heart. I want to be with you forever. I don't give a damn what your face looks like. I only care what your heart and soul look like. I want to be your wife and I want to be your wife now. Are you ready?"

Andy nodded his head. Cathy smiled and kissed his cheek. She turned to the door with a shining smile. "We're ready!"

"I don't know how I can top that!" the Chaplain said as he walked through the door.

Robin and Karen held hands. They looked at each other and then at their daughter. Love and fierce pride swelled in Robin. He put his hand around Karen's waist, and she pressed his arm close to her as tears made their way down her cheeks. Still, Robin chuckled to himself and sent a silent message to Andy: *God help you, Andrew Jackson.*

Watch for more exciting books in the GOTU series from Mike McNeff.

Also from Booktrope Editions

Cathedral of Dreams, by Terry Persun (Science Fiction) A compelling tale of a dystopian future and personal heroism, pitting the outsiders against the mind control machine of New City.

Skull Dance, by Gerd Balke and Michael Larocca (Thriller) An atmospheric tale of international nuclear espionage, intrigue and heroism, twisted politics, terrorism and romance.

Paradise Junction, by Phillip Finch (Thriller) A web of crime and intrigue as two privileged thrill seekers set off a series of vicious crimes leading to murder. (coming soon)

Sugarland, by Phillip Finch (Mystery) An exotic action filled tale. An insurance fraud draws an investigator to the Philippines and into a maze of violence and romance. (coming soon)

Memoirs Aren't Fairytales by Marni Mann (Contemporary Fiction) a searing account of a young woman's heartbreaking descent into drug addiction.

Wolf's Rite, by Terry Persun (Adventure) A ruthless big city ad exec is sent on a spirit walk by mystical band of Native Americans. At the edges of sanity Wolf explores love and violence and finds a new self.

Deception Creek, by Terry Persun (Coming of Age Novel) Secrets from the past overtake a man who never knew his father. Will old wrongs destroy him or will he rebuild his life?

Sweet Song, by Terry Persun (Historical Fiction) This tale of a mixed race man passing as white in post-Civil War America speaks from the heart about where we've come from and who we are.

Sample our books at www.booktrope.com

Learn more about our new approach to publishing at
www.booktropepublishing.com